SLAUGHTER IN THE
SAPPERTON TUNNEL

By Edward Marston

THE RAILWAY DETECTIVE SERIES
The Railway Detective • The Excursion Train
The Railway Viaduct • The Iron Horse
Murder on the Brighton Express • The Silver Locomotive Mystery
Railway to the Grave • Blood on the Line
The Stationmaster's Farewell • Peril on the Royal Train
A Ticket to Oblivion • Timetable of Death
Signal for Vengeance • The Circus Train Conspiracy
A Christmas Railway Mystery • Points of Danger
Fear on the Phantom Special • Slaughter in the Sapperton Tunnel
Tragedy on the Branch Line
Inspector Colbeck's Casebook

THE HOME FRONT DETECTIVE SERIES
A Bespoke Murder • Instrument of Slaughter
Five Dead Canaries • Deeds of Darkness
Dance of Death • The Enemy Within
Under Attack • The Unseen Hand • Orders to Kill

THE BOW STREET RIVALS SERIES
Shadow of the Hangman • Steps to the Gallows
Date with the Executioner • Fugitive from the Grave
Rage of the Assassin

PRAISE FOR EDWARD MARSTON

'A master storyteller'
Daily Mail

'Packed with characters Dickens would have been
proud of. Wonderful [and] well-written'
Time Out

'Once again Marston has created a credible
atmosphere within an intriguing story'
Sunday Telegraph

'Filled with period detail, the pace is steady and
the plot is thick with suspects, solutions and clues.
Marston has a real knack for blending detail,
character and story with great skill'
Historical Novels Review

'The past is brought to life with brilliant
colours, combined with a perfect
whodunnit. Who needs more?'
The Guardian

SLAUGHTER IN THE SAPPERTON TUNNEL

EDWARD MARSTON

Allison & Busby Limited
11 Wardour Mews
London W1F 8AN
allisonandbusby.com

First published in Great Britain by Allison & Busby in 2020.
This paperback edition published by Allison & Busby in 2021.

A CIP catalogue record for this book is available from
the British Library.

10 9 8 7 6 5 4 3 2

ISBN 978-0-7490-2681-3

Typeset in 11/16 pt Adobe Garamond Pro by
Allison & Busby Ltd

Printed and bound by
CPI Group (UK) Ltd, Croydon, CR0 4YY

CHAPTER ONE

Spring, 1862

At a time when most of the nation was still slumbering, the locomotive steamed towards Kemble, its wagons creaking under the weight of their loads and clanking over the rails. Standing on the footplate, the driver and his fireman glanced at the silhouette of the little station that suddenly rose out of the gloom like a friendly ghost to acknowledge their arrival while simultaneously bidding farewell to its fleeting visitors. It was not long before the goods train plunged into the first stretch of the Sapperton Tunnel, emerging briefly into the fresh air after 350 yards or so before hurtling into the much longer stretch. As it burrowed again through the Cotswold escarpment, the darkness was relieved only by the glow from the firebox.

'I hate this place,' confided the driver.

'Why is that, Olly?'

'I keep thinking of the poor devils who built it.'

'They did a good job.'

'Yes, but it was so dangerous. Some navvies had terrible injuries. Just think of it. Working down here with no natural light and filling their lungs with dust every day. It must have been torture.'

'They got paid for it,' said the fireman, cheerfully. 'In any case, they were used to hard labour. Digging this tunnel was a challenge. I reckon they were glad to take it on.'

In the narrow confines of the brick-built structure, noise was amplified, and they had to raise their voices above the tumult in order to be heard. Neither of them was aware of the plaintive bleating towards which they were now thundering. As they strained their eyes to peer through the billowing smoke, they could see nothing to cause alarm. Then, without warning, it happened. As it neared the mouth of the tunnel, the locomotive smashed through the makeshift pen in which a number of sheep had been imprisoned, killing the animals instantly before hitting the boulders that had been piled up ahead on the track. Derailed on impact, the train keeled over and threw both men uncaringly off the footplate. Wagons splintered, overturned or jack-knifed crazily, shedding their loads everywhere. For what seemed like minutes, the sound of sheer chaos echoed through the tunnel and caused tremors in the earth above it.

CHAPTER TWO

When he let himself into the superintendent's office, Colbeck
found the man seated behind his desk, poring over an Ordnance
Survey map. It was only when the inspector walked across to
him that Tallis realised he had a visitor. Raising his head, he
gave Colbeck an unwelcoming glare.

'I did knock, sir,' said Colbeck.

'Not loud enough – didn't hear a sound.'

'You sent for me, Superintendent, but, since you are clearly
preoccupied, perhaps it would be better if I returned at a more
suitable time.'

'No, no,' said Tallis. 'Now that you're here, you can stay.' He tapped
the map with an irritable finger. 'I've been trying to find Sapperton.'

'It's in Gloucestershire, sir.'

'I know that, damn you, but I need a precise location.'

'Allow me.'

Walking around the desk, Colbeck looked over Tallis's shoulder at the map. It took him only seconds to find the elusive village.

'It's here, sir,' he said, pointing. 'Sapperton is in a beautiful area of the county. The tunnel that bears its name is, in my opinion, one of the most striking examples of railway engineering in the whole country.'

'You won't think that when you see it.'

'What do you mean?'

'I'm sending you and Leeming there immediately.'

'Is there a problem with the tunnel?'

'A goods train came off the rails there – after it had slaughtered some sheep.' Picking up the telegraph, he handed it to Colbeck. 'I still can't work out if it's a genuine call for help or a hoax.'

The inspector glanced at it. 'It's genuine, sir.'

'You haven't even read it.'

'I didn't need to,' said Colbeck. 'I saw the name of the sender. Stephen Rydall is a member of the GWR board. He's a landowner in the area. I daresay that the sheep would have belonged to him.'

'Do you *have* to be so annoyingly well-informed?' said Tallis, slapping his hand down on the desk. 'It's uncanny.' He sat up in his chair. 'How on earth did you come to meet Mr Rydall?'

'I didn't meet him, sir. I just heard that name more than once when Sergeant Leeming and I were investigating a murder in Swindon. Mr Rydall was spoken of with great respect.'

'What do you make of his telegraph?'

'It arouses my interest at once, sir,' said Colbeck, reading the terse message. 'I can't ever remember a case that involves the wanton killing of farm animals. The disappearance of Mr Rydall's shepherd is quite mystifying.'

'Not to me,' said Tallis, confidently. 'I'll wager that he's the man you'll end up arresting. There's obviously been bad blood between Rydall and this fellow. The shepherd probably took his revenge by causing mayhem at the tunnel before making a run for it.'

'I think that highly unlikely, sir.'

'It's as plain as the nose on your face.'

'Shepherds tend to love the animals they look after. And why should this man destroy the very sheep that provide him with his livelihood? Besides, the major crime here is orchestrating the accident. That's not the work of a shepherd who hates his employer,' argued Colbeck. 'It's much more likely to be the work of someone with a grudge against the Great Western Railway.'

It had happened so many times that Madeleine Colbeck had grown accustomed to it. Whenever he had to set off on an investigation that took him outside London, her husband always made sure that he sent her a letter by hand so that she knew exactly where he was going. His last case had been in the Lake District. Madeleine was relieved to discover he would not be quite so far away this time. Out of consideration for his wife, Colbeck had not only made her aware of his movements, he'd arranged for the missive to be delivered to their home in John Islip Street by Alan Hinton, a young detective at Scotland Yard.

'Did you know what was in this letter?' she asked.

'The inspector told me they were off to Gloucestershire.'

'Did he give you any details?'

'No,' said Hinton. 'He was in something of a rush.'

'That's nothing new, alas,' she sighed. 'However, since you were kind enough to act as a postman, would you care for some refreshment?'

'I'd care very much but I must get back to work.'

'That's a pity. Lydia will be here very soon.'

His mood changed at once. 'Oh, I see . . .'

Lydia Quayle was Madeleine's best friend. They'd met when Colbeck went to Derby to investigate the murder of her father. Hinton had also met Lydia as the result of a crime, though one less serious in nature. She'd been troubled by a stalker and the detective was able both to protect her and arrest the man who'd been harassing her. As a result, Hinton and Lydia had been drawn together. Meetings between them, however, were all too rare and treasured as a result. It took Hinton a matter of seconds to change his mind.

'In that case,' he said, 'perhaps I *will* accept your kind invitation.'

Madeleine smiled. 'I had a feeling that you might, Alan.'

Ordinarily, train journeys with Victor Leeming followed a set pattern. He complained when they arrived at the station, moaned when they boarded the train and, if they were travelling in a full compartment that made a private conversation impossible, he'd stare balefully out of the window as if watching his hopes drift past in the opposite direction. The moment they were alone, he was prone to voice his many objections to the notion of train travel. This time, miraculously, it was different. When first told of their destination, he gave no protest and even managed something resembling a smile.

Leeming was a solid man in his thirties with the kind of unsettling features more appropriate to a desperate criminal. He looked shifty, malevolent and thoroughly out of place wearing formal attire, especially when he stood beside Colbeck, the acknowledged dandy of Scotland Yard. His frock coat was ill-fitted, and his baggy trousers had a stolen look about them.

As they took their seats in an empty compartment, he was actually exhibiting a measure of enjoyment. Colbeck soon learnt why.

'This train stops at Swindon,' said Leeming.

'Yes, it does, Victor.'

'I have fond memories of the place.'

'Yet we had some fairly gruesome encounters there.'

'I was thinking of the Queen's Tap, sir. It had comfortable beds, a friendly landlord and served a wonderful pint of beer. I don't suppose . . .'

'No,' said Colbeck, firmly.

'But the pub is no distance at all from the station. We could nip across there to renew our acquaintance with Mr Wells, enjoy a drink, then catch the next train. You said that they run regularly.'

'They do, indeed, and I'm sure that Hiram Wells would give us a cordial welcome. But getting to the Sapperton Tunnel is our priority. We're going to the site of a dreadful accident, remember. The damage is extensive, the tunnel is blocked indefinitely, and it may even be that the driver and fireman are murder victims. Really, Victor,' said Colbeck with a note of reproach, 'this is not a time to be thinking about a pint of beer.'

'You're right, sir,' said Leeming, lowering his head in penitence. 'It was wrong of me. I apologise. Work comes first, naturally.' When he looked up again, there was a hopeful look in his eye. 'We could always pay our respects at the Queen's Tap on our way *back* to London.'

'Address your mind to the matter in hand,' ordered Colbeck. 'And answer this question. When I gave you what scant information we have about this case, what was your reaction?'

'I felt sorry for the sheep.'

'So did I.'

'Why did they have to be killed like that?'

'I don't know, but I wonder if there's some religious aspect to their death.'

Leeming gasped. '*Religious?*'

'They could have been sacrifices.'

'What sort of sacrifices?'

'We'll have to ask the person who put them there.'

The light was good and the temperature warm. Conditions were ideal for the man. Having carefully chosen his spot, he sat down on a tree stump and opened his sketchbook. As he worked carefully away, the devastation around the mouth of the tunnel came slowly to life on the blank paper.

CHAPTER THREE

To Alan Hinton's delight, Lydia Quayle soon arrived at the house. Tea was served in the drawing room where they exchanged news. The detective felt a stab of guilt when he thought how Superintendent Tallis would react if he caught one of his officers relaxing with friends while on duty, but that fear was soon removed by the sheer pleasure of seeing Lydia again. To his eyes, she looked more poised and beautiful than ever. For her part, she was equally thrilled at the unexpected encounter. She was also interested to hear the message that Hinton had brought to the house.

'Sapperton?' she repeated. 'I've been there.'

'Really?' said Hinton.

'When I was a child, we used to visit an aunt who lived close to Cirencester. She often took us for a ride in her carriage to one of the villages nearby. Sapperton was among them.'

'What was it like?' asked Madeleine.

'I can't remember too much about it, to be honest. It was a long time ago. But I do recall that it was very pretty and there was this wonderful sense of space.'

'We don't get that here in London.'

'That's inevitable in a city as big as this one.'

'There are compensations,' said Hinton. 'London is always bustling with activity. There's never a dull moment here, whereas nothing ever happens in a quiet Cotswold village.'

'Something has certainly happened in Sapperton,' noted Lydia.

'It's the exception that proves the rule.'

'I'll be interested to hear more about the case.'

'So will I,' said Madeleine, 'though I'm wrestling with a big problem at the moment. Father always likes to know what Robert is up to and, as a rule, I'm happy to tell him. This time it's different.'

'Why is that?' asked Lydia.

'His son-in-law will be helping the Great Western Railway.'

'Oh dear! I see what you mean.'

'Since he worked all those years for a rival railway company, he hates everything about the GWR.'

'I don't see why,' said Hinton. 'I think that Brunel was a genius. Your father must surely accept that, Madeleine.'

'If only he did,' she said, sadly, 'but he despised the man. He's never said a good word about him. On balance, I fancy, it might be better if I told him that Robert had been sent somewhere on the eastern side of the country.'

'You'd *lie* to him?' said Lydia in disbelief.

'It would spare me another bruising lecture.'

'But he's bound to learn the truth eventually.'

'Yes,' added Hinton. 'When he speaks to Inspector Colbeck again, he'll be told all about the case.'

'That will make him angrier than ever,' Lydia pointed out.

Madeleine grimaced. Deceiving her father might not be the best course of action, after all. When he did learn the truth, she'd have to face his resentment as well as his fury. That was a daunting prospect. She decided that she'd have to think again.

Because they were climbing a gradient, the train had slowed down slightly. Leeming was unaware of any change, but Colbeck noticed the lower speed at once. He drew his companion's attention to it.

'Some locomotives struggle to get up this incline so they go double-headed. The alternative is to lessen the load they're pulling.'

'You mean that they'd detach some carriages?'

'Only if it were necessary,' explained Colbeck. 'And there is a danger involved.'

'Danger?'

'I remember reading about an incident on this line that occurred not far from here. The driver of a goods train was struggling to cope with the gradient so he split the wagons into two halves, intending to take the first lot to Gloucester before returning to pick up the others.'

'What happened?'

'They didn't stay where he'd parked them. The brakes failed

and the wagons careered back down the incline before crashing into some stationary carriages and coming off the rails.'

'Were any of the passengers in the carriages hurt?'

'There were no fatalities, but there were several minor injuries. Also, of course, they had a nasty shock.'

'I have one of those every time I see the superintendent.' They shared a knowing smile. 'When do we reach the site of *our* accident?'

'The tunnel is blocked so we'll have to get out at the eastern portal and go to the other end overland. I'm assuming that the GWR will have arranged some sort of transport for us. If they haven't,' said Colbeck, 'there'll be a lot of very angry passengers. Most of them have tickets for Stroud or beyond.'

Ten minutes later, the train began to slow down so that it could stop at Kemble station. A number of passengers got off, but nobody was waiting to get on. After its brief stay, the train set off again but at a much reduced speed. It soon slowed down so dramatically that they seemed to be creeping forward, as if the driver was eyeing the track ahead with misgiving. It made it easier for the passengers to enjoy looking at the sunlit countryside on either side of them, but it also started to worry them. Even though they'd been warned about the problem on the line, they couldn't understand why they were now moving at a snail's pace.

'What's happening, sir?' asked Leeming.

'We have to be patient.'

'I could walk as fast as this.'

'You may well have to do that before long.'

The prediction was soon proved correct. After stuttering

along for several minutes, the train came to a decisive halt, jerking the passengers as it did so. Voices were heard outside, then uniforms came into view. Railway policemen were opening doors and telling people to get out, helping them to do so with outstretched arms. Colbeck and Leeming were among the last to descend to the ground.

The first thing they saw as they alighted was the gaping mouth of the tunnel over a hundred yards away. They then noticed the fairly steep sides of the cutting either side of them. Climbing up the grassy bank would involve an undignified scramble. Fit and able-bodied, the detectives would have no trouble, but there were much older passengers as well as a number of women. Colbeck summed up the situation at once.

'They could do with men at the top, lowering ropes to haul people up. Come on, Victor,' he said. 'Some of the passengers will never get up there unaided. Let's give them a helping hand.'

Alan Hinton had left an hour ago, but Lydia was still there, enjoying her role as an unofficial aunt and dandling Madeleine's baby daughter, Helena Rose, on her knee. The child was burbling happily.

'It was a lovely surprise to see Alan again,' said Lydia.

'That's why I asked him to stay.'

'Thank you, Madeleine.'

'I had a feeling you'd be pleased.'

'Did he tell you what he was working on at the moment?'

'If he has any sense,' said Madeleine, teasingly, 'he'll be trying to devise a plan to see you more often. That's more important to him than anything else.'

'Oh, I don't know about that.'

'You're too modest, Lydia. He's devoted to you. What he'd really like, of course, is to work with Robert. That would suit all of us. We'd be able to invite him here on a regular basis as we do with Victor Leeming. You could . . . just happen to be passing.'

Lydia laughed. 'Stop it!'

'I'm simply being practical.'

'You can be so naughty sometimes, Madeleine.'

'Is that a complaint?'

Before Lydia could reply, they heard the doorbell ring. She saw the grim look that suddenly appeared on her friend's face and guessed what had put it there.

'You're expecting your father, aren't you?' Madeleine nodded. 'What have you decided?'

'I suppose that I'll have to tell him the truth.'

'It's the best thing to do.'

'I'm afraid that you're right,' said Madeleine. 'Brace yourself, Lydia. My father is about to lose his temper again.'

They heard the front door being opened and a brief exchange of voices. Short, wiry and beaming, Caleb Andrews was then shown into the drawing room by the maid. Madeleine stood up to give him a welcome, but it was his granddaughter who offered the warmest greeting. Jumping off Lydia's knee, she ran across to him to receive an affectionate hug and to tell him her news. It was minutes before they were able to sit down. After a nervous glance at Lydia, Madeleine cleared her throat. Before she could even mention her husband's name, however, Andrews slapped his knee in delight.

'I've heard some marvellous news,' he cried. 'The Sapperton Tunnel is blocked. It's yet another disaster for the GWR.'

'Who told you?' asked his daughter.

'Word travels fast on the railway, Maddy. You should know that. Whenever there's a major accident somewhere on the network, news of it spreads like wildfire. I burst out laughing when I heard.'

'Then you should be ashamed of yourself, Father.'

'Why?'

'When that train crashed, the driver and fireman might have been seriously hurt, if not actually killed.'

He blinked at her. 'How do you know about the crash?'

'Robert has been sent to investigate it.'

'*What?*' He was livid. 'My son-in-law is working for the GWR?'

'He'll solve crimes on the railway no matter where they are.'

'And I admire him for doing so,' said Lydia. 'Madeleine is right to question your response to the news, Mr Andrews. As a former engine driver yourself, I'd have thought you'd show sympathy for anyone who works on the footplate.'

'I do,' he insisted, 'and I'm sorry for those two men. In fact, I'm sorry for anyone forced to work for the GWR.'

'Father!' scolded Madeleine.

'Brunel was to blame. He and his father designed that tunnel. If it had been built much wider then it couldn't have been so easily blocked when a train was derailed. One track might have remained in use.'

'Robert will find out the full details,' said Lydia, trying to calm the old man down. 'Until then, it's pointless to speculate on what went wrong. But I must say that it's unfair of you to blame the late Mr Brunel.'

'I agree,' said Madeleine. 'It's unfair and unkind.'

'I don't want to hear of any drivers or firemen being hurt on the railway,' he said. 'I've been badly injured myself, so I know how dangerous it is to work on the footplate. But I still think that this latest accident is typical of the GWR because it . . .'

His voice tailed off as he saw the look in his daughter's eye.

'Let's talk about something else,' said Madeleine, firmly. 'What will Helena think of her grandfather if all you can do is to crow over a rival railway company? She's been dying for you to come.'

As if to reinforce the point, the child grabbed a doll from the sofa and put it into the old man's arms as a kind of peace offering.

Andrews had the grace to look shamefaced.

CHAPTER FOUR

The detectives worked as hard and unstintingly as the railway policemen. Having lugged their valises to the top of the bank, Colbeck and Leeming went back down again to offer an arm to anyone in difficulty and help them negotiate the steep climb. Once they'd reached the top, they repeated the process time and again, assisting others unable to manage on their own. One elderly lady needed both of them to steer her safely up the incline. Eventually, all the passengers had reached the summit where an array of vehicles awaited them. First class passengers were offered open carriages, while those in second class were guided to a phalanx of traps. Third class travellers had to settle for an assortment of carts, hastily assembled from nearby farms and covered in a thick layer of straw to hide the muck and stifle the stink.

'What about us?' asked Leeming.

'I'm sure that Mr Rydall will have organised some transport for us, Victor.'

'I hope it's not one of those carts. I can smell them from here.'

'One can't be too selective in an emergency,' said Colbeck. 'If you'll forgive a naval metaphor, it's a case of all hands to the pumps. Ah,' he added, as a thickset man with a greying beard walked across to them, 'it looks as if we've been recognised.'

'Inspector Colbeck?' asked the newcomer, looking from one to the other.

'That's me,' said Colbeck, 'and this is Sergeant Leeming.'

'I'm Sidney Walters, and I'm to take you both to Mr Rydall.'

'Thank you very much.'

'Follow me, please.'

Walters set off with the detectives at his heels. He was polite and well-spoken with a distinctive Gloucestershire burr. Judging by his manner and appearance, Colbeck guessed that he was employed by Rydall in a senior capacity. As he opened the door of an open-topped carriage for them to get in, the man confirmed it.

'I manage the estate,' he explained. 'As a rule, Mr Rydall would have sent someone else to meet you, but there's nobody available. All of our labourers have been drafted into the team trying to clear the line and that goes for some of the servants from The Grange as well. It's a crisis. Everybody has to do his share. It will take days, if not a week or more.'

Colbeck and Leeming clambered into the carriage and put their luggage on the seats opposite them. Ahead of them, the last of the passengers were being driven away. Hauling himself up into his seat, Walters flicked the reins and the horse set off. The carriage bounced its way across the grass.

'We understand that your shepherd has disappeared,' said Colbeck.

'Yes, he has,' said Walters over his shoulder.

'Does anyone know why?'

'Edgar just went. It is most unlike him. I fear trouble.'

'Why is that?'

'He loves what he does, and, in any case, he has a family to support. Edgar would never let us down. Clearly, he went against his will.'

'What about his sheepdog?'

'Blackie has vanished as well.'

'Has anyone searched for them?'

'Will is doing that right now. He's Edgar's son. His sister, Annie, went with him. If he's anywhere on Rydall land, they'll find him. They know every inch of the estate.'

'Has he ever gone off like this before?'

'Never,' said Walters, grimly. 'He'd be too afraid of me to do anything so stupid. That's why I'm worried about him. What Edgar Smayle has done is quite out of character.'

Alan Hinton was in luck. He not only got safely back to Scotland Yard before his absence was noted, he was instantly recruited to assist in making an arrest. A man responsible for a string of burglaries had been finally traced to his lair. Since

Hinton had helped to amass the evidence against him, it gave him a feeling of deep satisfaction to be involved in catching the man. It was not, however, a simple operation.

Even though he had a sergeant and another detective constable with him, the arrest was fraught with difficulties. The burglar's den was in a tenement in one of the more insalubrious districts of the city. It was a place where policemen – especially those in plain clothes – were reviled. When they arrived, they collected angry stares and muttered expletives from other residents. To their delight, the man they were after was at home, in bed with a prostitute he'd picked up for company. Startled by the arrival of three detectives who forced their way in, he jumped naked from the bed and began to fight them as if his life was in danger. The woman screeched and pummelled away at them with puny fists, before using her nails as claws. It was all they could do to subdue the pair and lead them, partly clothed, out of the building in handcuffs. The detectives were jeered at by passers-by.

It was only when their prisoners were in custody that the three of them could assess the damage. Hinton had got off lightly, sustaining only a scratch on his nose and a torn sleeve. The other detective constable had facial bruises and was completely dishevelled, but it was the sergeant who'd suffered the most. Since he'd been the one to grapple with the naked burglar, he was bitten on the cheek, given a shining black eye and had his whole face covered in vengeful spit. Needing to attend to his wounds and appearance, he gave Hinton the privilege of reporting their success to the superintendent.

Like most people at Scotland Yard, Hinton approached Edward Tallis's office with a degree of hesitation, fearing what he might find on the other side of the door. The fact that he was actually bearing good news was no guarantee that he'd escape without criticism. Tallis was bound to notice the ugly scratch on his face and the torn sleeve. After taking a deep breath, Hinton tapped on the door, heard a growled command to enter and went into the office. Tallis was in the act of stubbing out his cigar, smoke still curling in the air around him like mist encircling a mountain peak.

'What is it?' he demanded.

'Sergeant Vaughan sent me to report an arrest, sir.'

'Then don't just stand there, man. Do as you were told.'

Having rehearsed what he was going to say, Hinton delivered the report succinctly. Tallis remembered the spate of burglaries and was glad that the culprit was now behind bars. There was, however, no word of praise or congratulation. Hinton had learnt not to expect it. Some fifteen or more months earlier, he'd been instrumental in saving Tallis's life when the latter was abducted by two former soldiers from his old regiment. And there were other ways in which the young detective had been of enormous help to the superintendent. It was rarely acknowledged, and Tallis would sometimes walk past him without even recognising Hinton.

Waiting to be dismissed, the visitor hovered.

'Your sleeve is torn,' said Tallis, disapprovingly.

'The prisoner and his . . . female acquaintance resisted arrest, sir.'

'What's that on your nose?'

'In the course of a fight, it was scratched.'

'Get it seen to.'

'Yes, sir.'

'And the same goes for that sleeve.' Tallis flicked his hand to send the detective constable on his way then changed his mind. 'Wait!' Hinton raised an enquiring eyebrow. 'You've done well – exceptionally well – and I'm not referring to today's exploits. Thank you very much.'

Hinton walked out of the office with a broad smile on his face.

In other circumstances, they might have enjoyed the drive through the beautiful wooded valley of the River Frome. Every so often, a carpet of wild daffodils would come into view, swaying gently in the wind and lending an extra radiance. As they picked their way along, glorious vistas greeted them, but there was only limited time to admire them. They suddenly came out of the trees, reached the cutting and looked down at the western portal of the Sapperton Tunnel. Even though they had some idea what to expect, Colbeck and Leeming were shocked. What confronted them was a scene of utter devastation.

Looking forlorn and wounded, the locomotive lay on its side with the coal from its tender scattered far and wide. Behind it were a number of wagons that had also been derailed and deprived of whatever freight they'd been carrying. The bulk of the rolling stock was still inside the tunnel, and they could only imagine what destruction had been caused there.

'Is the tunnel itself badly damaged?' asked Colbeck.

'Yes,' replied Walters. 'A lot of the brickwork was badly chipped. Navvies will have to make extensive repairs to the walls, but they can't even start to do that until the mess inside the tunnel is cleared away.'

'It's reminiscent of a case we had in Scotland. Do you remember, Victor? In that instance also, the whole train had been deliberately derailed to cause maximum damage.' He turned to his companion. 'Don't you agree?'

But Leeming hadn't even heard him. His attention was fixed elsewhere. After the initial shock of viewing the hideous scene outside the tunnel, his gaze had drifted to the canal that ran parallel with the railway. Narrowboats were being pulled by horses and skimmed the water, blithely unconcerned at the tragedy that had happened not far away. The contrast could not have been starker, and it prompted a comment from the sergeant.

'Water is a safer way to travel,' he murmured.

Dozens of people were working hard around the stricken locomotive and its overturned wagons, moving debris away and retrieving the freight that had been spilt across the grass before placing it in a series of piles. A hundred yards down the track, the last of the passengers from the train on which Colbeck and Leeming had travelled were climbing gratefully into the carriages of a replacement that would take them on to Stroud, Stonehouse, Gloucester or Cheltenham. What they'd leave behind them was a scene of frenetic activity.

Standing in the middle of it and imposing whatever control he could was Stephen Rydall, a tall, striking man in his sixties with a bushy moustache and an air of unforced authority. He'd been there for long, punishing hours, refusing to have a rest or pause for refreshment because he was driven on by a sense of duty. The outrage had occurred on his doorstep and caused untold damage to property owned by the railway company in which he held an important position. What had been inflicted upon them, therefore, had great personal relevance to him.

Having yelled orders to all and sundry, Rydall broke off to help one of his farm labourers move a heavy spar of timber out of the way. When he pulled himself back up to his full height, he noticed two figures striding towards him. Realising who they must be, he felt a surge of relief. Identifying at a glance which one of them was the senior detective, he shook Colbeck's hand with an edge of desperation, then exchanged a handshake with Leeming.

'I'm Stephen Rydall,' he said. 'I cannot tell you how grateful I am to see you, gentlemen. I've had glowing reports of the way you solved that murder in Swindon.'

'We've had failures as well as successes,' warned Colbeck.

'The GWR is eternally gratefully for what you did there.'

'We grew to like Swindon,' Leeming put in. 'We stayed at the Queen's Tap where they serve the best—'

'Mr Rydall is not interested in our memoirs,' said Colbeck, cutting in and shooting the sergeant a warning look. He turned back to Rydall. 'When exactly did it happen, sir?'

'It must have been close to six o'clock this morning, Inspector. It was the first train of the day through the Sapperton Tunnel.'

'Who raised the alarm?'

'That would be Peter Doble, the landlord of the Daneway Inn. It's by the western portal of the canal tunnel,' said Rydall, pointing a finger. 'As you can imagine, there was a terrible noise. Others further afield would have heard it – I certainly did – but Doble was the first to react.'

'That's a job for you, Sergeant,' said Colbeck. 'Make your way to this inn and interview Mr Doble. Mr Walters will show you the way. Find out exactly what the landlord saw when he came over here.'

'Yes, sir,' said Leeming.

'And bear in mind that you are not there to discuss the quality of his beer but to investigate a crime that's had the most terrible consequences. Is that understood?'

'Yes, of course, Inspector.'

'When we first saw the wreckage,' said Colbeck as Leeming walked away, 'we both had the same reaction. We wanted to take off our coats and join in the clearance work.'

'You're far better employed finding out who caused this havoc,' said Rydall. 'It hasn't just torn up our timetable on this stretch of the line, it's going to be very costly. Much of the freight has been damaged beyond repair. One of the wagons was carrying boxes of fruit when it smashed into the side of the tunnel. Everything was squashed flat. The wagon looks as if it bled to death.'

'The GWR will be bombarded by claims.'

'That's only the start of it, Inspector.'

'The safety of your employees is of paramount concern,' said Colbeck. 'Your telegraph mentioned injury to the driver and fireman.'

'They're both still alive, thank God – more or less, anyway.'

'Were they badly hurt?'

'The one consolation was that they were hurled clear of the

engine itself, so they were not crushed beneath it. Nevertheless, they both suffered serious fractures and Treece, the fireman, is still in a coma.'

'Is the driver in a state to be interviewed?'

'I think so.'

'Where is he?'

'I had both men moved to The Grange – that's my home. It's fairly close and, luckily, there's a doctor in Frampton Mansell. Wyatt is a good man and a neighbour of mine. He spent twenty years as an army doctor. You can imagine the hideous sights he must have seen during the Crimean War. He saved the lives of soldiers with horrific injuries. I hope he can do the same with his latest patients.'

'I look forward to meeting him,' said Colbeck. 'First, however, I'd like to know why those sheep were killed.'

'So would I,' said Rydall, ruefully.

'Putting them in the path of a train seems so unnecessary.'

'It was an act of unforgivable cruelty.'

'How many of them were there?'

'Seven.'

Colbeck was startled. It was a number with biblical significance.

CHAPTER FIVE

Caleb Andrews was not a man given to introspection. Active, outgoing and passionately interested in the operation of the railway company for which he'd worked, he rarely had the time – or the need – to address a problem by thinking deeply about it. That had now changed. When he talked about the blocking of the Sapperton Tunnel, his scorn for the Great Western Railway had been roundly criticised by his daughter. Her friend, Lydia Quayle, had also shown her disapproval of his attitude. While he still enjoyed the pleasure of seeing his granddaughter, a shadow descended over his visit to the Colbeck residence. Andrews felt quashed, uneasy and in disgrace. He vowed to be less ready to criticise the GWR so routinely.

On his way back home, his sense of guilt increased. He was particularly sorry for the flippant comment he'd made about the driver and fireman of the train. They were men who did exactly what he'd done for so many years and deserved to be treated as kindred spirits. He'd known colleagues who'd been flung from their locomotive when it was derailed. In some cases, he'd attended their funerals and saw the effect that their deaths had had on their respective families. There'd been scant compensation for such searing losses.

Andrews recalled his own experience. When a train he was driving was flagged down and robbed, he'd refused to do what he'd been told and had been knocked senseless. He thought of how he would feel if he'd been told that employees of the GWR had laughed with glee at his plight simply because he worked for the London and North Western Railway. In reality, there'd been no mockery from anywhere. He'd received nothing but pity from other railwaymen. Why had he been unable to find the same sympathy for victims of a criminal act on a GWR line?

By the time he got home, his guilt had hardened into something far more insistent than simple remorse. Somehow Andrews had to make amends. The only way he could do that, he decided, was to visit the site of the crash and see the full extent of the damage. Even though it meant travelling on the broad gauge track he despised, he'd go to the place where his son-in-law was trying to identify those responsible for the attack on the Great Western Railway. It would be a form of atonement.

It did not take long for Victor Leeming to reach the Daneway Inn. Situated beside the Thames and Severn Canal, it was a long, low building of local stone, comprising three houses that had been joined together. Before he went towards it, he stopped to admire the portal to the tunnel, a minor work of art with crenellation worthy of a small castle. A narrowboat was moored nearby. Tethered to stakes, four horses were nibbling at the grass. In the little garden at the front of the inn were some tables and benches. A small group of bargees was sitting there over a half-eaten meal. Leeming climbed up from the canal and exchanged a greeting with them. Before he could go into the inn, the landlord came out with a tankard of beer in his hand. When Leeming tried to introduce himself, Peter Doble stopped him with a raised palm.

'I know who you are,' he said. 'Mr Rydall told me that he'd sent for you and you're very welcome. Sit yourself down, sir, and sample this.'

Doble lowered himself onto an empty bench and put the tankard on the table. Leeming needed no more encouragement. He took his place beside the landlord. Doble was a sturdy, bearded man in his fifties with the kind of friendly face that put newcomers at their ease. He waited until Leeming had sampled the beer and given a nod of appreciation.

'The Daneway is at your disposal, Inspector.'

'Actually, I'm only a detective sergeant – Victor Leeming.'

'I'm Peter Doble. Me and Molly, my wife, run this place.'

'It's a lovely spot,' said Leeming, shaking hands with him. 'How long is the canal tunnel?'

'Over two miles, Sergeant. When it were built seventy years or more ago, it was the longest tunnel of any kind in the whole country.'

'That's impressive.'

'Taking a boat through it is thirsty work. That's why there's an inn at both ends of the tunnel. After legging that distance, you need a drink.'

'Legging?'

'Haven't you noticed something about the canal?'

'No,' said Leeming. 'What was I supposed to see?'

'The towpath stops at the portal. Horses can pull the barges up to this point then it has to rely on strong pairs of thighs. That's why they fit wings to the bows.'

'Wings?' echoed Leeming. 'Is it going to fly?'

'A wing is a flat piece of board, rigged for the purpose. Two men lie on them and use their legs on the side and roof of the tunnel to keep the barge moving. It's back-breaking work.'

'I believe you. I could never do it.'

Doble chuckled. 'It would ruin that coat of yours.'

'What about those horses?' asked Leeming.

'They'll be taken overland to the eastern portal in Coates. Later on today, the bargees you see here will be quaffing their beer at the Tunnel House Inn. From that point on, the horses will take the strain, working in pairs and moving at a steady canter.'

'It sounds like a hard life to me.'

'They get used to it,' said Doble. 'Anyway, you didn't come to talk about the canal. It's the crash that interests you, isn't it?'

'Yes,' said Leeming. 'I gather that you raised the alarm.'

'I ran all the way to the tunnel and saw what had happened. It made my stomach heave, I can tell you.'

'What did you do?'

'I looked to see if the driver and fireman were still alive, then raced back here and saddled my horse. I galloped straight to Mr Rydall's house and told him what I'd discovered.'

'Before you left the railway tunnel, did you see anyone?'

'The place was deserted – apart from the two injured men, that is.'

'How much light was there?'

'Oh, it'd just broken through.'

'So, if someone had been there, you'd have spotted them.'

'I daresay I would've, but the place was deserted. It's no more than I expected. I mean, why *should* there be anyone there?'

'There's a simple answer to that.'

'Is there?'

'Someone might have wanted to gloat over what they'd just done.'

Stephen Rydall was reluctant to leave the site of the crash, but he knew how important it was for Colbeck to question the driver of the doomed train. He therefore took the inspector to a waiting trap and invited him to climb in. As they took their seats, Rydall noticed the spots of mud on his passenger's shoes and trousers.

'I'm sorry that you had to climb up that embankment,' he said, 'but we had to get you to this end of the tunnel somehow.'

'It would have been much easier for us to get off at Kemble.'

'That was not possible, I'm afraid.'

'You could have had us picked up there.'

'Nothing would have pleased me more,' said Rydall, 'but Kemble is only an interchange station. There's no road access out of it. Passengers who alight there catch the train to Cirencester on the branch line.'

Colbeck was surprised. 'It's not a proper railway station?'

'Squire Etheridge made it a condition that no station should be built on his land. He also insisted that the railway south of the junction should pass through a cut-and-cover tunnel so that he couldn't see it from his house. Unfortunately, we were forced to comply. When he sits up there in Kemble Court,' said Rydall with asperity, 'he can pretend that the railway doesn't exist.'

'Was he really so uncooperative?'

'Etheridge drove a hard bargain, Inspector. You won't believe the amount that the GWR had to pay him for the land he so grudgingly sold to us. I was involved in the negotiations so I know just how obstructive and demanding he was.'

Having set the horse in motion, he went on to describe how the section of line around Kemble was finally built. Colbeck had warmed to the man the moment he met him and was impressed by the work Rydall had clearly done on behalf of the GWR. His companion was a mixture of gentleman farmer and railway pioneer, tending the huge acreage that had been in his family for generations while embracing the commercial opportunities of the latest developments in transport.

'This local squire can't stand in the way of progress,' said Colbeck. 'Railways are here to stay. Surely, he can see the benefits they bring.'

'All that he can talk about is the disruption.'

'What manner of man is he?'

'He's a very strange one, Inspector. Some people make allowances for his eccentricity, but the majority find him rude, domineering and nakedly self-interested.'

'How much power does he have in the area?'

Rydall gritted his teeth. 'Far too much,' he said. 'Maddeningly, he refuses to accept the advances that railways represent. They're truly revolutionary. When I was a young lad, I once travelled with my father from Gloucester to London by canal. Our average speed was . . . leisurely.'

'What's that in miles per hour?'

'Eight at most – we had to go through an endless series of locks. I loved it at the time, of course, but the journey was interminable. Express trains can now do it in well under four hours.'

'That obviously doesn't impress Squire Etheridge.'

'He simply complains about the noise and smoke we generate.'

'How will he react to news of the crash?'

'Frankly,' said Rydall, turning to him. 'I wouldn't like to be there when he finds out.'

Gilbert Etheridge was a tall, angular man of seventy with a gaunt face featuring a hooked nose that kept two dark, smouldering eyes apart. He was, by inclination, a night hawk, working or reading well into the small hours, then sleeping until early afternoon. Neither his wife, who occupied the adjoining bedroom, nor his servants dared to rouse him from his slumber. They had to wait patiently until he stirred enough to reach out for the bell beside his four-poster.

When the distinctive tinkle was finally heard that day, a servant knocked on the door before going into the bedroom.

'Good day to you, sir,' he said.

'What kind of weather do we have?'

'It's a lovely spring day, sir.'

Etheridge sat up in bed. 'Is there any news to report?' he asked.

'There's been a bad accident on the railway.'

'How bad?'

'The Sapperton Tunnel is completely blocked, sir.'

'And?'

'A goods train has come off the line.'

Etheridge laughed with satisfaction.

When he talked about life on the canal, Peter Doble spoke a foreign language. Terms like 'breast', 'chalico', 'galley beam', 'gauging', 'keb', 'risers', 'stud' and 'trow' left Victor Leeming bemused. One word made him blink.

'Gongoozler?' he repeated.

'That's right, Sergeant.'

'What does it mean?'

'A gongoozler is an idle person who stands staring for a long time at anything sort of out of the ordin'ry. In other words, there's something not right about a man like that.'

'Have you ever seen a gongoozler around here?'

'Oddly enough,' said Doble, 'I have.'

'When was this?'

'It was earlier this week. A man stood down by the portal and stared at it for ages. He was dressed like a proper gentleman, but there was something strange about him. We were very busy that day so I couldn't pay much attention to him, but my wife saw him take out this notebook and draw something in it.'

'What was it, do you think?'

'We've no idea. After a couple of hours, he sneaked off.'

'Didn't he come here for a drink?'

'It was as if he hardly noticed The Daneway,' said Doble.

'How old would he be?'

'Much older than you, I'd say.'

'Was he on foot?'

'We didn't see a horse or a trap,' replied the landlord. 'He was just there. That's why I'd call him a gongoozler. He came out of the blue and just stared in silence.'

Leeming made a mental note of the incident so that he could report it to Colbeck. He then turned to a person who was of greater interest to him.

'Does Edgar Smayle ever come here?'

Doble nodded. 'He comes whenever he can.'

'He likes his beer, then.'

'Edgar likes it far too much, Sergeant.'

'What do you mean?'

'He sometimes has one pint too many and turns nasty. He usually ends up trying to pick a fight with a bargee.'

'That isn't a wise thing to do,' said Leeming, glancing at those nearby. 'They look like strong men to me. I suppose they'd have to be if they work on the canal.'

'They swear at Edgar, but they never dare to tackle him.'

'Why not?'

'He always has Blackie with him – that's his sheepdog. If anyone takes a step towards his master, Blackie will bare his teeth and let out this growl. It's enough to make any man back away.'

'It sounds to me as if Smayle makes enemies very easily.'

'It's true,' said Doble. 'Fair's fair, Edgar is the best shepherd in the county. You can't fault him. When he is at work – and he is on duty seven days a week – he never steps out of line.'

'That's what Mr Walters told us.'

'And there was something else he did well. His son, Will, came into this world without much between his ears. It's a sad business, really. Will's nickname is Badger Brain. Edgar is wonderful with him. He knows how to get the best out of the lad and treats Will as if there's nothing really wrong with him.'

'That shows a good side to Smayle.'

'Oh, he certainly has that. Once he's taken a drop, it's a different story. Every so often, I ban him for a month or two. When he comes back, he is on his best behaviour for a while. Then it'll start all over again. He'll get into an argument with another bargee.'

'Did you know that he'd disappeared?

'Yes – Mr Walters told me.'

'What do you think has happened to him?'

'I wish I knew,' said the garrulous landlord.

On the journey to his house, Stephen Rydall had also been talking about the shepherd. He told Colbeck that he feared the worst. Smayle would never have dreamt of hurting any of his sheep, and his dog would have fought hard to protect them. The only way that the man would have disappeared was if someone had taken him prisoner. Walters had reached the same conclusion.

'Why would anyone do that?' asked Colbeck.

'It might have been an act of revenge.'

'Does your shepherd have enemies?'

'Not so far as I know,' said Rydall, 'but *I* certainly do. Getting rid of a man on whom I rely so much is a means of striking at me.'

'I'll need the names of these so-called enemies.'

'I'll be happy to provide them, Inspector.'

'Is it conceivable that Squire Etheridge is one of them?'

'There's certainly no love lost between us, but I refuse to believe that he'd stoop to anything like this. It's the work of some madman who hates me and who knows that the way to hurt me most is to damage the GWR as much as possible.'

'I disagree, Mr Rydall.'

'Really? I'm shocked to hear you say that.'

'I've been thinking it through,' said Colbeck. 'I believe that the person responsible for the crash did have a conscience. They deliberately arranged for the disaster to involve a goods train. If they'd wanted the GWR to suffer even more, they'd have picked a passenger train instead. All we have to worry about is the two men on the footplate. If a train with hundreds of people aboard had gone haring through that tunnel, there'd have been carnage.'

'It could be pure coincidence that it was a goods train.'

'There's no coincidence here. What I see is evidence of careful planning. If they'd wanted to target a passenger train, it would have been easy to do so. They could simply look at the timetable. What they *couldn't* do, however, was to consult a timetable for goods trains.'

Rydall was alarmed. 'What are you suggesting, Inspector?'

'The person must have had help from someone employed by the GWR,' said Colbeck, 'someone who knew exactly when that goods train would be coming through the Sapperton Tunnel.'

CHAPTER SIX

Will Smayle was a sturdy young man of twenty, wearing a shepherd's smock and a battered hat. His eyes, two pools of dismay, seemed to be too large for his face and his mouth was agog. Walking alongside him was his sister, Annie, older, slighter and clearly in charge of the search. From time to time, she called out for her father, but there was never an answer. As they came to some bushes, Will used his crook to push them apart and his dog, Meg, took it as a signal for her to plunge into the undergrowth. She began to bark excitedly, but all she managed to do was to flush a rabbit out of its hiding place. Meg went tearing after it, but her master wanted her beside him. As soon as he whistled, she skidded to a halt and trotted obediently back towards him.

'You should have let Meg catch it,' said Annie. 'We can always do with a tasty rabbit to eat.'

'We came for Father,' argued her brother, the words tumbling slow and misshapen from his mouth. 'He's all that matters, Annie.'

'I know. You're right.'

'Must find him . . .'

Will pressed on with the dog at his heels. His sister followed in his wake. Her father's disappearance had been a shock, but it seemed to have had one positive result. It had given Will a determination he'd never shown before. Because of his limitations, Annie was still in charge, but her brother was nevertheless striding ahead purposefully. Their search had been long and thorough, covering all the places where their father would go on a regular basis. After hours on their feet, however, they hadn't found the slightest trace of him or of his dog.

Seeing that Will was becoming more agitated, Annie caught him up so that she could walk beside him and try to calm him down. It was a futile exercise. Nothing could take away the nagging fear he had for his father's safety. Will couldn't remember a time when his father had left the house without telling them where he was going. It was something Will needed to know all the time. As a rule, Edgar Smayle took him almost everywhere. The one place Will was never allowed to go to was the Daneway Inn. His father didn't want him mocked by anyone because of his obvious shortcomings.

After crossing a field, they came to the edge of Rydall's property. The five-barred gate in the drystone wall was secured by a chain and padlock. After first shaking it, Will began to climb over the gate. Annie put a restraining hand on his arm.

'You can't go there,' she said.

'Why not?'

'It belongs to Packwood Farm. Look at that sign.'

'What does it say?' he asked, unable to read the words on the board in front of him. 'Tell me, Annie.'

'It says that trespassers will be prosecuted.'

'Father might be there.'

'He'd have no reason to go anywhere near Packwood Farm.'

'He could be there, Annie,' insisted Will, climbing over the gate. 'I've got to keep looking till I find him.'

When he landed on the other side of the gate, Meg joined him by creeping under it. Anxious to widen the search, her brother pressed on, and Annie was left standing there, not knowing quite what to do.

While the landlord went back into the inn, Leeming took the opportunity to take out his notebook and record many of the things he'd been told. His brief insight into the lives of canal folk had inspired him to learn more, and he was soon chatting with the bargees. Doble eventually reappeared with a fresh tankard. When he put the beer on the table in front of the sergeant, the latter raised both hands.

'I can't drink that,' he protested,

'It's on the house.'

'That makes no difference.'

'You drank the first pint quickly enough.'

'I know. I admit it.'

'Don't you like our beer?'

'I love it,' said Leeming, 'and that's the problem. I'm not allowed to drink alcohol on duty. It's a strict rule.'

'Who's going to know what you do?'

'I am, and I'm feeling guilty enough already.'

'Just take a few sips,' advised the other, nudging him. 'Then you won't feel guilty at all. Go on, Sergeant. You deserve it.'

'Stop trying to lead me astray.'

With his notebook open, he fired another salvo of questions at the landlord and jotted down his answers. All the time he was doing it, he could see the tankard out of the corner of his eye.

The Grange was a sprawling manor house on the edge of Frampton Mansell. To get to it, they had to drive past a row of weavers' cottages, built centuries earlier when sheep farmers and wool merchants had flourished and made the Cotswolds famous. Rydall pulled the horse to a halt on the drive. As he climbed out of the vehicle, Colbeck was struck by how many outhouses there were. The main building had a solid, almost utilitarian appearance though there were a few architectural features that lent it a degree of charm.

Before they reached the front door, a servant opened it so that they could step into the hallway. A grey-haired man in his late fifties came down the corridor towards them. He'd removed his coat and rolled up his shirtsleeves. A gold watch protruded from his waistcoat pocket. Rydall introduced Colbeck to Dr Roland Wyatt, who was already extending a hand to the inspector.

'I'm very pleased to meet you, Doctor,' said Colbeck as they shook hands. 'How are your two patients?'

'One is in a considerably better state than the other, I fear,' replied Wyatt in a deep, educated voice. 'The fireman is still in a coma and all I've been able to do is to make him reasonably comfortable. The driver, Poulter, has splints on his fractures. He also had so many bruises that even his wife wouldn't recognise him.'

'Is he able to talk?'

'It's impossible to stop him, Inspector.'

'May I speak to him?'

'If you can get a word in,' said Wyatt, chortling. 'When I came to this village, I thought I'd retired then, all of a sudden, I'm roused from my bed at dawn for an emergency. It was just like old times. Thanks to you, Stephen, I've had the thrill of using my medical skills again. I feel useful.'

'You were far more than that,' said Rydall. 'By getting to the tunnel so quickly, you probably saved the fireman's life.'

'Not exactly – it's still hanging in the balance.'

'Is there no hope, Roland?'

'I've had to resort to prayer.'

'Where's the driver?' asked Colbeck.

'I'll take you to him,' said Rydall, indicating the corridor ahead of them then setting off. 'I had them kept on the ground floor. Getting them here was something of a trial. Poulter groaned the whole way. I didn't want him joggled about even more by carrying him up two flights of stairs. I thought it was important to get both men away from a scene they'd find very distressing. Dr Wyatt agreed.'

Colbeck followed him through a door at the back of the house and out into a yard. They went into a stable block that had been converted into servant accommodation. Rydall tapped on a door then opened it, ushering the inspector in before closing the door behind them. A sorry sight greeted them. Oliver Poulter was propped up in a single bed. An arm and a leg were in splints and his face and hands were covered in bruises. Blood had turned his fringe beard red. In spite of the pain it caused, he managed a brave smile.

'What's the news about Len?' he asked.

'He's doing as well as can be expected,' replied Rydall.

'When can I see him?'

'Treece is not ready for that yet.'

'Is he able to speak?'

'No,' said Colbeck, taking his cue, 'but you obviously are. My name is Inspector Colbeck. I'm a detective from Scotland Yard and I've been sent to investigate what is clearly a very serious crime.'

'I'll say it was,' attested Poulter. 'It damn near done for us.'

'Do you feel able to talk about what happened?'

'Yes, Inspector, I do. What would you like to know?'

'Everything you can remember.'

Travelling on the broad gauge of the Great Western Railway was in the nature of an ordeal for Caleb Andrews, but he forced himself to do it. When he'd bought his ticket, he'd been warned that the train would stop at the eastern portal of the Sapperton Tunnel and that he'd have to climb up a grassy bank if he wished to go beyond it. Andrews was not deterred. Having kept himself active, he was still sprightly for his age. In fact, he was looking forward to the challenge. It would help him to keep his mind off the smooth and comfortable journey he was now experiencing in a train belonging to a company he'd always detested.

Will Smayle went blundering on, searching desperately for his father. Meg danced around him as if they were playing some sort of game. Several yards behind him was his sister, Annie, unable to control her brother and afraid that they'd get into trouble. When he reached a copse, Will plunged straight in, looking behind every tree and bush. It was when he reached a clearing that he was brought to a dead halt. A tall, burly figure stepped out from behind an elm to block his way by raising his shotgun. The gamekeeper eyed him with suspicion.

'You must have seen the sign. Can't you read?'

Will tried to answer, but the words that dribbled out of him were incomprehensible. The man took a step closer.

'Talk English.'

Annie came running into the clearing and stood beside her brother. Will, meanwhile, made an effort to get some words out, but they made no sense to the gamekeeper.

'What's this idiot trying to say?' he demanded.

'Will is my brother,' she said, proudly, 'and he's not an idiot.'

'Both of you are trespassing.'

'We're looking for my father.'

'Don't tell me that *he's* here as well.'

'You don't understand. He's disappeared and we've no idea where he is. His name is Edgar Smayle, and he works for Mr Rydall as a shepherd.'

'So do I,' Will struggled to say.

'We've searched the whole farm from end to end. I'm sorry that we're on your land now. We don't mean any harm, sir.'

'Edgar Smayle,' said the gamekeeper, curling a lip. 'I met him once or twice at The Daneway and I can't say I took to him. In fact, we had words. But that doesn't mean I wish him any harm,' he added, voice softening. 'All I can tell you is that he's nowhere on Packwood Farm. I can *smell* intruders, and there's no whiff of him.'

'It's not the only terrible thing that's happened,' explained Annie. 'There's been a train crash that's blocked the Sapperton Tunnel.'

The man was shocked. 'Are you serious?'

'It's true,' she said. 'I swear it. The train was derailed. We saw the mess ourselves, but all we want to do is to find our father. He went off somewhere in the night and hasn't been seen since. We're desperate to find him.'

Though he talked at length, Oliver Poulter was able to tell them very little that had a direct bearing on how and why the tunnel had been deliberately blocked. Apart from anything else, he was still dazed by the experience. He was also guilt-ridden. As the driver of the train, he had responsibility for the safe delivery of the freight and feared that he'd be severely criticised.

'There's nothing you could have done,' Colbeck assured him.

'The GWR will place no blame on you,' said Rydall. 'If anything, we should be apologising. We take the safety of our staff very seriously.'

'It's my wife I worry about,' admitted the driver. 'Did you send that telegraph you promised, sir?'

'Not in person, as it happens, but I had it sent from the telegraph station at Stroud. Since both you and Treece live in Gloucester, it was addressed to the police there. They'll be in touch with your respective families.'

'Len's not married so there's no wife to break the news to, but I am, and Nancy'll be wondering why I didn't come home hours ago.'

'Word might well have reached her by now.'

'I'd hate her to see me looking like this.'

'Knowing that you're still alive will be a comfort in itself,' said Colbeck. 'The doctor obviously feels that you'll make a good recovery. His opinion should hearten Mrs Poulter.'

'I'll make sure I pass it on to her,' said Rydall. 'Meanwhile, you'll be kept here with Treece until the pair of you are well enough to be moved to hospital.'

Poulter was concerned. 'Me and Len don't want to impose, sir.'

'It's no imposition, believe me.'

'You're very kind, Mr Rydall.'

'Needless to say, I've been in touch with the relevant people in the GWR. They know that the pair of you will be unable to work for some time and are already organising replacements for your shifts. Once the tunnel is finally cleared,' he said, trying to inject a note of confidence, 'we'll carry on as if the crash was nothing but a bad dream.'

'You're forgetting something,' said Colbeck.

'Am I?'

'There's the small matter of a missing shepherd.'

* * *

Though his voice was gruff and his manner intimidating, the gamekeeper said that he would take no action against them for trespassing on the property. He also agreed to look out for their father and promised to send word if he found Edgar Smayle somewhere on Packwood Farm. Will and Annie trudged back to the wall that divided the two estates and climbed over the gate. Meg once again crawled beneath it.

Will was bewildered. 'What do we do now?'

'We go back home.'

'We need to look for Father.'

'They'll be worried sick about us, Will. They'll want news, even if it's bad news. And there's something else. Neither of us have eaten a thing today. We need food.' The dog yelped. 'And so does Meg.'

'You go back, Annie. I'll keep searching.'

'We must stick together.'

'I can manage.'

'No, you can't,' she said, firmly, 'and you know why. How would you have dealt with that gamekeeper if I hadn't been there to explain what we were doing? Alone with the sheep, you're fine. You do all the things Father taught you. With people, it's different. Some of them can be very cruel. That's why you need me there to protect you.'

His shoulders sagged. 'I know.'

'Let's go back home now.'

'But we've *failed*.'

'It's not our fault. Father has gone off somewhere, that's all.'

'He'd have *told* me, Annie.'

'We'll just have to hope that he comes back soon.'

'What are we going to say to everybody?'

'We tell them the truth,' she said, resignedly. 'Father's not here any more, and we haven't a clue where he's gone.'

When the train drew to a halt not far from the tunnel, Caleb Andrews was among the passengers who alighted before climbing up the embankment. Many people needed assistance, but he was proud of the fact that he got to the top without any help at all. A variety of vehicles was lined up to transfer them to the other end of the tunnel. On their way there, Andrews, sharing a trap, was interested to see passengers from the western end of the line coming towards them in a selection of carriages, traps and carts. Evidently, they would be travelling on the train that Andrews and the others had just abandoned. Though now operating a limited timetable on that line, the GWR was determined to keep it still functioning.

Arriving at his destination, Andrews got down from the trap and walked across to look down at the scene below. It made his stomach heave. Twisted metal and shattered wood littered the ground. Beneath it, he could see the mangled carcases of the sheep killed in the crash. Volunteers were still beavering away on the track, but they'd been joined by navvies now, men who'd helped to build the tunnel and were shaken when they saw the state it was in. Curious onlookers from nearby villages had also gathered, some with their eyes on the discharged contents of broken wagons. Railway policemen were guarding the entrance to the tunnel to keep out looters, but it would not be so easy to do that after dark.

Andrews stared at it all with a mingle of horror and shame. When he saw the engine tipped helplessly on its side, his heart went out to the driver and fireman. They were hapless victims of someone else's cruelty. He regretted what he'd said earlier about the GWR. Those who worked on the footplate were a special breed of men, united by their readiness to do a demanding job that was fraught with danger. He was sorry that he'd had to come all the way to Gloucestershire to be reminded of that. As he turned away, tears were coursing down his cheeks.

The temptation had been too great. Seated with Doble and the bargees, Leeming was soon caught up in the convivial atmosphere that developed. His hand went to the tankard for what he promised himself was a very small sip, then – without his even realising it – it drifted there again and again. Before he knew what was happening, he'd drunk over half a pint of beer.

'You'd make a good bargee,' said Doble. 'You've got the build for it. It's a good life when you get used to it. These men will tell you that.'

A ragged cheer went up from the bargees. Leeming shook his head.

'I like what I do, thank you very much,' he said.

'Isn't it dangerous?'

'I find that exciting.'

'Better you than me,' said Doble. 'I prefer a quiet life. I spend every day among friends.'

'Edgar Smayle wasn't very friendly. That's what you told me.'

'Drink up, Sergeant,' said the landlord, slapping him on the back. 'You're way behind everyone else. I took you to be a man who could hold his beer – especially if it was free.'

The bargees laughed, and Leeming joined in the merriment, his hand moving once again to the tankard. He was enjoying himself so much that he didn't see or hear the trap that emerged around the bend nearby. Even when it drew up next to the inn, he was unaware of its presence. It was only when a long shadow fell across the table that he realised Colbeck was standing there. Leeming was instantly sobered.

'Oh, I didn't see you there, Inspector.'

'So I observed,' said Colbeck, arching an eyebrow.

'I've . . . had a long talk to Mr Doble, the landlord.'

'That's me,' said Doble, getting up and offering his hand. Colbeck shook it. 'Can I offer you anything, sir?'

'I'm afraid not. Sergeant Leeming and I have work to do – if he's in a condition to leave, that is.'

'Of course, I am,' said the other, getting up at once. 'I'm fine, sir.'

He turned to Doble. 'Thank you for your help. I'm sorry to leave.'

The landlord grinned. 'Come back any time, Sergeant.'

'I will – goodbye, everybody.'

The bargees laughed and raised their tankards in farewell. Leeming followed Colbeck to the trap and climbed in beside him. As the horse trotted away, there was an ominous silence. It took Leeming a long time to find the courage to speak.

'Don't be misled by what you saw,' he began. 'I'd hardly touched that tankard of beer. The landlord more or less forced it on me. We had a long and very useful talk.'

'Please turn your head to the left when you speak,' suggested Colbeck. 'Then I won't have to inhale the smell of beer.'

Leeming quivered. 'Will you report me to the superintendent?'

'No, I won't.

'Thank you, thank you very much, sir.'

'If I did, he'd tear you limb from limb. At the very least, you'd be put back in uniform and reduced to the rank of constable. You're too good a detective to lose – when you obey the rules.'

'He forced the beer on me, sir,' protested Leeming.

'I didn't notice that there was any coercion involved. You seemed to be enjoying his company and that of those bargees. For their part,' said Colbeck, 'they all appeared to have accepted you as a drinking companion. They were obviously unaware of the fact that you were actually there to discuss a horrendous crime committed not that far away.'

'Mr Doble and I talked about nothing else.'

'I beg leave to doubt that.'

'Inspector—'

'Spare me your excuses. Just tell me what you learnt.'

While Colbeck concentrated on driving the trap along a winding track, Leeming fished out his notebook and flipped through the pages. He needed to compose himself before he was able to pass on the information he'd gathered. As he listened to it, Colbeck's face was impassive, but Leeming knew that the inspector was fuming inside. At the end of his recital, he tried to lighten the atmosphere.

'Do you know what a gongoozler is, sir?'

'I have a feeling that I might be sitting next to one.'

'It's a term used by bargees.'

'Is it in any way relevant to our investigation?'

'Well, not really . . .'

'Then I've no wish to hear anything about it.'

'Oh, I see.'

It was Colbeck's turn to recount what he'd found out. He talked about the visit to The Grange and his encounters with Roland Wyatt and Oliver Poulter. He'd seen the fireman for a few seconds and noted the extent of his injuries. Rydall had not only given them the use of the trap for as long as they needed it, he'd offered them accommodation in an annexe built near The Grange, and Colbeck had accepted when assured that he and Leeming would have their privacy respected there.

'What about meals?' asked Leeming.

'They'll be provided at our request. It transpires that Mr Rydall has an excellent cook and you'll be pleased to hear that – unlike the landlord of the Daneway Inn – he won't ever compel you to drink beer you don't really want.'

Leeming winced. 'Where are we going now, sir?'

'First of all, we'll drive to Stroud.'

'Why is that?'

'It has a telegraph station. I wish to contact the superintendent.'

'What about?' asked Leeming, nervously.

'*You* won't even be mentioned, I promise you. It's clear to me that this is going to be a complex and far-reaching investigation. I'll be asking for another detective to be assigned to the case.'

'Any help is always welcome, sir.'

'The person I'll request is Alan Hinton.'

'He'd be a good choice.'

'Let's hope that the superintendent agrees,' said Colbeck. 'Once we've sent the telegraph, we'll visit the family of the missing shepherd. We don't want them to feel neglected.'

As they drove on, they passed the crash site. Among the people gazing down at it, Leeming noticed someone who looked familiar.

'Isn't that your father-in-law, sir?' he asked.

Colbeck laughed. 'Don't be ridiculous.'

'Take a look for yourself.'

'There's no point.'

'He's very much like Mr Andrews.'

'Well, I can tell you now that it can't possibly be him.'

'Are you sure?'

'This is GWR territory,' said Colbeck, not even bothering to glance in the direction Leeming was pointing. 'My father-in-law would have to travel on Brunel's railway to get here. That would be anathema to him. Take my word for it,' he went on, confidently, 'the person over there is a complete stranger.'

CHAPTER SEVEN

None of the detectives at Scotland Yard liked to receive an urgent summons from the superintendent. More often than not, it meant that they'd receive harsh criticism rather than praise and creep away bruised and chastened. Alan Hinton felt the usual tremors as he knocked on the door and entered the room. Tallis was on his feet, adopting the stance he always used when about to excoriate one of his junior officers. Hinton ran his tongue over dry lips.

'What kept you?' demanded Tallis.

'I responded at once to your order, sir.'

'That was not my impression.'

'Then I apologise.'

'I expect an immediate response at all times, Hinton.'

'Yes, sir.'

'I've received a telegraph from Inspector Colbeck,' said Tallis, picking it up from his desk. 'He's in Gloucestershire.'

'Yes, I know.'

'Really?' Tallis glowered. '*How* do you know?'

Hinton regretted his mistake. If he told the truth, he'd be admitting that he'd taken time away from his duties to deliver a letter to Colbeck's wife. He'd not only be roundly condemned for doing so, Hinton would also get the inspector into trouble.

'Well,' said Tallis, glowering, 'I'm waiting.'

'I happened to see Sergeant Leeming as he was about to leave. He said something about a blocked tunnel in Gloucestershire. I don't know any of the details.'

'You soon will, Hinton.'

'What do you mean, sir?'

'Colbeck's telegraph contains a request for additional help. He names you. Do you think that you're equal to the challenge?'

'Yes, yes, Superintendent,' said Hinton, overcome with delight. 'It will be an honour to work with the inspector.'

'I'm not sending you there to be over-awed by his reputation,' warned Tallis, jabbing a finger at him. 'Colbeck doesn't want someone giving him applause all the time. He needs an able, committed officer who'll work twenty-four hours a day, if necessary, to catch whoever caused the disaster.'

'I won't let the inspector down,' promised Hinton.

'Don't you dare let *me* down either. I don't wish to find that I made the wrong decision in sending you there.'

'You won't have any cause for complaint, sir.'

'That applies to Colbeck and Leeming as well. When you meet up with them, please remind them of the standards I expect.'

Unable to keep a smile off his face, Hinton nodded. Tallis sat down again and reached for his cigar box. The detective was tentative.

'What are my orders, sir?'

'Disappear at once,' ordered Tallis. 'Get to the scene of the crime as soon as possible and show initiative. Above all else, justify the inspector's faith in you. This is a golden opportunity to show your mettle. Seize it with both hands, man.'

Hinton was out of the door in a flash.

When they reached the cottage, Leeming was startled. It seemed far too small to house the seven people they'd been told lived there. Built of local stone and coated with ivy, it had served generations of farm workers before it became the tied home of Edgar Smayle and his family. As soon as the trap pulled up outside the dwelling, Annie and Will came out with their mother. All three looked up hopefully for good news. After telling them that there was nothing to report, Colbeck introduced himself and Leeming, and assured them that every effort would be made to find the missing head of the family.

'Will and Annie went out looking for hours,' said their mother, Betsy Smayle, an emaciated woman whose red face was riddled with anxiety. 'They saw no sign of my husband.'

'It's true,' said Annie, sadly.

'He's gone,' added Will, eyes rolling and tongue distorting the words. 'We looked and looked.'

'Oh dear!' said Betsy, as if suddenly remembering the laws

of hospitality. 'We shouldn't keep you both out here like this. Will you come inside, please?'

'*I* will, Mrs Smayle,' replied Colbeck, getting out of the trap, 'but Sergeant Leeming can stay outside and talk to your children. They'll be able to tell him in detail about their search.'

'You do as the inspector says,' she told them. 'Let Annie do the talking, Will. She's got a better memory than you.'

Since he hadn't understood a word that Will had said, Leeming was relieved to hear that he'd only be questioning the girl. Stepping down from the trap, he took out his notepad. Colbeck, meanwhile, followed Betsy into the house and found himself in a cramped living room that obliged him to duck under low beams. Full of clutter, it had an unpleasant smell of stale food and dogs. Two other members of the family were there, Jesse and Mildred Smayle, an elderly couple who sat either side of the fireplace as if they were part of the furniture. Betsy introduced them by name, but they said nothing in response. Jesse was patently asleep and his wife, a gnarled, watchful crone, sat with skeletal hands folded in her lap.

'My own mother is an invalid,' explained Betsy. 'She stays upstairs most of the time, but we carry her down here for special occasions.'

She gave a wan smile, hoping that the detectives could provide such an occasion by finding her husband alive and well.

'Is he used to going out so early in the morning?' asked Colbeck.

'Oh, yes. He's on duty all the time. We've other shepherds – Will, for instance – but Edgar's in charge. He tells the others what to do and where to go.'

'When were you aware of his disappearance?'

'It would be not long after midnight, I suppose.'

'What did you do?'

'I did what I always do, Inspector,' she said. 'I turned over and went back to sleep.'

Colbeck didn't blame her. The woman needed all the rest she could get. Feeding and looking after the family put an enormous strain on her. The needs of her bedridden mother would be a particular burden. It was no wonder that Betsy looked so scrawny and careworn.

'Mr Walters spoke well of your husband,' he said. 'He told us that what's happened is completely out of character. Mr Smayle is dedicated to his job.'

'Edgar loves it.'

He lowered his voice. 'I'm sorry to have to ask you this,' he said, 'but it is important. Does your husband have any enemies?'

'No, he doesn't,' she said, quickly. 'Everyone likes him and looks up to him. Edgar is such a friendly man.'

'So, he has no reason to walk away from the farm?'

'None at all, Inspector – that's why it's so worrying.'

'It's a difficult time for Mr Rydall to lose the services of his senior shepherd,' said Colbeck, 'what with spring lambs being born in large numbers. Your husband must have his hands full.'

'That's never troubled Edgar. He likes hard work.' She reached out to grab him impulsively by the wrist. 'Tell me the truth, Inspector. My husband is still alive, isn't he?'

'I sincerely hope so, Mrs Smayle.'

Though his mother had told Will to leave all the talking to his sister, he felt impelled to add comments to whatever Annie said. Leeming found it distracting. While he sympathised with the young shepherd's all too obvious problems, he struggled to keep his temper in the face of the endless gabbled interruptions. Looking directly at her, Leeming seized on something Annie had told him.

'When you got to the tunnel, what was the first thing you saw?'

'It was our sheep,' she replied, gloomily. 'They'd been run over and mangled by that train.'

'How do you know that they were *your* sheep?' Will let out a wild laugh and pointed to his eyes. 'Well, let's be honest, one sheep looks very much like another.' Will shook his head violently. 'It does, surely.'

'There's different breeds, Sergeant,' said Annie, 'and you can tell them apart at a glance. Ours are Cotswold long-wool sheep. They've got this lovely golden fleece. Nobody within twenty miles keeps a flock like ours. It's the best in the county.'

Nodding enthusiastically, Will said something that only his sister could understand. It was evident to Leeming that they were very proud of their father and of his status on the farm. Will had been delighted to work alongside Smayle, doing something he loved and bringing in a small wage to supplement what his father earned.

'Seven sheep were slaughtered,' Leeming reminded them, 'and the man who looked after them has vanished into thin air. There's bound to be a connection between those two things.'

Will's face crumpled as he struggled to understand exactly what Leeming was implying, but Annie leapt to her father's defence at once.

'Father *loved* sheep,' she emphasised. 'He devoted his whole life to them. He'd never let them anywhere near the railway line in case they got hurt. That accident was nothing to do with him.'

'I agree,' said Leeming.

'Then what do you think has happened to him?'

'I don't honestly know. It may be that he is a victim of the person or persons who arranged that accident.' Annie shivered and Will's eyes widened in dismay. 'Since I know nothing about sheep farming, you'll have to answer the question that's troubling me.'

'What is it, Sergeant?' asked Annie.

'How did those sheep get into the tunnel in the first place?'

Colbeck believed that the more he learnt about Edgar Smayle and his family, the better. For that reason, he let the man's wife do most of the talking. Her father-in-law woke up from time to time and contributed an irrelevant piece of information, but he soon lapsed back into oblivion again. While she said nothing at all, Mildred Smayle listened to every word that was said, her eyes never leaving the person who spoke them. Colbeck was very much aware of the old woman's intense interest.

His interview with Betsy was brought to an abrupt end when they heard Will's voice raised in anger outside the cottage.

'I'll have to go,' she apologised, moving away. 'I know that sound. Something's made Will lose his temper.'

When Betsy hurried out of the room, Colbeck crossed over to her mother-in-law. The woman drew back defensively.

'Do you have anything to add, Mrs Smayle?' he asked, softly.

'No, I don't.'

'I sense that you do. There's no need to be afraid. Whatever you tell me, it won't get you into trouble. Now, then, did you agree with everything your daughter-in-law said?'

She shook her head. 'No, I didn't.'

'Why not?'

'My son *does* have enemies. There's an angry streak in him. You can see it in Will as well. They both flare up.'

'Does it ever lead to violence?'

'Not in this house,' she said, stoutly. 'I wouldn't stand for it.'

'Do you know who your son's enemies are?'

'I don't, I'm afraid.'

'That's a pity.'

'Remember one thing, sir.'

'What is it?'

'Edgar doesn't own this farm. He only works here.'

'We're very conscious of that, Mrs Smayle.'

'Mr Rydall rules the roost.'

'That's why we're coming to believe that the accident was arranged by someone with a grudge against him. He's admitted that he has enemies.'

'I know the worst one.'

'Who is that?'

'Michael,' said the old woman, darkly.

Colbeck was puzzled. 'Michael?'

'He used to be Mr Rydall's son.'

Having returned to the eastern end of the tunnel with the other passengers, Caleb Andrews knew that he had to wait until the next train arrived to take him back to London. He stared down at the eastern portal and was reminded of how much his former occupation relied unthinkingly on trust. Every time he set out on a journey in a locomotive, he trusted that it was in good working condition and that the track to his destination would be secure throughout, able to withstand the intense weight and friction that would be placed on it. Railway companies employed a vast number of people in a wide variety of jobs. Their trains worked on the blithe assumption that every employee knew his job and did it efficiently.

During all his years on the footplate, Andrews had trusted that, whenever he drove into a tunnel, he and his train would come out unharmed at the other end. The driver and fireman of the goods train earlier that morning had shown a similar unquestioning trust. It was woefully misplaced. At the other end of a dark tunnel running through solid rock, they'd met with calamity. If they both lived, the memory would haunt them for life. Andrews would have to contend with his own nightmare. He feared that he'd be haunted by the memory of the many years during which he'd thoughtlessly heaped contempt on the GWR with no respect for the decent human beings who kept its trains running.

They'd driven some way away from the cottage before Colbeck pulled the horse to a halt. He and Leeming began to compare notes. The sergeant was sorry that he'd unintentionally caused Will Smayle to shout in protest and wave his arms about as if having a fit.

'He was possessed,' said Leeming. 'It was frightening.'

'Luckily, his mother was on hand to calm him down.'

'I'm glad that somebody was. The boy simply exploded with anger. What do you think is wrong with him?'

'His defects, I suspect, are purely mental. He looks healthy enough and is able to do a job that requires both industry and judgement.'

'The poor lad can't speak properly and yet he's always dying to say something.'

'It must be very frustrating for him.'

'His eyes were burning like hot coals.'

Leeming went on to describe his chat with Will and Annie, both of whom insisted that their father was still alive. When he'd finished, it was Colbeck's turn. He talked about the endless hours that Smayle had worked during a normal week, and the range of abilities he needed to look after a large flock of sheep. Leeming was interested to hear how many people lived in the cottage and wondered how they could manage without even a trace of individual privacy.

'Our house feels crowded, but there are only four of us.'

'They make the most of what they have, Victor.'

'It must be so awkward for them.'

'They're just grateful to have a roof over their heads.'

'If you have a family, it really matters.'

'Without Smayle as their breadwinner, however, they'd struggle.'

'Surely, Mr Rydall wouldn't turn them out.'

'He might have no alternative.'

'But he'd feel sorry for them, wouldn't he?'

'Mr Rydall has an estate to run. To hold his job down, Smayle must have been a highly competent shepherd.

That's why he had so much responsibility. I can't see that son of his following in his footsteps. Can you?'

It was only when he got to the station that Alan Hinton realised he had no precise details about where he was going or how he'd get in touch with Colbeck and Leeming. The man in the ticket office solved the first problem, telling him that, if he bought a ticket for Stroud, he'd get to the western end of the Sapperton Tunnel by slightly unconventional means as a result of the accident, even though he wouldn't actually be going on to Stroud itself. Once on the train, he was able to lie back and meditate on his good fortune. Working with Colbeck made him the envy of his colleagues at Scotland Yard, but there was one person who'd take a different view. Lydia Quayle would be delighted at his minor triumph and it troubled him that he couldn't tell her about it before he left so that he could luxuriate in what he hoped would have been unstinting praise.

As the journey progressed, he came to see that he was letting his good fortune blind him to the reality of the situation. Hinton was, in fact, a rarity. Colbeck and Leeming almost never needed the assistance of another detective. It was an article of faith with them that they handled every case together without even considering additional help. The fact that they'd now done so meant that they'd learnt just how difficult the present investigation would be.

Hinton was not, therefore, going to take part in a case that was certain to end in success. He would be there, he decided, to shore up an already baffling investigation. It made him view his situation in a new light. He might soon return to London – with Colbeck and Leeming beside him – as part of a trio whose efforts had ended in abject failure.

Leeming was stunned by what he'd just heard from Colbeck. When telling the inspector who his worst enemies were, Rydall had somehow omitted to mention his own son. It seemed perverse.

'Does he have such a poor memory?' asked Leeming.

'I'm sure that he remembers Michael all too well. If a father and son fall out so completely,' said Colbeck, 'there must have been a serious dispute between them and it's one that Mr Rydall will never forget.'

'Why didn't he tell you about it?'

'Who knows, Victor? It could be sheer embarrassment.'

'Where is the son now?'

'I've no idea.'

'Why should he want to block that tunnel?'

'We don't know that he had the urge or the means to do so,' said Colbeck. 'All we have is the information from old Mrs Smayle that Michael *used* to be Mr Rydall's son. Note the past tense.'

'He still is, surely. Blood is thicker than water.'

'There's no point in speculating on the cause of the rift. We'll have to wait until we have more information. In the meantime, we can take a closer look at the two main enemies that Mr Rydall did name.'

'Who are they, sir?'

'The first is a man named Anthony Beckerton. He's a haulier who owns a series of barges that travel up and down the canals in

72

the south-west. Needless to say, he's not enamoured of railways. They've taken too much of his trade away.'

'What sort of person is Beckerton?'

'According to Mr Rydall, he's a vindictive one. Over the years, there's been a fair amount of petty vandalism on the line. Rydall is convinced that Beckerton organised it.'

'Destroying a goods train and blocking a tunnel is not what I'd call petty vandalism, Inspector.'

'I agree.'

'You'd have to be really evil to do that.'

'We'll tackle Beckerton tomorrow,' decided Colbeck. 'He's based in Gloucester. Mr Rydall described him as unduly forthright.'

Leeming grinned. 'We've dealt with someone like that before.'

'Indeed, we have.'

'Talking of the superintendent, do you think he'll agree to send Hinton to join us?'

'I hope so. We'll call at Stroud station again and see if there's a telegraph for us.' Colbeck pondered. 'I've just thought of something. Could there be something symbolic in this crime?'

'I don't follow, sir.'

'It involved a goods train that was doing something reserved for many years for canals. Water used to be the best way to move heavy freight. Might it be that Beckerton was sending a coded message?'

'You said earlier that there might be a religious significance.'

'I'm certainly not ruling that out. Do you know how many sheep were killed?'

'No, I don't, sir.

'Seven.'

Leeming shrugged. 'So?'

'It's a number that recurs time and again in the Bible.'

'I suppose it is.'

'How long did it take God to create the world?'

'Seven days.'

'Strictly speaking, it was six. The seventh day was the Sabbath, the day of rest. In other words,' said Colbeck, 'the number seven represents completeness and achievement.'

'What sort of a man sees killing those sheep as an achievement?'

'I don't know.'

'It's downright cruelty.'

'I agree, Victor. Sheep are the most harmless creatures.'

'This person has got a warped mind.'

'Mr Rydall said exactly that about Beckerton.'

'Yet from what you've told me so far about the man,' said Leeming, 'he doesn't sound very religious.'

'The other main suspect does.'

'What's his name?'

'Patrick Cinderby.'

'Did Mr Rydall tell you much about him?'

'He told me the most important thing, Victor.'

'Oh, and what's that?'

'The gentleman's full title is the *Reverend* Patrick Cinderby.'

The Royal Agricultural College had been in existence for less than twenty years, yet it had become a familiar landmark on the road out of Cirencester. Its impressive main building was designed in the Tudor style with rooms on two storeys and with attics above them. At the centre of the range was a five-storey tower that loomed over the whole college. A quadrangle had been constructed at the rear and the chapel was nearby. Farm buildings occupied the rest of the site, many of them housing animals. Attached to the college were well over four hundred acres of land, allowing students to get practical experience in every aspect of agriculture.

Patrick Cinderby seemed to be an embodiment of the place where he was the principal. He was big, solid, imposing and had the weathered look of a farmer. It was an optical illusion because, in fact, he was the son of a member of the royal household, a Cambridge graduate and an ordained priest. Now in his late thirties, Cinderby had a high forehead, curly black hair and a full beard. As he rose behind the desk in his office, he adopted the combative stance he always took when preparing himself for an argument.

There was a knock on the door, then it opened to admit a visitor.

'Thank you for coming at last,' he said with a hint of irony.

'I had to finish my lecture first,' explained the other.

'You could have left your students to discuss what you'd already told them, then resumed your lecture when you returned.'

'I prefer to do things my way.'

'That's one of the matters I wish to discuss.'

Vernon Redwood was Professor of Geology, Botany, Rural Economy and Natural History at the college, a scholarly man of middle years and medium height. He had the face of a startled badger and his bald head had finally won the battle against its remaining wisps of hair.

He put both hands on his hips and gave a truculent stare. 'I am not accustomed to censure,' he warned.

'Times have changed, Redwood.'

'What do you mean?'

'There have been complaints – many complaints.'

Redwood stiffened. 'From whom, may I ask?'

'They came from students who wish to remain anonymous.'

'Then they're nothing but contemptible mischief-makers.'

'They can't be dismissed that easily,' said Cinderby. 'Disapproval of a member of my staff is something that I'm duty-bound to investigate so that I can arrive at a fair judgement.'

'And what *is* this fair judgement?' demanded Redwood.

'Your teaching has fallen below the standards to which we aspire.'

'That's simply not true.'

'As a result – and after discussion with the board – I've decided to relieve you of the professorship of botany.'

Redwood was apoplectic. '*Botany?* I'm an acknowledged expert.'

'Agreed – but you have difficulty getting your expertise across.'

'My book on *The Natural History of British Meadow and Pasture Grasses* was well received. It's required reading on the subject.'

'I know,' said Cinderby, 'and that's why I took the trouble to read it myself. It's unquestionably first-rate. On the printed page, you have a gift for conveying the vast amount of information you gathered. In front of a room full of students, however, you lack conviction.'

'This is insufferable.'

'You've brought it upon yourself.'

'What I find most wounding,' said Redwood, 'is that the fact that you accept the malicious gossip from a couple of students without taking the slightest steps to confirm its veracity.'

'You malign me. As it happens, I took the trouble to stand outside the door during one of your lectures on botany and I heard the students sniggering at your mistakes.'

'Is this what it's come to?' demanded the older man. 'Am I to be spied on like this? It's conduct unworthy of a principal of this college.' He jabbed a finger in the air. 'May I remind you that I was appointed to my present post after a distinguished career as curator and resident professor at the Birmingham Philosophical Institution? My lectures were universally hailed.'

'I'm sorry that you couldn't manage the same feat here.'

Redwood was puce with anger. 'That's exactly what I *did* achieve.'

'I beg to differ.'

'Ah, I see your game. You're doing it again, aren't you?'

Cinderby smiled. 'I've no idea what you're talking about.'

'Last month you reduced Professor Avenell to tears, and now it's my turn. When your predecessor retired, we all hoped that he'd be followed by a man of equal standing and comparable learning.'

'Let's not resort to insults.'

'You've done nothing but insult me since I came here,' said Redwood, warming to his theme. 'You did it with Professor Avenell and others have suffered at your hands as well. I refuse to accept this reduction in my status. Botany is my first love. You won't find anyone with a greater knowledge of the subject.'

'We can certainly find someone more able to communicate effectively with the students. I'm an ambitious man, Redwood. My mission is to raise the standards in this college so that it can vie with any university in the country.'

'Does that have to entail showing disrespect to your staff?'

'Giving someone an honest appraisal of his work here is not a case of disrespect,' said Cinderby. 'It's an example of the search for improvement that I've initiated.'

'Ha!' exclaimed Redwood. 'I'd call it a search for scapegoats.'

'I invited you here for a sensible discussion about your position. It's my duty as principal to do so. And it's my *right*.'

'It's not a right that you're exercising – it's a malicious delight you take in exerting your power and undermining your staff.'

'I resent that charge.'

'I refuse to withdraw it.'

'You'd do well to consider the consequences.'

'When we lost our last principal,' said Redwood, vehemently, 'we lost a true friend. Instead of that, we now have a pompous, conceited, autocratic bully who enjoys eavesdropping on his staff in the hope of hearing something to their detriment.'

'I'll brook no criticism, Redwood.'

'You are a disgrace to the position you hold, Reverend Cinderby.'

'This discussion is at an end,' snapped the other.

'What discussion? You brought me here to issue an ultimatum.'

'That's nonsense. I sought to lighten your load as a lecturer by removing your responsibility for the teaching of botany.'

'It ill becomes you to lie so brazenly.'

'If you had the sense to realise it,' said the other, angrily, 'you'd see that I'm acting in your best interests.'

'Poppycock!'

'Moderate your language, please.'

'You are trying to demote me.'

'It's within my power to do so, Redwood.'

'That power is being cruelly misused.'

'Take care,' said Cinderby, icily calm. 'You're pushing me towards the point where I'll have to demand your resignation.'

'I will tender it with the greatest of pleasure. As for sniggering from the students,' he went on, 'you should hear what they do when forced to listen to one of your sanctimonious sermons. They snort and giggle all the way through them.'

Turning on his heel, he left the room and slammed the door behind him. Cinderby smiled contentedly. He'd achieved exactly what he'd hoped.

CHAPTER EIGHT

The train juddered to a halt, and Alan Hinton got out with the other passengers, noting that they'd stopped well short of the tunnel entrance. Railway policemen were shepherding everyone towards the steep embankment. Many passengers needed help to climb up, but Hinton scaled it with ease, encouraged by the sight of Victor Leeming urging him on from the top. The sergeant gave him a welcoming handshake.

'I remembered what you told me,' said Hinton, lifting his valise. 'Whenever you and the inspector go to a different location, you always take a change of clothes.'

'It's true. We're never really dressed for the country.'

'Where's the inspector?'

'He's gone off to talk to Mr Rydall, the man who summoned us here in the first place. They'll be at the site of the crash. I just hope that you've got strong nerves.'

'Why?'

'I'll be driving you there in a trap,' said Leeming. 'When the inspector holds the reins, the horse does everything that it's told to do. It's different with me. I have a job to control the animal.'

'Would you like me to take over?'

'Do you think you could?'

'I had an uncle who was a cab driver,' said Hinton. 'As a boy, I used to groom his horse for him. By way of thanks, he taught me how to handle his cab.'

'Then I'd be delighted to hand over the reins to you, Alan. You know, it's strange. I often thought that I'd like to be a cab driver, but I simply don't get on with horses.'

Hinton laughed. 'That would be a handicap.'

'Let's be on our way.'

'Have you made any progress?'

'Inspector Colbeck seems to think so,' said Leeming as he led the way to the waiting trap, 'but I feel as if we're groping in the dark. That's why we needed extra help.'

'I was so grateful that you picked on me.'

'You've earned it, Alan.'

'So, what exactly have you been doing?'

'My first job was to interview a Peter Doble. He's the landlord of the Daneway Inn by the entrance to the canal tunnel. When the train was derailed, Doble was the first person to get to the scene. He's a good man,' said Leeming. 'When I met him, he gave me a free tankard of beer.'

Hinton grinned. 'Pity we're not supposed to drink on duty.'

'I didn't think one pint would hurt. It gave me a chance to have a long chat with Doble. He told me some amazing things about life on the canal. I had no idea there was so much to learn.'

'Such as?'

'Well, to start with, bargees have their own language.'

'What sort of language?'

'It sounds like English but it's full of words I've never heard before. For instance,' said Leeming, eager to show off his new-found knowledge, 'do you know what a gongoozler is?'

Because the man was so busy supervising the work at the western portal of the tunnel, Colbeck had to wait some time to speak to Rydall. When the latter broke away to talk to the inspector, he was very apologetic. The two men moved well clear of the debris.

'I'm very sorry, Inspector,' said Rydall. 'I simply can't resist joining in the operation.'

'That's understandable, sir.'

'How may I help you?'

'Earlier on, I asked if you had any particular enemies, and you were kind enough to provide me with two names.'

'That's right – Beckerton and Cinderby.'

'I believe that there might be a third name.'

'There are probably a dozen or so more if I put my mind to it. I mentioned the two individuals who are the most antagonistic towards me. Beckerton makes no bones about his hatred of who I am and what I stand for. Cinderby prefers to conceal his animosity, but it's still there, believe me.'

'What about someone nearer to home, Mr Rydall?'

'I don't understand.'

'I'm told that you have a son.'

'I have two, as a matter of fact. Both of them run farms on their own and – thanks to the GWR – send their livestock to market by train.'

'Which one of them is Michael?'

Rydall bridled. 'Where did you get that name from?'

'It came into my ear somehow,' said Colbeck, evasively.

'The person you mention is no longer my son. We parted by mutual consent over five years ago. His ties with the family were completely severed.'

'May I know what brought all this about, sir?'

'It's not relevant to the investigation,' said Rydall, dismissively.

'It might be if there's unfinished business between the two of you. Rifts of this kind can fester over the years. Your manner suggests that, after all this time, it's still a burning issue for you.'

Rydall took a deep breath before speaking. 'There were faults on both sides, Inspector,' he said, choosing his words with care, 'and that's all I'm prepared to say. Beckerton will be a far more fruitful source of interest to you. He once challenged me to a duel.'

'Were you tempted to accept?'

'I refused to take him seriously.'

'Why was that?'

'Wait until you meet him,' suggested Rydall, 'then you'll understand. Beckerton's idea of a duel is a bare-knuckle brawl behind one of his warehouses. Only a fool would fight him on those terms.'

'Quite so,' said Colbeck. 'May I ask if other members of the family are estranged from Michael?'

The question was unsettling. Rydall needed a few moments to regain his composure. His response was emphatic.

'They've chosen to follow the path that *I've* taken.'

'Do you know where Michael is at the moment?'

'Frankly,' said Rydall, showing real anger for the first time, 'I don't know, and I don't care.' He looked Colbeck full in the face. 'Does that answer your question?'

Arriving back at Paddington station, Caleb Andrews was still in a mood of contrition. News of the accident had now found its way onto the front page of the evening paper. When a vendor waved a copy in his face, Andrews brushed the man roughly aside.

'I know,' he said, bitterly. 'I've been there to see it.'

St Peter's Church stood at the heart of the village of Rodmarton. It was a building of Norman origin though nobody was able to put an accurate date on its construction. It was built of rubble and rough ashlar, its most arresting feature being the high, square tower topped by a spire that pointed towards heaven with Christian resolution. When he arrived, the man got down from his horse and tethered the animal to a bush before taking a long, searching look at the church. Every detail delighted him. Having chosen a vantage point, he sat on a tree stump and started to bring the inspiring image alive in his sketchbook.

* * *

Two centuries earlier, the Crown Inn had been a cider house, but it had long been converted into a village pub of bewitching charm. As they enjoyed a drink there that evening, the three detectives discussed the case and accepted that it posed all kinds of problems. Hinton had to absorb a vast amount of information before he felt confident enough to ask a question.

'Wait a moment,' he said, finally breaking his silence. 'Why should we bother with the Reverend Cinderby? A clergyman would never be involved in an outrage like the killing of sheep and the blocking of that tunnel. It's against everything he believes in, surely.'

'We've met strange clergyman before,' said Leeming as he recalled an earlier investigation. 'The one we met up in the north of England was really weird.'

'I don't think that Cinderby compares with him,' said Colbeck. 'Apart from anything else, he's too busy running the Royal Agricultural College. If Rydall is to be believed, it was an appointment engineered by Squire Etheridge, who is a close friend of Cinderby's.'

'Birds of a feather,' muttered Leeming.

'We know that Etheridge hates railways, notwithstanding the fact that he made so much money out of the GWR when he agreed to sell them land. Cinderby might share his disdain. And since Mr Rydall felt it was important to name him,' decided Colbeck, 'the reverend deserves a visit. That's a job for me.'

Leeming was relieved. 'Good – I always feel guilty when I talk to clergymen. What am *I* to do, sir?'

'I think you're the man for Anthony Beckerton. You can talk his language. Take a train to Gloucester and seek him out. As for you, Alan,' he continued, turning to Hinton, 'you can join in the search for the shepherd. That will mean finding your way to Smayle's cottage. Talk to old Mrs Smayle and see if you can find out why one of Mr Rydall's sons is no longer considered to be a legitimate member of the family.'

'Couldn't you ask Mr Rydall himself?' asked Hinton.

'I did exactly that and came up against a blank wall.'

'Why was that, sir?'

'I'd very much like to know.'

'It sounds as if he has a guilty secret to hide,' said Leeming.

'Possibly,' said Colbeck. 'But while we're on the subject of sons, there's Will to consider. He's the shepherd's son, a young man with many handicaps. Victor will explain.'

'I think Will knows far more than he realises,' said Leeming. 'The trouble is that his brain is addled, and you won't understand a word he says.'

'Handle him with care, Alan.'

'How do I get to the cottage?' asked Hinton.

'Take a trap,' said Colbeck. 'Mr Rydall said that I can borrow a horse whenever I wish. I'll ride to the college.' He looked around. 'How do you find this inn?'

'I like it here. It's very comfortable.'

'Good – I chose it because it's so close to The Grange. Walters, the estate manager, reckons that The Bell in Sapperton is better but we'll settle for this one. It has real character. Mix with the local people, Alan, and listen to their gossip. Gather as much information as you possibly can. We can never know enough about a place.'

'Yes, sir,' said Hinton.

'Could *I* stay here as well?' asked Leeming, hopefully.

'No, Sergeant.'

'Why not?'

'It's because we've already accepted Mr Rydall's hospitality. I didn't feel that I could ask him to find room for a third person. Now,' he continued, turning to the other, 'what are your first thoughts?'

'I'm still trying to sort everything out in my mind,' confessed Hinton, scratching his head. 'I was interested in what you told me about a possible religious angle to the crime. That might bring in Reverend Cinderby, I suppose.'

'We may be completely wrong on that score,' said Colbeck.

'I agree,' added Leeming. 'Beckerton is a much more likely villain. He's fought against the building of a railway from the start and seems to blame Rydall for its existence.'

'Then why hasn't he struck before?'

'Perhaps he has, sir. There was all that vandalism.'

'We've no proof that Beckerton was behind it.'

'And there's no evidence that he wasn't.'

'What about this shepherd who's disappeared?' asked Hinton. 'By the sound of it, he has a lot of responsibilities. His work and his family are right here. Nothing would have torn him away from the farm. And the same thing goes for that dog of his. Where the devil is Blackie?'

Laughing and teasing each other, the children tore off their clothes and jumped straight into the canal. Undeterred by the fact that it was dark, cold and armed with occasional pieces of driftwood, they splashed about happily. It was only when one of them dived beneath the water that the fun stopped. Resurfacing at once, the boy let out a cry of terror and swam towards the bank. The others quickly followed and hauled themselves out of the water. The boy who'd raised the alarm shivered uncontrollably.

'What's wrong?' asked someone.

'There's a dead dog down there,' he replied.

Having spent long hours on his feet, Stephen Rydall finally succumbed to fatigue. Work continued at the crash site and he felt able to leave the supervision to GWR engineers who'd brought cranes and other equipment to the tunnel. Rydall slipped away. Now that he was able to relax for the first time, he realised what a heavy toll the day had taken on his energy. Hauling himself into the trap took a real effort.

His wife was waiting patiently for him at home. Catherine Rydall was a handsome woman with the kind of beauty that had defied the passing of years. She had poise, intelligence and an ability to control her emotions in a crisis. When she welcomed her husband with a kiss, she was calm and supportive.

'It's so good to see you back home at last,' she said. 'What's the situation at the tunnel?'

'It's heart-rending,' he replied. 'Men have been working there for a whole day without making any perceptible difference. A fresh team of navvies will arrive later on and they'll work throughout the night with the help of lamps.'

'What about the labourers you were using?'

'Walters has sent them back to the farm. Their work is done.'

'Come and sit down,' she advised, guiding him across the drawing room. 'You look exhausted.'

'That's putting it mildly, my love. I've been given a salutary reminder of just how old I really am.' He lowered himself down on the sofa and she sat beside him. 'Today has been an ordeal from start to finish.'

'Let someone else take over.'

'That's exactly what I have done, Catherine. I will now concentrate on helping to find the villains who are behind this.'

'Isn't that Inspector Colbeck's job?'

'He can't do it properly without my guidance.'

'I met him earlier,' she said. 'He came to see if there'd been any improvement in the condition of the two victims. Dr Wyatt introduced him to me. I was very impressed. The inspector is clearly a cut above the policemen with whom we've had dealings in the past.'

'He's a . . . remarkable man,' he said, slowly. 'Inspector Colbeck and Sergeant Leeming have worked hard from the moment they got here, and they've now brought in a third colleague to lend assistance.'

She studied him. 'What's wrong, Stephen?'

'Nothing is wrong.'

'You were so pleased to be able to summon Inspector Colbeck here. It was the one thing that lifted your spirits. Yet now that he's actually here, there's a note of doubt in your voice. Have you so soon lost confidence in him?'

'No, my love,' he said, trying to sound more positive. 'I still believe that he's the only man who can bring to justice the devils behind this disaster. Like me, he loves and understands railways. Colbeck is patently a brilliant man and very thorough – perhaps *too* thorough.'

'That's impossible, surely.'

'He's found out something that has nothing whatsoever to do with this business. I had to make that clear to him. I daresay you can guess what it is.'

She heaved a sigh. 'Michael.'

'I'm ashamed to say that his question caught me off balance.'

'What did he ask you?'

'He wanted to know where Michael was and if he harboured any spite towards us. Apart from admitting that we'd broken our links with our son, I told him very little. You must do the same, Catherine.'

'Why should *I* be involved?'

'He may try to prise more detail about Michael out of you. Tell him nothing whatsoever. Do you understand?'

'Yes, I do.'

'The subject is closed.'

'On the other hand—'

'I don't even want to hear his name again,' he said, interrupting her. 'He's no longer a member of this family, and we must treat him as the stranger that he's become of his own volition.'

'If that's what you prefer, I'll do as you say.'

'It's not a question of *my* preference, Catherine. You have to be convinced that it's the right thing. When he . . . did what he did, you were as angry with Michael as I was.'

'Yes, I was.'

'I'm still seething about his behaviour. Aren't you?'

'I've tried to forget it altogether,' she said, firmly. 'Brooding on what happened all those years ago achieves nothing.

Michael has gone, and that's that. You were right to tell the inspector that what happened in our family is not germane to his investigation.'

She met his gaze calmly, but her mind was in turmoil.

When they'd climbed as fast as possible out of the canal, the children had dried themselves then put on their clothes again. They scampered along the towpath until they came to the Daneway Inn. Peter Doble listened to what they were trying to tell him through chattering teeth. He then rushed across to the boat moored nearby.

'I need to borrow a keb,' he said.

'Why?' asked the bargee.

'Just give it to me, man. It's important.'

The bargee handed over a long, iron rake that he kept for fishing things up from the bottom of the canal. With the children around him, Doble hurried to the place where the discovery had been made. The boy who'd dived into the drowned animal pointed to what he felt was the right spot. Doble poked around with the keb until he made contact with something solid. He could feel that it was very heavy and knew that it must be tied to something to anchor it below the water. Telling the children to stand back, he swung the rake out of the water and created a miniature waterfall in doing so. As soon as he lowered the carcase onto the towpath, he saw that some rope had been tied around it and attached at the other end to a sizeable boulder. The dog was instantly recognisable.

'Dear God!' he exclaimed. 'It's Blackie.'

* * *

Dr Wyatt not only checked his patients regularly, he welcomed the families of the two injured men and tried to still their fears a little. Oliver Poulter's wife and brother were shaken to see the state he was in but reassured by his smile. There was good news for the parents of Leonard Treece, an elderly couple who owned a small shop in Gloucester and who'd been horrified when told what had happened. Like Poulter's visitors, they were over-awed by the sight of The Grange and felt completely out of place. Dr Wyatt greeted them with the information that their son had come out of his coma and was in good spirits. The doctor was now able to predict that driver and fireman would make full recoveries in due course. For their part, each of the patients was lifted by the sight of their families. Treece was still only half-awake, but Poulter couldn't stop talking about the accident with the zeal of a survivor.

The three detectives were still deep in discussion at The Crown when the door burst open and a man came in, panting for breath and putting his hand on the back of a chair to steady himself. Colbeck recognised him as one of the servants from The Grange.

'What's happened?' he asked, on his feet at once.

'Mr Rydall's had a message,' gulped the servant. 'They've found Edgar Smayle's dog in the canal. It's dead. You're to come at once, Inspector.'

A small crowd had gathered on the towpath. The dead sheepdog had been divested of its rope and covered by tarpaulin. When Colbeck and Leeming arrived together, they found Rydall peering into the water. Everyone else was doing exactly the same. The newcomers soon understood why. There was a big splash as Doble came to the surface, took some deep breaths and wiped the water out of his eyes. He shook his head.

'He's not there,' concluded Doble. 'I've raked the bottom of the canal with a keb and searched it by hand over this whole stretch, but there's no sign of him.'

When the landlord swam to the bank, a bargee offered him a helping hand and pulled him out. Colbeck and the others saw that, before plunging in, Doble had stripped to the waist and taken off his shoes and socks. His sodden trousers were stuck to his legs. His wife, Molly, was there to wrap a towel around his shoulders. After thanking him for undertaking the search, Rydall drifted across to the detectives.

'Some children were swimming in there and found Blackie.'

'How did the animal die?' asked Colbeck.

'See for yourself,' said Rydall, pulling back the tarpaulin.

Leeming gasped at the gruesome sight. 'His skull has been smashed in,' he said. 'Why didn't the killer simply shoot him?'

'The sound of a gunshot in the middle of the night would have carried a fair distance,' observed Colbeck. 'The landlord and his family would certainly have heard it, not to mention anyone moored beside the canal.'

'I've sent word to Smayle's wife,' said Rydall, lowering the tarpaulin. 'This is what I feared most.'

'What is, sir?'

'If his dog is dead, then so is Edgar Smayle.'

'Not necessarily,' said Colbeck. 'Don't give up hope so easily.'

'The killer would have no reason to keep him alive.'

'I'm still struggling to understand why anyone should want him dead. Smayle has his detractors – which of us doesn't – but we've found no evidence of someone with a desperate urge to take the man's life.'

'Edgar loved his dog above all else.'

'Then killing the animal would be a way to wound him deeply.'

'Why stop at wounding when he could be murdered?'

'Perhaps someone wanted him to stay alive so that he could *suffer*,' suggested Colbeck. 'My advice would be to wait and see until we know what really happened during the night.'

'Look,' said Leeming, pointing a finger, 'we've got company.'

Heading towards them along the towpath was a horse and cart. Will Smayle was driving. His mother and sister were huddled together on the vehicle. The women looked as if they were already in mourning, but Will had the wild-eyed look of someone bent on revenge. Curled up at his feet was his own dog, Meg. As the cart drew to a halt, the animal leapt up and started barking.

Will jumped to the ground and walked across to the tarpaulin with Meg at his heels. The women watched tearfully from the cart. Lifting the tarpaulin, Will gazed down at the corpse of his father's dog before letting out a roar of anger. He then buried his face in his hands.

'I know how you must feel,' said Colbeck, sympathetically. 'This is an atrocious thing to do, and I promise you that we'll hunt down the person responsible. I should tell you, however, that the canal has been searched for a human body and none has been found. Did you hear me, Will? *None* has been found.'

All that he got by means of a reply was a grunt.

'Tell your mother and sister, please. It might bring them some comfort. Meanwhile, don't give up hope. I haven't done so. Have faith.'

It was not clear if Will actually heard the words. He certainly didn't respond to them. Lost in a private world, he lifted the dripping body of the dog in his arms and laid it with almost reverential care on a sack on the back of the cart. Meg hopped up beside Blackie and began sniffing the dead dog, then curled up beside the animal in its customary position. Will turned to Colbeck as if wishing to speak to him, but no words would come out. They could see the desperation in his face. The detectives watched as Will got slowly into his seat again before driving off in the direction of home.

CHAPTER NINE

Madeleine Colbeck was pacing up and down the drawing room. Knowing that her husband would be away from home that evening, she'd invited both Lydia Quayle and her father to join her for dinner. As it happened, Lydia had a prior engagement, but her father had willingly agreed to visit the house again. Yet he still hadn't turned up. Caleb Andrews had become increasingly forgetful of late, but he'd never let his daughter down so completely before. She feared that he'd fallen in with his old railway friends who drank at a pub near Euston. With a couple of pints of beer inside him, he'd probably lost track of time and would arrive, full of apologies, much later. It was the only explanation.

When it was well past an hour of the appointed time, Madeleine's concern turned to irritation, then gradually matured into full-blown anger. Apart from anything else, Helena had been put to bed in tears because the promised visit of her grandfather had not materialised. Andrews had managed to upset both mother and child. Finally, she heard the bell ring and the sound of a maidservant going to answer the door. Rising to her feet, Madeleine was seething. When her father came into the room, she took a step backwards and waved away the kiss he tried to bestow on her.

'What sort of time do you call this?' she demanded.

'I know I'm late, Maddy.'

'I invited you for dinner this evening, not for breakfast tomorrow.'

'There's no need to be sarcastic,' he complained.

'Do you know how long I've been waiting?' she asked. 'Where have you been, Father?'

'Gloucestershire,' he said.

She was taken aback. 'Could you say that again, please?'

'I took a train to Gloucestershire, Maddy. And yes, it did mean I had to travel on Brunel's railway, but I forced myself to do it. I felt that I just had to see it with my own eyes.'

'What are you talking about?'

'It's that accident in the Sapperton Tunnel. What I saw was bad enough,' he explained, 'but what I couldn't see inside the tunnel itself would probably have been worse. A whole goods train was destroyed. I felt so sorry for the driver and fireman.'

'Let me get this right,' she said, adjusting to the

information. 'Are you telling me that you've been out of London for most of the day?'

'Yes, I have. You and Lydia are to blame.'

'Why?'

'The pair of you made me feel so guilty at the way I'd enjoyed the idea of trouble on the GWR. So I bullied myself into going to see with my own eyes how serious the crash had been. It stunned me, Maddy,' he confessed. 'I've been wandering around in a daze ever since. I'm so sorry for keeping you waiting. I just didn't realise how quickly time was going by.' His eyes looked hopefully upwards. 'Is Helena still awake?' Madeleine shook her head. He was forlorn. 'So I've let down my granddaughter as well.'

'She'll forgive you, Father,' said Madeleine, moving close enough to plant a kiss on his cheek, 'and so do I. What you did must have taken such an effort for you. I can't remember a time when you weren't complaining about Mr Brunel and the GWR.'

'They're enemy territory. At least, I thought so until today.'

'What's changed to make you say that?'

He lifted his shoulders. 'I grew up, Maddy.'

'That would be a relief to all of us,' she said under her breath before raising her voice. 'Did you see Robert while you were there?'

'No, I didn't. I was too shocked even to look for him.'

Studying him more closely, she noticed how pale, weary and ill at ease he was. The glint had disappeared from his eye and he'd lost all of his usual alertness and energy. Madeleine was concerned.

'Have you eaten at all today?' she asked.

'I haven't touched a thing since breakfast.'

'Then let's get some food inside you,' she said, taking him by the arm. 'I'm sorry I was so tetchy with you. Now that you've told me where you were, *I'm* the one who feels guilty. It's time for dinner. Come on,' she added, leading him out of the room, 'I want to hear every detail of what you saw on your travels.'

Midnight found the navvies still there, working by the light of lamps to clear away the wreckage. Fires had been lit outside the mouth of the tunnel to provide more illumination. Since so many of the wagons had been smashed to bits, there was an unlimited supply of timber to feed the flames. Railway policemen were on duty at strategic points in case looters came in search of plunder. Clouds obscured the moon.

Two figures emerged from the gloom and crept stealthily towards the scene. They paused to take stock of their position and saw how quickly they'd be able to flee from it. Colbeck and Leeming had become furtive criminals so that they could see how easy it was to go to and from the tunnel in the half-dark. Further down the line, they'd stumbled on a pile of small boulders lying well away from the track. Some of them, they realised, had helped to derail the goods train. Leeming spoke in a whisper.

'How did the sheep get here?'

'I think that Edgar Smayle brought them,' replied Colbeck.

Leeming was shocked. 'He deliberately *led* them to their death?'

'No, of course he didn't. But they were definitely sheep from his herd, and Blackie was an expert at rounding them up. That could only have happened if someone was holding a gun on the shepherd,' said Colbeck. 'A pen must have been set up beforehand by the western portal to the tunnel. Blackie guided the animals into it.'

'Once he'd done that,' said Leeming, reconstructing it in his mind, 'he was of no further use, so he was killed and dropped in the canal.'

'That's what I'm coming to believe.'

'So am I.'

'But what about Smayle himself?'

'I think he's dead, sir.'

'I have my doubts about that, you know.'

'There was no point in keeping him alive.'

'Yes, there was,' said Colbeck, thoughtfully. 'He might still have some value to his kidnapper.'

'What sort of value?'

'He could be used to extort a ransom.'

'Who from?'

'Mr Rydall. His shepherd is of prime importance to the farm.'

'I can understand that,' said Leeming. 'There are sheep almost everywhere on his land. But all those years working outdoors must have sharpened Smayle's instincts for danger. How could he possibly be lured out of his bed in the middle of the night?'

Colbeck was honest. 'That's the bit I haven't worked out yet.'

Dawn had yet to break when Catherine Rydall opened her eyes and became aware of the fact that she was alone in bed. After wondering what time it was, she shook her head to bring herself fully awake, then pulled back the sheets so that she could get up. When she'd put on a dressing gown and slippers, she left the room and padded downstairs. Hearing a noise in the kitchen, she went quickly down the corridor towards it and saw light spilling out from under the door. Catherine entered the kitchen as her husband was finishing a piece of toast.

'What are you doing up so early?' she asked.

'I have to get back to the tunnel, my love.'

'They can manage without you, Stephen.'

'I need to feel that I'm helping,' he said.

'What happened was a horrible crime, but you mustn't think you have a personal responsibility to get embroiled in clearing up the mess. That's a job for the GWR.'

'I'm a member of the board, Catherine. I feel it's my duty.'

'Leave it to people who actually work on the railway.'

'They need someone to bark at their heels.'

'Must it be you?'

He took her in his arms and gave her a reassuring squeeze. Rydall had hoped to have a hasty breakfast and make a quick departure before his wife had even woken up. Instead he'd robbed her of sleep and made her very anxious.

'It isn't just my obligation to the GWR,' he told her. 'There's a deeper commitment for me. Edgar Smayle is one of my most reliable men, and he's disappeared. I owe it to his family to find out why.'

'They must be worried sick.'

'They are, Catherine. I could see it in their faces. When they came to pick up Smayle's dog yesterday, I could read their minds. They think that Smayle himself must be dead too.'

'Isn't that very likely?'

'That's what I thought,' said Rydall, 'but Colbeck disagrees. He thinks that we must retain hope. Until we find a body, he says, we must believe that Smayle could be alive. He'll never get the family to share his belief.'

'No, I suppose not.'

'In their minds, they'll never see Smayle alive again. They fear that he was murdered in the same callous way as his dog.'

On the previous day, the family had been rocked. A much-loved sheepdog had been hauled out of the canal. They had gone to reclaim him. No words had been spoken on the journey back to their cottage. All three of them were too stunned by the turn of events to speak. When they'd arrived back at their cottage, they saw Edgar Smayle's downcast parents shuffling out into the fresh air. One glance at the body of the dead dog was enough to confirm their fears. They would never see their son alive again. Without being asked, Will took over as the man of the house and lifted Blackie off the cart with care before moving him to a spot in the front garden. The others had watched in silence as he fetched a spade and began to dig feverishly. Annie took the older members of the family indoors, then emerged again to hold her mother's arm. The two of them looked on in dismay as the hasty burial took place. Will's dog, Meg, whined piteously. Only when her best friend had been covered by three feet of earth did she slink away to mourn in private.

On the following morning, very little was said. The members of the family went through their established routines, hoping to find some comfort in them. Desperate to take over his father's duties, Will left early with his dog. His grandfather trailed after him, making light for once of his aching bones and his advanced age. Aided by her daughter, Betsy made breakfast for the remaining members of the family though she was unable to eat or drink anything herself.

Annie was worried. 'You must have something,' she urged.

'What's the point?'

'We have to keep body and soul together.'

'If I touched any food, it would make me sick.'

'Then at least *drink* something,' said Annie. 'Shall I make another pot of tea?' Her mother shook her head. 'I'll make it, anyway. You might feel like it in a while.'

'I won't,' insisted her mother. 'It will be a waste of time.'

Before Annie could reply, she heard the clip-clop of a horse's hooves and the rattle of a trap. She peered through the window and saw the vehicle pulling up outside. The driver was a well-dressed young man who jumped down and tethered the horse before appraising the cottage. Annie went out to meet him.

'Can I help you, sir?' she asked, politely.

'I hope so,' he replied. 'I'm Detective Constable Hinton, and I've been sent here by Inspector Colbeck.'

Annie's hand went to her heart. 'Is it about Father?'

'Indirectly, I suppose that it is.'

'You've found his body, haven't you?'

'No, that's not why I'm here.'

'I'd rather you told us the truth. We're strong enough to bear it.'

Hinton was impressed by her ragged beauty and by the bravery with which she jutted out her chin. She sought confirmation of something she dreaded in order to break the news to the rest of the family. She obviously believed the shock would be lessened coming from her, rather than delivered by a complete stranger.

'I really came to talk to Mrs Smayle,' he said.

'Mother is inside, sir. Will you step in?'

'Actually, it's *old* Mrs Smayle I want.'

'Oh, I see . . .'

Colbeck enjoyed the bracing ride on a fine morning. It took him past Sapperton and on through Oakley Wood. He knew that Cirencester had been a provincial capital during the Roman occupation and that many relics survived from that period. The town was also the place where two famous Roman roads – Fosse Way and Ermine Street – actually met. Much as he'd like to have explored Cirencester, he knew that any leisure activities were out of the question. His sole purpose in heading for the town was to interview the Reverend Patrick Cinderby, who, in spite of his status as an ordained priest, might conceivably be a suspect in the case that had brought Colbeck to the area.

The Royal Agricultural College eventually rose up to his right, and he was able to admire the sense of purpose that it seemed to represent. The closer he got, the more striking it seemed. Pulling his horse to a stop outside the main building, he dismounted to take a long look at the facade.

A porter came bustling out to meet him.

'May I help you, sir?' he asked.

'Yes, I've come to speak to the principal.'

'That's not possible at the moment, sir. He's at a meeting of the staff. It won't last all that long,' he added by way of encouragement, 'but, for obvious reasons, I can't interrupt.'

'I wouldn't dream of asking you to do so,' said Colbeck, handing the reins to him. 'I'd be grateful if you could take care of my mount. While I'm waiting, I'd like to have a wander around the grounds and perhaps meet some of the farmers of tomorrow.'

'May I tell the principal who wishes to speak to him?'

'My name is Inspector Colbeck of Scotland Yard.'

'Am I allowed to know what's brought you here, sir?'

'It's a private matter between Reverend Cinderby and me. Thank you for your help,' said Colbeck. He waved an arm. 'Look at all this space. As a city dweller, I'm intensely envious of your students. They're learning their trade in a veritable Garden of Eden.'

Talking to Mildred Smayle turned out to be a difficult assignment. When the old lady was finally coaxed downstairs, it was evident that she'd been crying. A handkerchief was still clutched in her hand. Another handicap for Hinton was the presence of two other women, a daughter-in-law and a granddaughter, respectively. Since he didn't feel that he could ask them to leave what was, after all, their own home, he hoped that they might be able to add something to what the elder member of the family told him. Waiting for Mildred to lower herself into her chair, Hinton felt like an intruder at a funeral. He was about to ask the wrong thing in the wrong place at what was patently the wrong time.

As three pairs of eyes stared at him, he cleared his throat.

'When the inspector came here yesterday,' he said to Mildred, 'you told him something that might be very important in this investigation.'

'I never spoke a word to him,' she said, warily.

'He was asking if Mr Rydall had any enemies.'

'I don't remember that.'

'You gave him a name, Mrs Smayle.'

'You're wrong, young man.'

'Inspector Colbeck has an excellent memory,' said Hinton. 'More to the point, he wrote down the name you gave him in his notebook.'

'Who was it?' asked Betsy. 'I didn't hear any name.'

'That's because you went outside when you heard an argument taking place, Mrs Smayle. The inspector was left alone in here with your mother-in-law.'

'I don't remember that,' said Mildred, stubbornly.

'You must do. It was only yesterday.'

'If I can't remember it, it's best forgotten.'

'I agree,' said Betsy. 'I'm sorry that you made the journey in vain, Constable Hinton. Whatever was said couldn't have been that important.'

'It might have been very significant,' insisted Hinton. 'What your mother-in-law told the inspector was that Mr Rydall had a sworn enemy.'

'I didn't, I didn't,' wailed Mildred.

'It was his son, Michael.'

Betsy rounded angrily on the old woman. 'Is that what you said?'

'No, no,' bleated Mildred, 'it's a lie.'

'Mr Rydall doesn't have a son called Michael, does he?'

'No, he doesn't, Betsy. You're quite right.'

'There you are, Constable,' said Betsy, turning to him with her arms folded. 'The inspector is wrong. We've never heard of anyone called Michael.'

Hinton assessed the situation at once. The source of information was being closed down abruptly. Betsy was plainly annoyed that her mother-in-law had let the name slip out. Living in a tied cottage meant being respectful at all times to the man who owned it and who could evict them whenever he chose. They had to do as they were told. As far as the Smayle family were concerned, Michael Rydall didn't exist. Hinton was curious to know why.

Victor Leeming had gone further afield than either of his colleagues. He caught a train that had disgorged its passengers at the eastern end of the tunnel, then waited for those who'd been driven overland from the other end. After stops at Stroud and Stonehouse, they pulled into the much larger station in Gloucester. Leeming took a cab to the offices of Anthony Beckerton and Son Ltd. Because they were located in the docks, Leeming found himself in the middle of some intense activity: carriers were coming and going, cranes were at work, ships of all sizes were being loaded and unloaded, passengers were boarding or disembarking, sailors and dockworkers were everywhere, and the hungry, wheeling gulls added to the general pandemonium.

Leeming had expected a wait before he could see Beckerton, but, as soon as his name was passed on, he was immediately summoned to the latter's office. It was a large, low room that looked as if it had been hit by a blizzard of paperwork. Every shelf, table and available surface was covered by untidy piles of papers. The desk behind which Beckerton was standing was all but invisible beneath a small mountain of files. There was an acrid but unidentifiable smell in the air. On the wall behind the desk was a plan of the canal system.

Anthony Beckerton was in his natural habitat. He was a big, broad, untidy man in his sixties with crumpled clothes, dishevelled hair and abundant side-whiskers that looked as if they were about to form a pact to develop into a full beard at any moment. When they exchanged a handshake, Leeming felt the raw power of Beckerton's grasp.

'Who are you, and what do you want with me?' asked Beckerton, lowering himself onto his chair and indicating that his visitor should also sit. 'I'm a busy man, Sergeant. Be brief.'

'I'm here in connection with the railway disaster, sir.'

'Railways are a disaster in themselves.'

'I'm talking about the Sapperton Tunnel.'

'What about it?'

'It was blocked when a goods train was deliberately derailed.'

'Really – when did this happen?'

'Yesterday morning. You must have heard the news.'

'I'm only interested in what happens on the canals. They're much safer than railways. They don't kill people the way the GWR does.' Closing an eye, he scrutinised Leeming with the other. 'Why are you bothering me?'

'Your name was given to us as a person of interest.'

'That's because I'm a very interesting person,' said the other with a sudden guffaw. 'Over forty years ago, I started out with little money but lots of ambition, and I'm now the richest haulier in the south-west. Hard work and hard bargaining got me where I am today, Sergeant. While I'm talking to you, I've got barges galore sailing on the Stroudwater, the Thames and Severn, the Gloucester to Sharpness and the Herefordshire and Gloucestershire Canals. I reach places the railways still can't touch,' he added, tapping his chest. 'I'm known for reliability.'

'You've obviously built a reputation for yourself, sir.'

'Competitors are envious of my success. They're always looking for ways to take me down a peg or two. Which one of the bastards gave you my name?'

'It wasn't a haulier, sir.'

'Then it must have been that snake-in-the-grass, Rydall. Don't believe a word he tells you. Stephen Rydall hasn't forgiven me for the way I stopped him becoming a Member of Parliament for this city. I spiked his guns good and proper,' he said, chortling. 'Whenever he made a speech in public, I was there to heckle him with friends of mine who had very loud voices. We turned all his meetings into a shambles. I also gave money to the person who stood against him and who was a much better candidate. Yes,' he concluded, slapping his desk. 'it was Rydall who blamed me for this terrible crime. He would. The truth is that I didn't even know about it until you told me. Give him my regards when you see him, Sergeant, and tell him that I'm completely innocent.' He rose to his feet. 'Thank you for coming.'

'Well—'

'I bid you good day.'

Before he knew what was happening, Leeming was being hustled to the door and shown out. He stood there for several minutes wondering if he should make another attempt to question Beckerton or simply give up and slink away. One thing, however, was clear to him. The haulier's name had to remain on the list of suspects – probably at the top.

Colbeck did not have to wait long at the college. After he'd walked around the quadrangle and spoken to a couple of students about the curriculum, he drifted towards the farm buildings. Before he reached them, he was summoned by the porter he'd met on his arrival. The man led him into the main building and along a corridor to the principal's office. Colbeck knocked and went into the room. It was impressively large and just as impressively neat and tidy. Patrick Cinderby stood behind the desk to welcome his visitor. There was no offer of a handshake. Each took a moment to study the other before sitting down.

'I commend the initiative of the GWR,' said Cinderby, 'in sending for a detective from London. It is far beyond the competence of railway policemen to find the culprits behind this outrage.'

'I'm surprised to hear praise for the GWR coming from your lips, Reverend Cinderby,' replied Colbeck. 'I was given to understand that you were not uncritical of the railway system.'

'That is correct, Inspector.'

'May I ask what your objection is?'

'Essentially, it's a man-made eyesore amid the beauties of nature. When we have the benefit of glorious countryside all around us, why go out of our way to deface it with ugliness, pollute it with billowing smoke and deafen it with mechanical clamour?'

'Some of that clamour may soon be coming to agriculture,' said Colbeck. 'Mechanisation is inevitable. You can't resist it.'

'We believe that the old ways are still the best.'

'Is this what you teach your students?'

'Why do you ask that?'

'Many of them, I venture to suggest, came to Cirencester on a train. We've long moved on from the days of the stagecoach.'

'Argument is an essay in futility, Inspector. We obviously have entrenched positions from which neither of us will budge. I must say,' he went on, looking down his nose at his visitor, 'that you are not what I imagined when I heard that a detective was asking to speak to me. I thought you'd be less assured and more deferential.'

'I see no need for deference, sir.'

'Perhaps you should. I am, after all, principal of a college with royal patronage, and I also happen to be a graduate of the University of Cambridge.'

'I am a graduate of the University of Oxford,' said Colbeck, easily, 'so you'll understand why I don't genuflect in your presence.'

Cinderby winced. 'What do you want of me, Inspector?'

'I was hoping for straight answers to straight questions.'

'Be so good as to put them to me, but bear in mind that I have other demands on my time.'

'Yes, Mr Rydall told me you'd taken on additional

responsibilities here. I understand that, unlike your predecessors, you have the power to hire and fire your professors.'

'Yes, I do – and rightly so.'

'It was the issue on which you and Mr Rydall disagreed.'

'There were several others.'

'But it was the one that caused him to resign from the governing body,' said Colbeck. 'Otherwise, he'd still be making an important contribution to the operation of this college. He must surely be accounted a great loss.'

Cinderby sniffed. 'That's a matter of opinion.'

'I believe that he was one of the pioneers behind the decision to build this college, the first of its kind – never let us forget – in the entire world. Cirencester will for ever be synonymous with the notion of agricultural enterprise, and Mr Rydall was partly responsible for that.' Colbeck looked him in the eye. 'Are you happy to lose the intelligence and experience that a farmer like Mr Rydall can bring to the table?'

'We have men of equal merit in the governing body.'

'Yet none with his sense of dedication, I fancy.'

'Stephen Rydall is no longer content with farming,' said Cinderby, wrinkling his nose in disapproval. 'He has other irons in the fire. Being a member of the GWR board, I know, weighs far more heavily with him than monitoring our activities here at the college. A man should surely know which of his competing interests takes precedence.'

'And which does in *your* case?'

'I beg your pardon!'

'Well, your obligations to the church must inevitably come before any work you do here. That goes without saying. You have to be a good shepherd to your flock before you turn to your more mundane duties as the principal of this college.'

'Your irony is both misplaced and bordering on flippancy,' said Cinderby, rising to his feet with righteous indignation. 'I'll hear no more of it.'

'Then we can move on to a real conversation. One more thing, however,' said Colbeck. 'Mr Rydall has worked on the family estate throughout his entire life. In the interests of learning everything possible about agriculture, he has not been afraid to get his hands dirty.' He paused for effect. 'Do you actually *have* any experience of farming to pass on to your students?'

Cinderby scowled.

CHAPTER TEN

After his visit to the Smayle cottage was rudely curtailed, Alan Hinton arrived at Stroud station much earlier than he'd planned. He'd agreed with Leeming beforehand that he'd wait there to pick him up when the sergeant returned from Gloucester. The station, which followed the standard GWR pattern, consisted of two platforms connected by a bridge. Hinton noticed that a new padlock had been fitted to the door of the stationmaster's office. Wearing his uniform with pride, the stationmaster was consulting the large watch that he'd just taken from his waistcoat pocket. Hinton walked over to him and pointed to the door.

'What happened?' he asked.

'Someone broke in, sir.'

'When was this?'

'Three nights ago,' said the other. 'We had to change the lock.'

'Was anything stolen?'

'No, sir – nothing was touched.'

'Is anything of value kept in there?'

'Only the ticket money, and that's locked in the safe.'

'Did the intruder try to force it open?'

'No,' replied the stationmaster. 'He went to all the trouble of smashing the lock to get in, then left everything exactly as it was. If you ask me, he just did it for fun.'

Now that they'd each got the measure of the other, Colbeck and Cinderby sparred for several minutes as they looked for openings to exploit. The principal eventually decided to bring the preliminaries to an end.

'You are wasting your time, Inspector,' he said, peremptorily. 'What is more galling from my point of view is that I am wasting *my* time as well. We both know why you're here.'

'Do we?'

'You came as a result of a vendetta that Mr Rydall believes exists between us. It's a figment of his imagination. I bear him no ill will. You might care to assure him on that score.'

'How did this phantom vendetta arise?'

'I disagreed with him. That's all it took. What began as a grudge against me hardened into something that eats into his very soul. Rydall is a man who simply cannot bear defeat in argument.'

'That's not a judgement of him that I'd make.'

'Unhappily, I know him far better than you.'

'I can hear a sharp edge in your voice.'

'Stephen Rydall put it there.'

'Is he such an ogre in your eyes?'

'He *uses* people, Inspector. You're his latest victim.'

'I am nobody's pawn,' said Colbeck, stoutly, 'and I never would be. I am here in the Cotswolds to arrest the person or persons responsible for devising the derailment of a goods train and, possibly, for the murder of a shepherd. Given the seriousness of those charges, I have neither the time nor the patience to get drawn into this little game you appear to be playing with Mr Rydall.'

'It's not a game, Inspector.'

'Then what would you call it?'

'It's a fundamental difference of belief.'

'As a man of the cloth, you'd have the advantage there.'

'I'm not talking about religion,' said Cinderby, 'but about the philosophy that underlies the building of this college. In essence, it was intended to be an extension of secondary school education for the sons of yeoman farmers.'

'That's a laudable objective, I'd say.'

'And so would I, Inspector, but it is also a limited one. We should aim higher. This college should attract more talented and intelligent students so that we can vie with the best universities. I see no reason,' he continued as if addressing a large audience, 'why this institution should not transform agriculture in this country by producing graduates of a standard equivalent to that of Cambridge.'

'Or even that of Oxford,' said Colbeck, 'an older academic foundation.'

'You take my point?'

'I do, but I find it irrelevant to the crimes that bring me here.'

'Stephen Rydall sent you out of spite against me. Be honest, Inspector,' said Cinderby. 'Do I look like the sort of person who would kill sheep and derail a train?'

'No, you don't.'

'Then go back to Rydall and tell him that.'

'He already *knows* that you don't look like that sort of person.'

'Then why bring my name up at all?'

'Perhaps he feels that you're capable of hiring someone who *does* look like the sort of villain we're talking about.' Eyes bulging, Cinderby was back on his feet at once. 'That's pure supposition on my behalf, mind you. Attach no importance to it.' Colbeck also got up from his chair. 'May I ask a question?'

'You've asked too many, as it is.'

'Where do you preach on Sunday?'

'I'll be at All Saints' Church in Kemble.'

'Is that anywhere near Kemble Court?'

'It's right next door, Inspector.'

'In that case, Squire Etheridge may be present.'

'He certainly will be,' said Cinderby. 'I'm there as his guest.'

'I look forward to seeing you both in church, then.'

Cinderby was unsettled. 'Your attendance at Morning Service is not compulsory, Inspector.'

'Oddly enough,' said Colbeck, 'I feel that it is.'

* * *

117

Expecting a wait of well over an hour or more, Alan Hinton was delighted to see Victor Leeming step out of a train from Gloucester in half that time. The sergeant looked decidedly glum.

'How did you get on?' asked Hinton.

'Beckerton more or less threw me out.'

'What was he like?'

'He reminded me of the sort of people I used to arrest for affray when they'd drunk themselves stupid. The difference is that Anthony Beckerton was as sober as a judge.'

As they strolled towards the waiting trap, he gave Hinton a brief description of his interview with the haulier. Leeming was disappointed to have learnt so little of the man.

'You learnt that he doesn't like being questioned by the police,' said Hinton. 'And you learnt something new about Mr Rydall.'

'He and Beckerton hate each other.'

'It's a case of railway versus canal.'

'Rydall is a farmer.'

'I saw the way he was working at the crash site when I dropped you off there earlier. He's not employed by the GWR, yet he was giving orders as if he was Brunel back from the grave.'

'That's true,' said Leeming. 'When we met him yesterday, he'd been in charge of the clearance work since the alarm was raised. He's convinced that the derailment was a form of punishment for *him*.'

'Is Beckerton the kind of man who'd want to punish someone?'

'It's the sort of thing he'd love, Alan.'

When they reached the trap, Hinton untied the reins from

a post and climbed into the vehicle. Leeming sat beside him, and they set off. He asked Hinton what had happened at Smayle's cottage.

'The old woman changed her tune.'

'What do you mean?'

'When I reminded her of what she'd told the inspector,' said Hinton, 'she denied ever speaking to him. Her daughter-in-law was there and so was that pretty young girl. They were looking daggers at the old woman.'

'Why?'

'She spoke out of turn.'

'You mean that she said something she's forbidden to say?'

'They're *all* forbidden to say it, I reckon. Mr Rydall is to blame. I think he ordered them to keep their mouths shut about this son of his. Michael has been outlawed. Nobody dares to say his name.' Hinton offered his companion the reins. 'Would you like a turn?'

'No thanks – the horse would probably bolt.'

'I find him very biddable.'

'Then *you* drive the trap, Alan.'

Hinton suddenly remembered his chat with the clerk at Stroud station and told his companion about it. When he heard about the break-in, Leeming snapped his fingers.

'That could be it,' he decided.

'What are you talking about?'

'The person who broke in *did* want something, after all.'

'But nothing was taken.'

'Yes, it was, Alan. The stationmaster's office probably contained a timetable of goods trains as well as passenger trains. All that the burglar had to do was to find out what time the first train would come through the tunnel yesterday morning. He *knew* it'd be a goods train,' said Leeming, 'so he could round up those sheep and put those boulders on the line in time to cause the crash. Well done, Alan,' he went on, slapping him on the back. 'I think we've solved a problem. I may have failed with Beckerton and you drew a blank with old Mrs Smayle, but we're not going back to the inspector empty-handed.'

Mildred Smayle sat alone in the living room of the cottage in the chair reserved for her. She cut a wretched figure. She was mourning the death of her son and wondering what was going to happen to her and the rest of the family. At the same time, she feared the anger of her daughter-in-law. Mildred was in disgrace. In mentioning the name to Colbeck, she'd broken an iron rule and been chastised for it. She knew that it was inexcusable. When she saw Betsy coming back into the house, therefore, she drew back as if to avoid a blow. It never came. Instead of striking her, the younger woman put a consoling arm around her shoulders.

'I'm sorry I was so angry,' she said.

'I did wrong, Betsy. I know it.'

'Let's try to forget it.'

Mildred was anxious. 'Will you tell Mr Rydall?'

'No, of course I won't. It would get us all into trouble.'

'I don't know what made me speak to the inspector.'

'Try to forget it,' said Betsy, 'and don't ever – *ever* – mention Michael's name again. It's what we promised to do.'

'It just . . . slipped out.'

'The inspector is sure to have mentioned it to Mr Rydall.'

'That's what I'm afraid of,' said the old woman.'

'We'll just have to hope that he didn't say where he got his information from. Mr Rydall is a kind man,' said Betsy. 'He's been good to us over the years.'

'Yes, he has.'

'But if he knew one of us had talked about Michael, he might turn nasty.'

Catherine Rydall was an essentially honest woman who had been devoted to her husband since the day when they married. She accepted without question his right to make all the decisions even if she didn't always agree with them. For the most part, it had been a happy and fulfilling marriage. Only one sad development had led to friction between them. Michael, the youngest of their sons, had behaved in such a way that his father exiled him from the family. While she had definite qualms about the decision, Catherine had no power to change it, and she'd found herself put into an awkward position. Ordered to forget all about Michael's existence, she found the maternal instinct too strong to renounce him entirely.

Apart from the servants, she was almost alone in the house. Dr Wyatt was so pleased with the state of his patients that he didn't feel it necessary to hover over them. Promising to be back in an hour or so, he went home to his wife. Catherine's husband was preoccupied at the site of the crash and wouldn't be home until much later. She felt confident that she wouldn't be disturbed. Going upstairs to the master bedroom, she unlocked the secret compartment in her wardrobe where she kept her jewellery box. A second key was needed to open it.

Removing the items one by one, she put them on the dressing table before lifting the false bottom out of the box. Concealed below was a collection of treasured letters held together by a pink ribbon. Most of them were *billets-doux* from Rydall, written during their courtship, but it was a more recent letter that she extracted. It had been sent from Canada to a friend in England who could be trusted to pass it on to Catherine in secret. When she'd first read it, she'd had mixed feelings, pleased that Michael was coming back to England while simultaneously terrified that her husband might find out.

The missive was far too dangerous to keep. After reading it one more time, she walked across to the fireplace, set the letter alight, then dropped it into the grate. A bitter family tragedy sent wisps of smoke curling up the chimney.

Lydia Quayle's mouth fell open, and her eyes widened in disbelief.

'Have you made this up, Madeleine?'

'No, it's absolutely true.'

'Your father actually *went* to Gloucestershire?'

'Yes,' said Madeleine, 'and it was thanks to us, apparently.'

'What did *we* do?'

'We made him feel guilty. That's never happened before, even though I've had to reproach him time and again about his attitude towards the GWR. Yesterday – somehow – we caught him on a raw nerve.'

'And what exactly did he see?'

Madeleine repeated what her father had told her, stressing the fact that he'd stayed at the site of the crash longer than he'd originally intended. In fact, he'd been tempted to climb down the cutting in order to help with the clearance work.

'Luckily, he realised that he was too old for that.'

'I daresay that he wasn't dressed for manual work either.'

'He certainly wasn't, Lydia.'

'How did you react when you heard where he'd been?'

'When the news had sunk in,' said Madeleine, 'I was glad. I was also proud of him. I've never heard my father say a good word about the GWR before, but he was genuinely sorry for the company. What he's really hoping for is the news that the driver and fireman survived the crash. That would come as a relief to him.'

'Is Robert likely to tell you that when he writes?'

'It's more than probable. Concern for the two men on the footplate will be uppermost in his mind.'

'If they die, they'll become murder victims.'

'If it had been a passenger train, there would have been terrible injuries for lots of people and, most likely, some fatalities.' She gritted her teeth. 'I hope that Robert catches whoever was responsible very soon.'

After his lively encounter with the principal of the college, Colbeck resisted the temptation to ride into Cirencester in order to explore the town. Putting duty before pleasure, he headed back in the direction of Frampton Mansell and reflected on his visit. The Reverend Patrick Cinderby was clearly a highly intelligent and able man if he could hold down such an important position. What Colbeck objected to most was his arrogance underpinned, as it was, by his sense of entitlement. A member of the clergy might be expected to have a more pleasant and tolerant manner than Cinderby had exhibited. There was a spiky quality to the principal that would not be welcomed by the students at the college or, for that matter, in the churches where he preached.

Colbeck tried to be dispassionate. Disliking someone was not a reason for assuming the worst about them. Cinderby was an unlikely suspect for the calamity at the Sapperton Tunnel and yet he'd been named by Rydall as an enemy of his. To what lengths would that enmity drive him? And how close was his relationship with Squire Etheridge, the man whose hatred of railways had been taken to the point of absurdity? What would either stand to gain from an act of sabotage?

By the time that The Grange came within sight, he had not found the answers to his questions. His attention was in any case diverted by the sight of two people talking to Dr Wyatt outside the house. Colbeck guessed at once that the man and the woman in late middle age were the parents of the injured fireman. Shaking the doctor's hands, they looked so pathetically grateful. The father helped his wife into the waiting trap before he got in beside her. He then drove off.

Wyatt waited outside the house until Colbeck trotted up to him.

'Mr and Mrs Treece?' asked the inspector.

'Yes,' replied Wyatt, 'They came to see their son for the

second time. He's still dazed by what happened, but he rallied when his parents turned up.'

'What sort of mood is he in?'

'He's as chirpy as a bird, even though he must be in great pain. Mrs Poulter, the driver's wife, has been here as well. She perked her husband up at once. Having loved ones beside you is the best medicine of all.'

'You must take a lot of credit, Dr Wyatt. It was a stroke of good fortune that there was a doctor in the village.'

'Actually, I'm a *retired* doctor, or, at least, I thought I was. Being back in the harness, so to speak, has been oddly exciting. And when you only have two patients to look after, you can give each of them individual attention.'

'How long will they stay here?'

'I can't give you an exact time,' said Wyatt. 'Mr Rydall assures me that they can stay as long as is necessary. He's also provided me with a servant to act as a nurse. Somehow he feels obscurely responsible for what's happened to the two men.'

'That's because he believes that whoever engineered the crash was acting out of malice against him personally.'

'Is that your view as well?'

'I'm keeping an open mind.'

'That's very wise, Inspector.'

'We're still at the stage of gathering background information.'

'That must be very time-consuming.'

'It's the reason I sent for additional help.'

'Yes, I noticed Sergeant Leeming going off in a trap this morning with a young man.'

'That was Detective Constable Hinton,' said Colbeck.

'He seemed very eager.'

'He's eager, intelligent and has boundless energy. All three qualities will be needed for this investigation.'

'You sound as if you're confident of success.'

'I am, indeed, but I'm also aware that it may take time. We're fully prepared for that. We'll stay here as long as is necessary.'

Victor Leeming realised that there was a way to make amends for their respective failures. While he'd been given a dusty answer by Anthony Beckerton in the Gloucester docks, Hinton had been baulked at the Smayle cottage. However, all was not yet lost.

'I can see a way to kill two birds with one stone,' he said.

'What do you mean, Sergeant?'

'We simply call at the Daneway Inn.'

'Why?' asked Hinton.

'It's beside the canal. Peter Doble, the landlord, will certainly know Beckerton. I'd value his opinion of the man. Since he and his wife have been at The Daneway so long, he'll also have an idea why Michael Rydall was expelled from the family.'

'What sort of man is the landlord?'

'He's very friendly,' said Leeming, rolling his eyes. 'In fact, he was too friendly. I made the mistake of accepting that free pint from him. When the inspector saw me with a tankard in my hand, he tore strips off me.'

'It's difficult to refuse a free pint.'

'Nevertheless, it's what we have to do. If I'm caught in the act again, I'll be sent back to London immediately.'

'But you're a close friend.'

'Rules are rules – even for me.'

He told Hinton which route to take, and they soon picked up the canal, crossing it at a bridge then heading along the towpath. Doble was pleased to see Leeming again and shook him warmly by the hand. When he was introduced, Hinton also qualified for a handshake. The landlord took his visitors into the bar and signalled to his wife who was behind the counter.

'Two free pints, please, Molly.'

'They're on their way,' she replied.

'No,' said Leeming, waving a hand, 'we didn't come to drink your excellent beer. What we need is information.'

'Then you've come to the right place,' she said, cheerily. 'Peter and I are aware of everything that goes on around here.'

'Since you're part of the canal community, you must know a man named Anthony Beckerton.'

Molly grimaced. 'Yes, we do.'

'How would you describe him?'

'He's the most successful haulier in the county,' said Doble, 'and he lets everyone know it. That's not a criticism. Beckerton deserves to be where he is. He worked very hard to get there. His rivals claim that he's done it by bullying and cheating and that may be true. I don't know. He's a bit of a rough diamond, but that's not a problem in the canal trade.' He chuckled. 'I suppose we're all a bit like that.'

'Why does he seem to hate Mr Rydall?' asked Hinton.

Doble laughed. 'He doesn't *seem* to hate him. He loathes the man.'

'What about his sheep?'

'He hates absolutely everything about Mr Rydall.'

'Does that include his shepherd?' said Leeming.

Before he could reply, Doble was hailed by a group of noisy bargees who came into the bar and shook hands with him in turn. The detectives turned to Molly instead.

Leeming was curious. 'Do you share your husband's opinion of Beckerton?'

'More or less,' she said.

'How would *you* describe him?'

'He's fine when there's someone else in the room with you, but he's very different when a woman is left alone with him. I keep well clear of Anthony Beckerton. That's all I'm going to say.'

'Then let me ask you about someone else, Mrs Doble.'

'Call me Molly. Everyone else does.'

'I believe that Mr Rydall had a son called Michael, who is . . . well, no longer part of the family, it seems.'

'You'll have to excuse me, Sergeant,' she said, as the bargees surged forward. 'These lads have just legged their way through the tunnel. They'll have a real thirst on them . . .'

By way of confirmation, the bargees gave a loud cheer.

The Reverend Patrick Cinderby was very glad to see his visitor. After his uncomfortable conversation with Colbeck, it was a relief to talk to a friend, especially one to whom he could pass on good news.

'Professor Redwood has resigned,' he told the man.

'Really? What brought that about?'

'There was some adroit manipulation on my part.'

'Is that a polite way of saying that you sacked the man?'

'I was much more subtle than that. I manoeuvred him into a position where he effectively sacked himself.'

'Well done, Patrick!'

Squire Etheridge had called at the college to see the man he had helped to secure the position of principal. In return, Cinderby had done his friend a favour.

'We will soon be advertising the post,' he said. 'I rely on you to advise your nephew that we'll be interviewing candidates before too long.'

'Darley is supremely well-qualified for the professorship. I know that he doesn't have the experience that Redwood had, but he more than makes up for it in other ways.'

'He's a fellow graduate of Trinity College, Cambridge, and that's the best qualification of all in my mind.'

'I agree,' said Etheridge.

'It's heartening to see you again,' said Cinderby. 'After a rather fraught exchange with Redwood yesterday, I had an inspector from Scotland Yard here earlier today, trying to harass me.'

'What on earth brought him to the college?'

'Can't you guess? Rydall whispered my name in his ear.'

'But why is he in this part of the country?'

'It appears that Inspector Colbeck has a reputation for solving crimes related to the railway system.'

'The railway system is a crime in itself,' snapped Etheridge. 'It's a concept that should've been strangled at birth. So, Rydall sent for him, did he? What sort of person is the inspector?'

'He's the opposite of what I expected. I thought he'd be an earnest but rather plebeian individual who knew his place in society. What I got with Colbeck was a dandy who claimed to be an Oxford graduate and who showed scant respect for my position as priest or principal.'

'Is he clever, do you think?'

'He's extremely clever.'

'Then it might be sensible to have him watched.'

'I agree.'

'In your place,' said Etheridge, 'I'd have refused to see him.'

'That would have been foolhardy. I'm glad that I did see him. One should always know one's potential enemies. He's no lackey of Rydall's. Colbeck is a man of independent mind. That's what worried me the most.'

'Rydall will have told him all kinds of nonsense about us.'

'I had clear proof of it. The inspector had the gall to challenge me about decisions I'd made with respect to this college. It was insufferable. What happens inside this institution is none of his business.'

'I'd have chosen stronger language than that, Patrick.'

Cinderby smiled. 'I suffer the restraints of my calling.'

'Let's hope that he doesn't come back.'

'Oh, he won't give up easily, I'm afraid. As a matter of fact, he was interested in meeting *you* as well.'

'Why?'

'He'll tell you when he comes to church to hear me preach.'

Etheridge was aghast. 'He's coming to All Saints'?'

'Colbeck's methods are unusual.'

'I'd say that they were positively bizarre.'

'It's so annoying,' said Cinderby. 'Rydall has set him onto me out of spite, and I hate the thought of being under surveillance. The inspector is much more than a nuisance. He's a positive danger. We must somehow find a way to shake him off completely.'

CHAPTER ELEVEN

When they met as arranged in Colbeck's room at The Grange, the three of them had a lot to discuss. The inspector went first, telling them about his visit to the college and his clash with its arrogant principal. Hinton was impressed by the way that he'd stood up to the man, but Leeming took a different view.

'I'm not sure that you should have bothered with him, sir.'

'I was given strict instructions to do so, Victor,' said Colbeck. 'Mr Rydall knows the gentleman far better than I do. If he believes that the Reverend Cinderby is worthy of investigation, then I have to follow his advice.'

'I still have my doubts,' said Leeming.

'Why?'

'A man in his position wouldn't stoop to a crime like this, surely. What would he gain? Nothing, as far as I can see. I think you've been led astray.'

'I don't feel that somehow.'

'Think of those sheep slaughtered by the train. A man who is principal of an agricultural college would have every reason to *save* farm animals – not to kill them.'

'That's a fair point, Victor, and one that I've considered. Yet, at this early stage, I can't dismiss the Reverend Cinderby as irrelevant. He would never soil his hands by getting directly involved but he might issue orders to someone who did. And so might Squire Etheridge. However,' he went on, 'that's enough of *my* adventures. What have *you* found out?'

'Beckerton is a much more likely suspect, sir.'

'Why do you think that?'

Leeming told him about his brief and inglorious meeting with the haulier, ending, as it did, in his rather unceremonious departure from the man's office. The sergeant then went on to explain that he and Hinton had gone to the Daneway Inn.

'And before you ask,' said Leeming, 'we didn't touch a drop of beer. I just thought it was important to talk to Doble and his wife. They've met Beckerton many times. His boats go past their inn every day. Doble was careful not to criticise him, but it is clear that he doesn't actually like the man. His wife, Molly, was more forthright. She hates the sight of him because the haulier pesters her whenever he finds her alone.'

'Did she think Beckerton capable of this crime?'

'Yes, she did – when we had a chance to talk to her properly, that is. Some bargees interrupted us for a while, so we had to bide our time. Molly reckons that Beckerton has been in trouble with the police in Gloucester many times, but he's never been prosecuted.'

'Was that because of insufficient evidence?'

'It's either that or someone's taking bribes.'

'Beckerton is a rich man, apparently,' said Hinton, 'so he can afford to dangle a lot of money in front of the police. If they're paid as little as I was in uniform, they could be tempted.'

'Let's not condemn them without proof,' warned Colbeck. 'I'll make contact with the Gloucester constabulary and find out a little more about their dealings with Beckerton.' He glanced at Leeming. 'Is there anything else to report?'

'I've said my piece, sir, but Alan has news about Stroud station.'

'Oh?'

Taking his cue, Hinton told him about his discovery that the stationmaster's office had been broken into, but nothing had been taken. Though he found the news interesting, Colbeck was not ready to jump to any conclusions, reasoning that the burglar could simply have been interrupted and fled the scene.

'While I agree that the break-in *might* have been a means of consulting the timetable,' he said, 'I think we should exercise caution. What I really wish to know,' he went on, 'is how Alan fared at Smayle's cottage. Did you speak to the shepherd's mother?'

'I tried to, Inspector,' said Hinton, 'but she was too

scared to answer my questions. Old Mrs Smayle denied ever talking to you.'

'Her memory can't be that bad.'

'It was nothing to do with her memory. Her daughter-in-law and her granddaughter were there at the time and kept giving her warning looks. They seemed shocked that she'd spoken to you about Mr Rydall's son. After I'd left,' he went on, 'I fancy that the pair of them would have vented their anger on the old woman.'

'They've been sworn to secrecy, I fancy,' decided Colbeck. 'Old Mrs Smayle spoke out of turn.'

'That's when I came up with the idea of calling at the Daneway Inn,' said Leeming. 'Doble and his wife know this area like the backs of their hands. Every whisper of scandal comes into their ears.'

'Is that what it was – a scandal?'

'I'll let Alan tell you.'

'It took time to get Doble away from those noisy bargees,' recalled Hinton, 'but we finally managed it. All I had to do was to mention Michael's name and out it came.'

'Go on,' urged Colbeck, listening intently.

'The landlord didn't know the full details – nobody outside the family does, it seems – but he said that Michael had been a problem for some time. He was a rebel. Unlike his elder brothers, he didn't want to run his own farm. As a result, he and Mr Rydall had constant arguments. Michael seemed to be doing things deliberately to vex his father.'

'My boys are like that sometimes,' moaned Leeming.

'We were told that Mr Rydall objected strongly to his

son's choice of friends – especially his female friends.'

'Now we're getting somewhere,' said Colbeck.

'When he got involved with one young woman in particular,' continued Hinton, 'Mr Rydall refused to have her in the house. That was a crushing blow for Michael, it seems. Before the rest of the family knew it, he disappeared one night and has never been heard of since.'

'What about this young woman?'

'She disappeared with him, Inspector.'

'But she had a family of her own, presumably.'

'She did and she didn't,' said Hinton. 'According to Doble, she moved into the area when her parents died and lived with an aunt who barely had enough money to feed herself.'

'That would hardly recommend her to Mr Rydall,' said Colbeck. 'He's a wealthy man who's proud of his position in society.'

'Exactly, sir – he didn't want his son associated with a penniless girl who had little education. The idea that Michael would defy him and run away was too much to bear. From that point on, his youngest son was no longer a member of the family. Doble said that it is a strange way for Rydall to behave. It is as if Michael never existed.'

'Where is he now?'

'Doble couldn't tell us that,' said Leeming. 'And he didn't know if this young woman was with him any more. Nobody seems to have heard a word about Michael Rydall since the day he ran away.'

'It made me wonder . . .' began Hinton, tentatively.

'Speak out,' encouraged Colbeck. 'Never be afraid to voice an opinion.'

'Well, I think that Michael Rydall needs to be on our list of suspects. When he left home, he must have been seething with hatred of his father. If he wanted his revenge, he couldn't take it in a better way than by causing that derailment. It hurt Mr Rydall in two ways.'

'Yes,' said Leeming, 'as a farmer and as a member of the GWR board.'

'In a short space of time, his shepherd disappeared and some sheep were killed. Having lived here for so many years, Michael would have been familiar with the geography of the estate and of the railway line. He'd also have known that he could get access to details of goods traffic from Stroud station.'

'Don't let your imagination get the better of you, Alan,' cautioned Leeming. 'We've no proof that Michael is anywhere in the vicinity.'

'He may not even be in the country,' Colbeck pointed out. 'If he'd eloped with this young woman, he wouldn't be the first disaffected son to search for a new life abroad.'

'How can we find out where he is?'

'Mr Rydall won't even talk about him.'

'Is there anyone else you could approach, sir?' asked Leeming.

'There might be,' said Colbeck, thoughtfully, 'but I'd need to be very careful. The last thing I want to do is to anger Mr Rydall.'

Stephen Rydall had finally handed over the task of supervising the clearance work to the GWR itself. He forced himself to leave the Sapperton Tunnel and turn his attention to the estate. Glad to see him back in the farmyard again, Walters was concerned about his employer's appearance.

'You look absolutely exhausted,' he said.

'I've been burning the candle at both ends,' admitted Rydall.

'It's time you had a good rest.'

'There's no chance of that happening, Sidney. There's far too much to do on the estate. I can't leave everything to you. As for the crash,' he went on, 'I know that I got rather obsessed with it, but it was an education for me.'

'In what way?' asked Walters.

'Well, I didn't realise that some people actually *live* in the tunnel?'

'How did you find that out?'

'I talked to one of the railway policemen guarding the wagons against looters. He told me that, when he first got there, he noticed that there'd already been pilfering. Using a lamp, he went deeper into the tunnel and found rudimentary bedding.'

Walters was appalled. 'That's shocking,' he said. 'You'd have to be desperate to live in there in the dark. Think of the trains speeding past. It's not a risk I'd dare take.'

'Nor me,' said Rydall. 'But let's turn to the estate. I should imagine that everyone's stunned by the disappearance of Edgar Smayle.'

'They are. Why would anyone want to kill him?'

'We're not sure that he's dead.'

'I am,' said Walters, firmly, 'and so is everyone else. That son of his keeps searching for him but all to no avail. Smayle is gone for good. My guess is that he was murdered along with his dog.'

'Inspector Colbeck thinks that we shouldn't assume that. He has hopes that Smayle might still be alive.'

'Then I strongly disagree with him.'

'He's handled cases like this before, remember. Colbeck has learnt to keep all options open, however unlikely.'

'Smayle is dead,' said Walters, emphatically.

'Then we've lost a good man.'

'He's among the best we employ. It's going to be very difficult to replace someone with his skill and experience.'

'I agree.'

'His disappearance raises an awkward question, Mr Rydall.'

'I know, Sidney.'

'What happens to the family?'

Annie Smayle had been searching high and low for her brother. She eventually ran him to earth at the very edge of the estate. Will was using his crook to poke about in some bushes.

'There's no point, Will,' she said.

'Yes, there is.'

'Come back with me.'

'Father's here somewhere.'

'He's not.'

'I won't give up till I find him.'

'You're needed to look after the flock,' she pleaded. 'I can't do it on my own. It's what Father would have wanted us to do. Mr Rydall needs to see that we can manage. Don't you understand?'

'Go away.'

'Do you want us all to be turned out of the cottage?'

Will looked at her with despair in his eyes. The thought of losing his home and his job rocked him. He felt completely helpless. Annie took him by the arm and led him gently away.

'Listen to me, Will,' she said, softly. 'I know what's best.'

Alan Hinton was at once pleased and disappointed. His first reaction to Colbeck's decision was to produce a broad grin. It slowly faded away when he realised that, in being sent back to London, he was being moved away from the sphere of action. Instead of communicating with Tallis by means of telegraphs, Colbeck had elected to send him a full written report to be delivered by hand. There were two sources of consolation for Hinton. As well as visiting Scotland Yard he'd be carrying a letter for Madeleine Colbeck and could hope that Lydia Quayle might be at the house when he called there.

More importantly, he'd be returning to the Cotswolds the moment that his errands had been done. He'd be straight back in the middle of a perplexing but stimulating case beside Colbeck. It was a chance to show his worth and to learn from a master of his trade.

The inspector, meanwhile, had taken a train in the opposite direction and enjoyed the scenic views on the way to Gloucester. As soon as he arrived, he took a cab to the police station and found that the duty officer there was Sergeant Miller, a tall, slim, watchful man in his forties with a solemn voice. Colbeck introduced himself, but Miller's only response was a grudging deference.

'I'm here to ask about Mr Anthony Beckerton.'

'Ah, yes,' said Miller, sniffing, 'we know Anthony Beckerton. We know him very well.'

'You don't sound as if it's a happy relationship.'

'He's a rogue, Inspector, an out-and-out rogue.'

'Yes, but he's never been taken to court, I hear.'

'Every time we arrest him, he wriggles out of the charges.'

'And what sort of charges are they?'

'Take your pick,' said the other, lugubriously. 'He's been hauled in here for drunkenness, causing an affray, indecent behaviour, allegedly bribing an auctioneer and knocking a man to the ground before urinating over him.' He tapped his chest. 'I arrested him on that occasion.'

'Then he should have been prosecuted.'

'The man he punched refused to press charges.'

'Was he afraid of Beckerton?'

'Let's just say that he knew there'd be consequences. A rival haulier who did try to take him to court had a nasty accident. He had to be fished out of the canal one night. He'd been beaten up.'

'How can you let Beckerton get away with things like that?'

'He has the best lawyer in the city. Then, of course,' said the sergeant, 'there are his charitable activities. Most people here love him for his generosity. He puts money into schools and libraries. Also, he sponsors a children's festival every year. It's difficult to put a local hero behind bars.'

'I gather that he can be a nuisance to women.'

'There's that, too.'

Colbeck asked him for details of Beckerton's business dealings and got an impressive list of achievements in return. The sergeant would not be drawn on whether or not everything that the haulier did was within the bounds of the law. Colbeck changed tack.

'Who is the senior officer here?' he asked.

'That would be Inspector Neil, sir.'

'What was his reaction to the disaster at the Sapperton Tunnel?'

'He thought we should have been summoned to investigate.'

'The police station in Cirencester is closer to the site.'

'So is the one in Stroud, and that's been ignored as well.'

'You sound aggrieved.'

'We think we have every right to be,' said Miller. 'We're very proud of our reputation, sir.'

'What have you done to achieve it?'

'We've kept the streets safe for the citizens of Gloucester.'

'I don't think that the man who was urinated over would agree,' said Colbeck. 'He didn't even have the satisfaction of seeing Beckerton fined for the offence.'

'You underestimate us, Inspector.'

'In what way, may I ask?'

'The Gloucester constabulary is an experienced and effective police force,' boasted the other. 'We've dealt with murders.'

'Did you *solve* them?' asked Colbeck, bluntly.

The sergeant responded with sullen silence. After thanking him for his help, Colbeck went off in search of Beckerton. If the man had evaded prosecution for a string of offences, there had to be a reason beyond his having an excellent lawyer. Colbeck wanted to find out what it was.

* * *

Victor Leeming, meanwhile, had been given the task of finding out more about the departure of Michael Rydall. On the principle that landlords of local inns would be fruitful sources of information, he decided to visit them in turn. It posed a problem. The only way to get around was to use the trap, and Leeming was not at all confident that he could control the horse. It took him minutes to find the courage to climb into the vehicle. In the event, the animal behaved extremely well, trotting along paths that it knew by heart and responding to the driver's every command.

He got off to a disappointing start in The Crown in Frampton Mansell. The landlord had only been there for three years, well after the time when Rydall's youngest son had left. All that he could do was to confirm rumours about Michael. Leeming drove on to Sapperton and had more luck at The Bell. The landlord's wife, a motherly woman in her fifties, had little to say in favour of Michael.

'He was a handsome young devil,' she said, 'with no care for other people. When he'd had too much to drink, he could be foul-mouthed and awkward. My husband had to throw him out more than once. We had to ban him in the end. Other customers were complaining.'

'Did he come in here with friends?'

'He was a ladies' man, Sergeant, except that the ones he brought here were not always ladies. They never seemed to last long, and I don't blame him for that. Those young women were . . . not really his sort.'

'When he was banned from The Bell, where else would he go?'

'Oh, I'm told he went further afield,' she said. 'Most of his father's estate stretches in the direction of Stroud, and that's a big place, much bigger than Gloucester, in fact. Michael would've had much more choice of places to eat and drink there.'

'Can you suggest any inns where I might start?'

'You could try The George. It likes to call itself a hotel and so does The Lamb. They're among the best. Michael had plenty of money so he'd take his lady friends to places that would impress them.'

'You said that your husband threw him out of here.'

'That's right – three or four times in all.'

'Why did you allow him back in after the first time?'

She was honest. 'That was my fault, Sergeant.'

'What did you do?'

'I believed in his apologies,' she admitted. 'Each time he caused trouble, he'd come back next morning to say how sorry he was, offering money to pay for any damage he'd caused. Michael Rydall was cunning. He'd always bring a gift for me – flowers, usually.'

'You didn't have to accept them.'

'I couldn't turn him away, Inspector,' she said with a defensive smile. 'It wasn't in my nature. As I said earlier, he really was a handsome young devil.'

'Did you persuade your husband to give him another chance?'

'Yes, I did – again and again.'

'How do you feel about it now?'

'It was a big mistake.'

* * *

144

Alone in her bedroom, Catherine Rydall was in a quandary she found excruciating. A letter written by her estranged son had found its way to her well over a month ago. It meant that Michael was certainly back in England again though she had no indication in which part of the country he intended to settle – and with whom. He'd only told her that he himself would be returning. There was no mention of the woman with whom he'd left the country in the first place. Had the couple parted? Could she have died? Was there another woman in his life? If so, why was there no reference to her in the letter?

It was very frustrating. Catherine was feeding off crumbs of information. She still didn't know if he'd married the woman with whom he'd left or – and the idea appalled her – if they'd been living in sin abroad while posing as man and wife. Whatever the truth, her son had caused her pain and acute embarrassment. He'd also sown the seeds of potential discord between Catherine and her husband. Rydall had effectively killed their youngest son and forgotten that he'd ever been part of the family. And yet – in spite of his glaring faults – he was still very much alive in his mother's mind. His letter might have been destroyed but she could remember every single word of it.

What Michael had not explained, however, was his reason for coming back to his native country. Could it be that he blamed his father for driving him away in the first place and had returned to exact some sort of revenge? The first time that the thought had wormed its way into her mind, Catherine had dismissed it summarily, but it kept coming back and causing her deep anxiety. Supposing that Michael *was* somehow connected with the horrors of the train crash?

However remote the idea seemed, should she at least raise the possibility by telling Colbeck that her youngest son was back in the country? Or should she remain silent in order to retain her husband's love and trust? If Rydall knew that she'd kept in contact with Michael, he'd be furious with her. From that point on, marital life would be torture. If, however, it turned out that their son *had* been implicated in some way in the disaster at the tunnel, Catherine would have been protecting a criminal. She felt paralysed by fear.

As soon as he met the man, Colbeck made it clear that he wouldn't be hustled out in the way that Victor Leeming had been. He straightened his shoulders and looked Anthony Beckerton in the eye.

'Before you tell me that you're a busy man,' he said, 'let me warn you that we could have this conversation at the police station rather than in the relative comfort of your office.'

'Stay as long as you wish,' said Beckerton with a grin. 'I'm sorry that I couldn't give your sergeant more time. I liked him. He's the sort of man I'd enjoy talking to over a pint of beer.'

'I don't think that he'd say the same about you.'

'That's as may be, Inspector.' He gestured towards a chair and Colbeck lowered himself into it. 'Now then, how can I help you?'

'Why don't we start with an explanation? I've been talking to Sergeant Miller. It seems that you're not unacquainted with the police station.' Beckerton laughed. 'Having committed a number of offences, you've somehow evaded prosecution.'

'Of course, I have. You'd have done the same in my position.'

'I very much doubt it.'

'I'm a businessman, Inspector. That means I'm always in search of good publicity. It brings in more trade.'

'Relieving yourself over a man with whom you fought is not what I'd characterise as good publicity.'

'That's because you don't know the full details,' said Beckerton, affably. 'One – it wasn't a fight, it was a bit of fun. Two – I didn't knock him to the ground, he tripped and fell. And three – I didn't piss over him at all. It started to rain.' He snapped his fingers. 'Case dismissed.'

'You have a very cavalier attitude to justice.'

'That's not true. I always work within the law.'

'Were you working within the law when you broke up meetings at which Mr Rydall was speaking? You boasted to Sergeant Leeming that you ruined his chances of getting elected.'

'I made a small contribution towards it, that's all.'

'Mr Rydall is entitled to have legitimate ambitions to become a Member of Parliament.'

'I wanted to rein in his power, Inspector. He's got dangerous plans. If it was left to him, railways would criss-cross this county until there was hardly a blade of grass visible.'

'You seem to forget that he is a farmer as well. He cherishes the land far more than you do. It provides his income.'

'Rydall inherited a small fortune. He doesn't need an income.'

'Having met him, I fancy that he'd regard his inheritance as an agreeable irrelevance. At heart, he's a born farmer. He's never happier than when he's dealing with his sheep.'

Beckerton smirked. 'He's got seven less of them to count now.'

'How do you know?'

'It's common knowledge.'

'Yet when the sergeant called here earlier,' said Colbeck, 'you claimed that you didn't even know there'd been a derailment.'

'I didn't,' said Beckerton with an easy smile. 'The moment the sergeant left I sent my secretary to buy the local paper. There was a long report about the incident. Seven sheep were killed, the driver was injured and the fireman is still in a coma.'

'Actually, he's recovered consciousness now.'

'I'm glad to hear it. When he and the driver are fit enough for work, I'll offer them jobs on the canals. It's a less hazardous way of life.'

Colbeck watched him carefully before he spoke again.

'Do you know Edgar Smayle?'

'I've never heard of him.'

'That's odd. His name must have been in the newspaper article you claim to have read. Smayle is Mr Rydall's shepherd. On the night of the crash, he vanished along with his dog.'

'Oh, yes, I vaguely remember the name now.'

'You remember the number of sheep correctly, yet you forgot the shepherd who looked after them.'

'My memory plays tricks on me sometimes.'

'I'm told that you're well known at the Daneway Inn.'

'And at every other pub on the canals,' boasted Beckerton. 'I make a point of getting around them.'

'Smayle often drank at The Daneway. There's a good chance that you'd have bumped into him there.'

'Maybe I did, maybe not.'

'We found his sheepdog yesterday. Its head had been smashed in before it was tossed into the canal.'

'That's terrible. What about Smayle himself?'

'He's still missing.'

'Then I'd say the chances are that he's dead.'

'Did you read *that* in the local paper as well?'

Beckerton grinned. 'Why are you trying to catch me out?'

'I'm a stickler for detail.'

'So am I when I'm dealing with something important.'

'Are you claiming that sabotage on the railway, and a possible case of murder, are *not* important enough to hold your attention?'

'They're irrelevant to me, Inspector.'

'So why did you send for the newspaper?'

'Sergeant Leeming aroused my interest,' said the other. 'If someone accuses me of something, I like to know what it is.'

'We haven't accused you of anything.'

'I'll bet that Rydall did.'

'You are simply one line of enquiry, Mr Beckerton.'

'Then I can save you the trouble of hounding me any more.' He put a hand to his heart. 'I swear that I did not cause that derailment.'

'Do you have any idea who did?'

The answer was unequivocal. 'No, I don't.'

Colbeck glanced around the office, then studied Beckerton. The man had obviously done very well in his chosen way of life. It was something in which he gloried. As a consequence, he felt that he'd put himself beyond the law.

'When were you last in the Daneway Inn?' asked Colbeck.

'Oh, it must have been – what – a month or so ago.'

'It's not far from the Sapperton Tunnel.'

'No, it isn't,' said Beckerton. 'I remember strolling across to it and wondering how many sheep I could pen in the way of a goods train.' His coarse laughter reverberated around the room. 'Any more questions, Inspector?'

CHAPTER TWELVE

Glad to be back in London, Alan Hinton was also keen to leave it again as soon as possible. He took a cab to Scotland Yard and went to the superintendent's office. Tallis was surprised to see him but grateful that he'd brought a report with him. He read every word with care before setting the sheets of paper aside.

'I don't detect a sign of progress in here,' he complained.

'Oh, it's certainly taken place, sir.'

'This report is typical of Colbeck. It's concise, well-written and full of promise while at the same time lacking clear evidence regarding the few suspects you've unearthed.'

'The investigation is still in its early stages, Superintendent.'

'That's no excuse.'

'There are still lots of avenues to explore.'

'Then be so kind as to tell Colbeck to explore them with greater speed and more vigour. Every morning newspaper carried a report of the derailment. Journalists somehow seem to have amassed more detail about it than my officers managed to do.'

'That's not true at all, sir.'

'What are your orders?'

'I must return to the Cotswolds as soon as possible.'

'Then you can pass on *my* orders,' said Tallis, raising his voice. 'I've been besieged by leading figures from the Great Western Railway. They're demanding action. Tell the inspector to get them off my back by solving the case as quickly as he can. If he continues to plod along,' he added, 'I may have to come to Gloucestershire myself to inject some speed into the investigation.'

Driving to Stroud was a real test of Leeming's nerve because he had to negotiate a variety of terrain. Bumpy at best, some of the tracks were downright treacherous, catching him out with hidden potholes and introducing adverse cambers that made the trap lean over at an angle. He had to hang on to prevent being tipped out. Miraculously, the horse trotted through it all without losing its pace or its patience. Leeming began to feel that his dream of becoming a cab driver might not be so unrealistic after all.

Stroud was built on a series of hills. In the previous century, there'd been a rise in the use of water power, and, as a result, the cloth industry had become centred on Stroud. In the

1820s, there had been over a hundred and fifty mills in and around the town. Some had perished during the depression in the next decade, but the mills remained the dominant source of employment and the population remained substantially in excess of that of Gloucester.

After enjoying a ride through open countryside with pleasant views wherever he looked, Leeming had to adjust to the noise and ugliness of industry. Back in an urban environment, his search began. By the time he finally located the George Hotel, he was glad of a rest and a chance to reward the horse with the nosebag he'd brought. At that time of day, the place was almost deserted. He had to duck under a low, undulating beam as he entered and made his way to the bar. Tempted to buy himself a tankard of beer, he decided to master his thirst so that he didn't antagonise Colbeck again. Leeming explained to the landlord who he was and why he'd come to the area. The latter, a bearded old man with a dramatic shortage of teeth, was delighted to be drawn into a police investigation. It would be something unusual to talk about that evening when his regular customers came in for their beer.

'What was the name?' he asked.

'Michael Rydall. He was the youngest son of Stephen Rydall.'

'Everyone knows Mr Rydall around here. As soon as you leave Stroud and drive through Chalford, you'll be on Rydall land.'

'I know. I've just come from that direction.'

'What was the name again?'

'*Michael* Rydall,' said Leeming. 'He was the youngest of three sons. I'm told that he used to come to Stroud of an evening.'

'When would this be, sir?'

'Oh, we'll have to go back five or six years.'

'That's putting too much of a strain on my old memory, Sergeant. I can remember my childhood very clearly but, after that, things are a bit blurred. Wait a moment,' he added as an idea popped into his head, 'I'll give Ellen a call.'

'Ellen?'

'She's my granddaughter. Ellen works behind the bar.'

He disappeared through a door behind the bar and Leeming was left to hope that the barmaid had a better memory and substantially more teeth than her grandfather. The old man took so long to reappear that Leeming began to wonder if he'd forgotten why he'd left the bar. At length, he did come back in, his voice filled with pride.

'This is Ellen,' he said, indicating the young woman who followed him in. 'She's worked here for the last . . . how many years is it?'

'Six,' she said. 'I came here after my accident.'

Leeming didn't need to be told about her accident because it was all too obvious. Ellen was a plain, pale-faced, full-bodied woman in her early twenties, handicapped by the loss of her left hand. Leeming noticed the stump peeping out from her sleeve.

'Ellen worked in a mill,' her grandfather explained. 'All she did was to look the wrong way and her hand got caught. But she's still got the use of the other one and does the work of two barmaids.'

She gave a wan smile. 'How can I help, Sergeant?'

'Do you remember someone called Michael Rydall?'

'I think so.'

'What can you tell me about him?'

'He wasn't the only member of the family that came in here, but he stood out from the others. He was so good-looking.'

'Was he alone when he came here?'

'Oh, no, there was always this young woman with him.'

'I'm told that he kept changing his women friends.'

'He only brought the same one here,' she recalled. 'She was very pretty and had lovely hair. They had a meal sometimes. I know that because I served them.'

'When was this, Ellen?'

'It was not long after I started working here.'

'Did he cause much trouble?'

'No, Sergeant, there was none at all.'

'We don't stand for any of that here,' said the old man. 'People know they must behave proper. If this man you're talking about became a nuisance, I'd have had him straight out of the door.'

'He was nice and quiet,' recalled Ellen.

'Are you sure that you're talking about Michael Rydall?'

'Oh, yes, the woman kept using his name. She looked at him fondly all the time, and he smiled back at her. I liked them,' she said with regret, 'but not for long. All of a sudden, they stopped coming.'

Alan Hinton couldn't wait to hand over the letter to Madeleine. After taking a cab to the house, he was let in by the maid. Hearing his voice, Madeleine came eagerly out of the drawing room. When she saw what he'd brought her, she was delighted.

'Thank you so much, Alan,' she cried. 'How ever did you come to get hold of this?'

'The inspector handed it to me in person.'

'But that would mean that you've been to see him.'

'I've done more than that,' he said, beaming. 'I've been assigned to help in the investigation. The inspector asked for me.'

'That's wonderful! Congratulations!'

'I have to travel back to the Cotswolds fairly soon.'

'If you can wait a few minutes, I'll read Robert's letter then dash off a quick reply. Oh, this is such a lovely surprise!' She led the way into the drawing room and opened the letter as she did so. 'This is the last thing I expected.' The doorbell rang. 'That may well be Lydia. Why don't you let her in?'

Hinton needed no second invitation. He almost bounded into the hall and reached the door before the maid could do so. He opened the door and greeted Lydia with a broad smile. Pleased to see him, she was thrilled when she heard that he was working with Colbeck on a major investigation. Madeleine, meanwhile, was reading her letter. While it gave her great pleasure, she saw that there was no hint that her husband might be coming back to London in the near future. Crossing to the desk, she took some stationery from the drawer and wrote a short but expressive letter to him. When she went into the hall, Hinton and Lydia were simply gazing happily at each other in silence.

'What a shame!' she said. 'Alan has a train to catch. But since you haven't had chance to speak to him properly, why don't the two of you travel to the station in the same cab? That will give you time to catch up on each other's news. What do you think of the idea?'

The two of them burst into laughter.

* * *

The train from Gloucester took him back to within a hundred yards of the scene of devastation. While the other passengers had to climb up the embankment before being driven to a waiting train at the other end of the tunnel, Colbeck took the opportunity to pay a visit to the Daneway Inn. The first thing he did was to congratulate Peter Doble on the way that he'd recovered the body of the dead sheepdog. The landlord was modest.

'It was no effort for me,' he said. 'I've been swimming in the canal since I was a boy. You'd be amazed at some of the things I've found down there.'

'In this case, you found something very important. It explained what had happened to the missing dog and moved the investigation on to a new stage.'

'Edgar Smayle is not dead,' insisted Doble.

'I never said that he was.'

'Everyone else believes that he's gone for good, but I just have this feeling about him. Edgar is a survivor. He'll have pulled through somehow.'

'I sincerely hope so. However,' said Colbeck, 'the person I really wanted to discuss with you was Anthony Beckerton.'

'I talked about him to the sergeant.'

'I want more detail. I had a long talk with Mr Beckerton and came away with the feeling that I wouldn't trust him for a second.'

'Lots of people do, Inspector. Yet he's very successful.'

'That's what he kept telling me. But it's *your* assessment of him that I came to hear. Sergeant Leeming had the feeling that you sang his praises without actually liking the man.'

'Few people *do* like him,' said Doble, guardedly, 'but we have to rub along with Beckerton. He's an important figure in the canal trade.'

'Yes, and he's worked hard to achieve that position. I'm more interested in his character. How far would such a person go to achieve his ends?'

'That depends what those ends are.'

'Mr Rydall wonders if Beckerton was involved in the derailment in the Sapperton Tunnel.'

'Mr Rydall is entitled to his view,' said Doble. 'I don't share it.'

'Why not?'

'Beckerton's not stupid. He knows when a risk is too big to take.'

'What about your wife?'

'Molly?'

'Would she agree with you or with Mr Rydall?'

'Molly and I are in business, Inspector. We don't have views that are likely to upset our customers. That doesn't go down well. As for my wife,' he went on, signalling to her, 'ask her yourself.'

'Did you want something?' asked Molly, coming over to their table. 'What can we get you, Inspector?'

'Thank you all the same, Mrs Doble, but I never drink during the day.'

'The inspector's been to see Anthony Beckerton,' said Doble.

'Better him than me.'

'I gather that you don't like the man,' said Colbeck.

'I don't like anyone who pesters me, sir.'

'Beckerton's feud with Mr Rydall seems to be an open secret.

I was asking your husband how far he thought Beckerton would go to hurt Mr Rydall.'

Catching a signal from Doble, she bit back what she was about to say.

'I agree with Peter,' she said.

'Is that because you and he speak with one voice or because you're afraid to accuse Beckerton?'

'Mr Rydall has other enemies.'

'We are looking closely at them, believe me.'

'This is not fair,' said Doble, reasonably. 'You're trying to make us condemn a man who brings a lot of trade to this inn. We don't *know* if Beckerton is behind what happened at the tunnel. You're the detective, Inspector. You know how to find out the truth. Don't ask me and Molly to solve the crime for you.'

'I appreciate the position you're in, Mr Doble.'

'We try to be friends with *everybody*,' said Molly.

'Then you have a life which suits both you and your husband. My situation is different,' said Colbeck with a wry smile. 'I spend my life in pursuit of people I could never bring myself to befriend. Someone who can abduct Edgar Smayle, arrange for some of his sheep to die in agony, then kill his dog before tossing him into the canal is not fit to live in civilised society. This person's name may or may not be Anthony Beckerton, but I'll find him in the end.'

When she'd been in her prime, Pamela Etheridge had been a tall, stately, beautiful woman who could turn every man's head at a ball. Half a century had left a cruel signature on her body. Bearing five children had taken its toll and a riding accident had left her with a permanent limp that brought an end to her days of moving gracefully on the dance floor. As she entered middle age, her bold, upright stance slowly dwindled away and left her with a pronounced hump. In spite of her deficiencies, she remained a lively and confident woman. What she saw in the mirror still brought her a degree of satisfaction, however, because she was careful to stand at a particular angle.

When her husband came into the drawing room, she was reclining in a chair near the fireplace. Etheridge saw the burning logs.

'It's a lovely day, darling,' he chided. 'You don't need a fire.'

'Please leave me to decide what my needs are.'

'Why not go for a stroll to blow the cobwebs away?'

'Do you see *any* cobwebs on me, Gilbert?' she challenged.

'I was speaking metaphorically.'

'That's an abuse of the English language. If employed in the correct way, it remains the finest means of communicating effectively.'

'Why are you in such a truculent mood this morning?'

'I think I've been remarkably serene. Has my voice been raised? Have my eyes blazed with anger? Can you recall any hostile gestures I've made? No, of course you can't. Stop exaggerating.'

'I'm sorry, my darling.'

'And so you should be,' she said. 'Have you written to Darley yet?'

'The letter went off in the post first thing.'

'Good – at least you've done something right.'

Etheridge smiled tolerantly. He was so accustomed to his

wife's barbs that they failed to annoy him, still less to cause any pain. Marriage to an outspoken woman meant that he had to make allowances.

'He and Patrick will get on well,' he said.

'There may be other candidates for the post.'

'Our nephew has a distinct advantage. My friendship with the principal means that the professorship already has his name on it. Patrick deliberately contrived the opening for him by easing Professor Redwood out.'

'I never liked the fellow. He could be peppery.'

'To be fair,' said Etheridge, 'he came with excellent qualifications.'

'Qualifications are meaningless if you lack the ability to inspire your students. Patrick was right to get rid of him.'

'Yes, Pamela.'

He smiled inwardly. His wife had just repeated, word for word, something he'd told her the previous day. It was a habit she'd developed recently, listening to what he said then regurgitating it at a later date as if it was her own freshly minted opinion.

'He's certainly made his mark at the college,' he told her. 'Patrick has taken control of all appointments and acted boldly in a number of ways. It's unusual behaviour in a clergyman. They tend to be cautious and guided by tradition. Think of the rectors we've had at All Saints' over the years – worthy men, every one of them, but lacking in imagination and readiness to accept new ways of doing things.'

'*Old* ways are often the best,' she declared.

'We'll have to disagree on that point.'

'Don't be so silly, Gilbert. If you wish to do something useful, poke the fire for me, then tell me about this detective you mentioned yesterday.'

'He is one Inspector Colbeck,' said Etheridge, using the poker to move the logs about then replacing it in the hearth. 'Patrick took against him on sight, and that rarely happens. He found the man prickly and disrespectful.'

'That's insupportable. Patrick should complain to his superiors.'

'I believe that he's already written to Scotland Yard.'

'Why should the inspector visit the college at all?'

'Stephen Rydall sent him.'

'That explains it,' she said. 'He's always causing trouble.'

'For some reason, Colbeck expressed a desire to hear Patrick preach at All Saints' tomorrow. He also showed an interest in me.'

'We don't want him here, Gilbert.'

'We can't defy a representative of the law.'

'Oh, yes, we can. The inspector has no business with us.'

'Perhaps he feels that he has.'

'In that case,' she decreed, 'you need to speak to the butler. If this dreadful individual dares to come to our door, he must be sent round to the servants' entrance. Policemen need to be taught their place.'

Having returned to The Grange to collect his horse, Colbeck rode to the farm from which the estate was run. Stephen Rydall was in his office, studying some figures in a ledger. Pleased to see the inspector, he offered him refreshment, then gave orders for it to be prepared. The two of them were soon relaxing in armchairs. Colbeck began by talking about his visit to Gloucester police station.

'Yes,' said Rydall, 'I'm sure that Inspector Neil was piqued when I didn't summon him. The same is true of the police in Stroud and in Cirencester, of course. Since they're both closer to the scene, they might have expected to be put in charge of the operation.'

'Why did you ignore them?'

'They lack the experience that you have, Inspector.'

'I can't say that I've ever dealt with a blocked tunnel before.'

'You have a reputation.'

'It's not one that meets with general approval,' said Colbeck with a smile. 'Local constabularies tend to resent me for stealing their opportunity to deal with a major crime on the railway. That's not always true, mind you. We've had much-needed cooperation in some parts of the country. As a rule, however, we're viewed as metropolitan poachers.'

'Tell me about your meeting with Beckerton.'

'Actually, it was more of a confrontation.'

Rydall laughed drily. 'I've had a few of those with him.'

Colbeck gave a brief account of his visit to the haulier, collecting a series of resigned nods from his listener. When he touched on the fact that Rydall had once stood for parliament, there was an awkward silence. Colbeck waited minutes before he eventually broke it.

'Did Beckerton really break up some of your meetings?'

'Most of the time, he hired thugs to do so.'

'Do you have any proof of that?'

'No, I don't, but it's typical of him.'

'I can well believe it, sir. However, if you'd wished to take legal action against him, you'd have needed cast-iron evidence that those gangs were paid by him to disrupt your meetings.'

'Beckerton was too slippery to be caught.'

'How many MPs does Gloucester return?'

'Two.'

'Do you intend to stand again at the next election?'

'Yes, I do,' vowed Rydall. 'Parliament needs people like me. I'll be more discreet about my public appearances next time, that's all.'

'Are you afraid that Beckerton might target you again?'

'I'm counting on you to make sure that he's not around to cause any more mischief for me. Now that you've met him, you must agree that he has to be the prime suspect for what happened inside the tunnel.'

'Yes, he is the prime suspect but not the only one. You also gave me the name of the Reverend Patrick Cinderby, though, frankly, I can't see what motive he'd have to perpetrate the crime.'

'He's driven by a hatred of me, Inspector.'

'Is that enough to make him go to such extreme lengths?'

'Cinderby wouldn't be operating on his own,' said Rydall. 'He's a close friend of Squire Etheridge. During the negotiations with him for the purchase of land on which the railway would run, we developed a fierce dislike of each other. Etheridge is one of those people who feel that they're born to rule. He treated me as if I was a kind of serf.'

'I'm hoping to meet him tomorrow.'

'Where?'

'I thought it might be instructive to see how Cinderby performs in the pulpit. He'll be at All Saints', Kemble.'

'Then you'll certainly get to meet Etheridge and his wife. She is even more supercilious than her husband, by the way. She expects people to bow or curtsy to her.'

'The lady will get neither from me. But let me ask you something else, if I may. When we first arrived here,' Colbeck recalled, 'you told us there'd been acts of vandalism on the line.'

'Beckerton's work – I'd bet anything on it.'

'What about Squire Etheridge? He detests railways with a passion. Is he capable of hiring people to cause damage of that kind?'

Rydall pondered. 'It's possible, I suppose.'

'Arranging the crash was not easy. It involved careful planning. I doubt if anyone could do it from scratch, so to speak.'

'They'd work up to it – as Beckerton must have done.'

'Tell me something about Etheridge. Has there ever been an incident when someone employed by him was implicated in trouble on the line?'

Rydall needed a few moments to consult his memory.

'Strangely enough, there was,' he said at length.

'Go on, sir.'

'I'd completely forgotten it, to be honest, because it was an isolated event.' Rydall frowned. 'Or perhaps it wasn't.'

'What happened?'

'A man was caught trespassing on the line not far from the other end of the Sapperton Tunnel. It turned out that he was a servant at Kemble Court and claimed that he'd lost his way.'

'Who caught him?'

'It was a couple of railway policemen on night duty. I remember hearing about it. They said that the man was very polite and seemed sincere, so they let him go with a caution. That was the end of it – or so they thought.'

'Do you believe that he might have trespassed again?'

'It's conceivable.'

'Then he might have done so on the night before the train crash,' mused Colbeck. 'The servant's first visit might have been exploratory. On the second occasion . . .'

As they enjoyed afternoon tea, Madeleine Colbeck and Lydia Quayle chatted amiably. Both were in a good mood. Madeleine had heard that morning that a painting of hers had been sold by the dealer who gave her work prominence in one of the windows of his gallery. For her part, Lydia was still basking in the pleasure of having sat close to Alan Hinton as the two of them took a cab to Paddington.

'What did you talk about?' asked Madeleine.

'Oh, it was only this and that.'

'It must have been more than idle chatter.'

'Alan talked about this new assignment. He was exhilarated.'

'Sitting beside you would have contributed to that exhilaration, Lydia,' teased the other. 'He adores you.'

'Oh, I wouldn't say that.'

'How many more clues do you need?'

'I've told you before, Madeleine. We're simply friends.'

'There's nothing simple about your relationship.'

'We . . . like each other.'

'Is that all?'

'You're being very wicked today,' said Lydia, smiling.

'Does that mean I was wrong to suggest you shared that cab?'

'Not at all – it was a very pleasant journey.'

'What happened when you arrived at the station?'

'Alan got out, and I waved him off.'

'Was there no farewell kiss? No, I'm sorry,' said Madeleine, penitently. 'I shouldn't pry. It's unfair of me. The truth is that Alan came here for *my* benefit, not yours. He delivered Robert's letter and is taking back a reply.'

'He told me that the hamlet where they're staying is delightful.'

'Robert said the same in his letter. Frampton Mansell is close to that place you went to with your aunt – Sapperton.'

'It was idyllic.'

'Then why don't we go and see both villages for ourselves,' suggested Madeleine with sudden excitement. 'We could take the train to Cirencester and call in on your aunt.'

'That's a wonderful idea,' said Lydia, 'but there's one snag.'

'What is it?'

'Aunt Gwendoline died fifteen years ago.'

Victor Leeming sighed with relief. What had promised to be an ordeal had turned out to be an adventure. He had not only discovered that he could drive a trap without actually overturning the vehicle, he'd picked up a scent and followed it. What he'd learnt at the George Hotel made him wonder if Michael Rydall had frequented any other inns in the town. He therefore visited The Lamb, The Golden Heart, The Swan and two other places. At each one, the landlord or his wife remembered Michael dining there of an evening occasionally. He'd always been with the same young woman. The barmaid at the Half Moon recalled that his companion's name was Edith, and that she was very shy as if unused to dining in such comfort. The Bell at Sapperton had only bad memories of Michael. It was heartening to find that he'd made friends at other hostelries. Every one of them had been sorry when their young patron and his female friend had abruptly disappeared.

On the drive back to Frampton Mansell, Leeming realised that he'd visited eight pubs in all yet not touched a glass of beer in any of them. He could imagine how his colleagues at Scotland Yard would react when he told them about his uncharacteristic sobriety. They'd laugh in disbelief.

When he got to back to The Grange, he left the horse and trap by the stables, then paid a visit to Oliver Poulter, the driver of the wrecked train. Leeming was surprised and pleased to see that Leonard Treece, the fireman, had improved so much that he'd been moved into the same room as his friend. All three of them were soon caught up in a lively discussion. Since both railwaymen pressed him for details of the investigation, Leeming assured them that steady progress was being made and that the arrest of those responsible would happen in the fullness of time.

'We didn't realise we'd killed some animals,' said Poulter. 'Everything happened so quickly. Dr Wyatt told us that seven sheep had been penned on the railway line.'

'That's cruel,' added Treece. 'What sort of cold-hearted bastard would let some poor animals get sliced to death like that?'

'I wish I knew,' said Leeming. 'Inspector Colbeck wonders if there might be some religious significance. Could it be some form of sacrifice?'

'It's a weird kind of religion, if you ask me,' said the fireman, angrily. 'Whoever put those sheep there has got no conscience. It's vile. I wish I knew where that devil is hiding.'

Bright sunshine made the Parish Church of St Matthew look at its best. Set a little apart from the village of Coates, it was of Norman origin but had been altered and embellished in succeeding centuries. After tethering his horse, the man glanced at the nearby rectory, then walked up the path between the gravestones. He knew exactly what he wished to see first, and he soon found it. High up on the south-west angle was an anthropophagus, a mythical cannibal in the act of swallowing the latest victim. It brought an approving grin to the man's face. Opening his notebook, he copied the carving with great care.

CHAPTER THIRTEEN

Colbeck found the visit enlightening. Having only seen Stephen Rydall in his guise as a member of the GWR board, it was interesting to watch him acting solely as a farmer. On the wall of his office was a large map of the estate, some of it broken up into tenant farms but the bulk of it was kept by Rydall.

'As you can see,' he said, pointing a finger at the map, 'we have a fair amount of arable land. We grow a variety of crops and have had satisfactory results with all of them. Sheep, however, are my passion so most of the land is set aside for them. They're wonderful animals, Inspector.'

'I'll have to take your word for it, sir.'

'They ask so little of us.'

'You must have been horrified by the sight of those dead sheep on the line. If, as I believe, your shepherd was forced to take them there, it would have been akin to torture for him.'

'Smayle has always tended the flock with love.'

'He may yet be able to do so again.'

Rydall sighed. 'I wish I could believe that.'

'I see no reason to abandon hope.'

'Of all the people I employ,' said Rydall, 'Edgar Smayle was the most important. He had a way with sheep that was almost magical. His disappearance is not simply a loss to me. The herd will soon become aware of it.'

'They'll miss Blackie as well.'

'That dog was remarkable. Smayle could make him do anything, simply by whistling. Blackie is irreplaceable.'

'Whoever killed the dog knew that.'

'Catch the people responsible, Inspector,' urged the other. 'I want to look them in the face.'

'You'll be able to do that one day, sir. I'm sure of it. Before too long, they'll make a mistake.'

'Meanwhile, I have to struggle on without my shepherd.'

'Who is looking after the flock now?'

'Will Smayle is doing his best, poor lad, but he has severe limitations. Then there's his grandfather, Jesse. He used to be a shepherd himself until arthritis crippled him. Unless a miracle happens and we get Smayle back, the future looks bleak for the whole family.'

Lambing was an aspect of his work that Edgar Smayle had liked best. Though he could be hard in many ways, he brought a tenderness and understanding to the work. It was something that he'd learnt from his father, but the latter no longer retained his skills. Hobbling around on a walking stick, he was in agony. If he bent over a sheep to ease a new lamb into the world, he was uncertain and heavy-handed. His grandchildren had to help him.

'Damn it!' he cried as he dropped his walking stick.

'Don't worry,' said Annie, moving swiftly across to the pen. 'I'll pick it up for you.'

'Wipe it clean first. It's covered in afterbirth.'

'You go back indoors, Grandad. Will and I can manage.'

'I must do my bit,' he insisted, watching her pick up a handful of straw to wipe his stick. 'There was a time when I could do this with my eyes closed.'

'It's too much for you.'

'Don't you dare say that to me, girl.'

'You're in pain. I can see it.'

'And I can feel it,' he said, taking the stick from her without a word of thanks. 'But I mustn't give in. Don't you understand? I have to show Mr Walters that I can do *something* – even if I have to crawl on my hands and knees.'

A sharp twinge in his hip made him let out a yelp. Annie's heart sank. Her grandfather was in real distress. He wouldn't be able to save them from eviction. Where could the family possibly go?

Since he had so much news to impart, Leeming waited at The Grange with growing impatience. When he heard the sound of hooves clacking on the cobbles, he came out of his room immediately. Seeing Colbeck dismount and tether his horse, he walked over to him.

'Where've you been?' asked Leeming.

'I've been to see how Mr Rydall runs his estate. Let's sit outside in the sun and I'll tell you all about it.' They moved to a bench nearby. 'Actually, I went to the Daneway Inn first.'

'Why was that?'

'Having met Beckerton for myself, I did what you had the sense to do. I talked to someone who knows him well. Doble was the obvious person. I got the same feeling that you did. The landlord is very careful what he says about Beckerton.'

He told Leeming about his visit to Gloucester and his subsequent talks with Peter Doble and with Stephen Rydall, especially the latter.

'One has to admire his energy,' he said. 'Mr Rydall is a man of many interests. Apart from running the estate and attending board meetings of the GWR, he has political ambitions and he also owns a factory in Cirencester that manufactures agricultural implements.'

'Does it make anything to scrape sheep dung off your shoes?'

'Just watch where you put your feet, Victor.'

'I tried that, but I still keep stepping into it. Anyway,' said Leeming, 'you don't have to say anything about Mr Rydall. I spent hours listening to people telling me what an important man he is in this part of the Cotswolds.'

'Where have you been?'

'I spent most of the time in Stroud.'

Colbeck was impressed. 'You drove all the way there and back?'

'I showed the horse that I was in charge and had no trouble.'

'What did you find out?'

'Oh, I learnt a lot about the Rydall family.'

'Did that include Michael?'

'It was mostly about him, sir.'

Leeming went on to talk about his pilgrimage from one inn to another, gathering information at each one but never – he was careful to stress – being tempted to drink alcohol. At all of the places he'd visited in Stroud, he got the same answer. Michael Rydall had dined at each one, always with the same young woman. Without warning, he'd then vanished completely.

'Landlords were very sad about that. Michael always behaved himself and he had plenty of money to spend. They welcome customers like that. As for Edith, his girlfriend, she seems to be the one who calmed him down – unlike at The Bell in Sapperton, where he was thrown out a few times. In each case, he had a different woman with him.'

'Yet in Stroud, he was always with this friend, Edith.'

'Yes, sir,' said Leeming as a broad grin spread over his face.

'Have I said something funny?' asked Colbeck.

'No, no, you haven't.'

'Then why are you beaming at me?'

'I've been saving the best bit until last. You heard me mention the Half Moon in Stroud.' Colbeck nodded. 'The barmaid there told me something that made the effort of going all that way worthwhile.'

'What was it?'

'He's been *seen*, Inspector.'

'Who has?'

'Michael Rydall.'

'Where?'

'It was near the railway station in Stroud. The barmaid said that he looked a little fatter and older than she remembered him, but it was definitely Michael. He was on his own and drove past her in a trap. In other words,' said Leeming as if he'd just solved the case, 'Alan Hinton was right. We have another suspect to consider – Michael Rydall – and, to my mind, he's far more convincing than any of the others.'

The train stopped more often than it had on the previous journey he'd taken to the Cotswolds. There was no complaint from Alan Hinton. In fact, he hardly noticed that it was taking longer. His mind was filled with happy memories of sitting beside Lydia Quayle in a cab and pressing gently against her. He could still hear her voice and smell her perfume.

It was not until their penultimate stop that he became aware of how far they'd come. Doors were opening and slamming shut as passengers got out at Kemble station so that they could take a train on the branch line to Cirencester. The station was simple to the point of being rudimentary. At every other station buildings had been of Cotswold stone and all kinds of trimmings had been added. With its absence of stone and its wooden platforms, Kemble looked half-hearted, as if it didn't have the courage to blossom into a typical GWR station. There was something pitiable and apologetic about the place.

Hinton made a mental note to ask Colbeck about it.

Arriving at the Daneway Inn, the man pulled the horse to a halt and got out of the trap. Molly Doble was bending over one of the outside tables to gather up plates and tankards. Beckerton's blood stirred immediately, and he had the urge to creep up behind her and feel her buttocks or slip his arms around her so that he could touch the full breasts. At that moment, her husband came out of the inn to assist her. When he noticed his visitor, Peter Doble blinked.

'What are you doing here, Anthony?' he asked.

'I came to speak to you.'

'Why?'

'Can't you guess?' Beckerton smiled at Molly as she carried her full tray towards the inn. 'You look as fetching as ever, Molly. Have you missed me?'

Saying nothing in reply, she went into the building and closed the door behind her. Beckerton turned to Doble and his manner changed.

'Don't fall out with me, Peter,' he warned.

'What do you mean?'

'I'm a good friend but a wicked enemy.'

'There's no need to threaten me, Anthony. I never fall out with anybody, least of all with someone like you.'

'Why did you set those detectives onto me?'

'I didn't.'

'First of all, it was that Sergeant Leeming, the one who looks as if he belongs on the other side of the law. I tied him in knots. Today it was the turn of Inspector Colbeck. He was much more trouble.'

'I didn't send either of them, honestly.'

'Don't lie to me, Peter.'

'It's the truth – I swear it.'

Beckerton stood over him and looked deep into his eyes. Holding his ground, Doble met his gaze directly. The other man eventually relaxed.

'Somebody gave them my name.'

'It must have been Mr Rydall.'

'They're both clever men, Colbeck more so than Leeming. Before coming to Gloucester, they'd have wanted to find out more about me. The obvious place is here. You know me better than anyone.'

'They did come,' admitted the landlord, 'but only *after* they'd been to see you. The sergeant came yesterday, and the inspector cornered me today.'

'What did they want to know?'

'They asked me my opinion of you.'

'And what did you say?'

'I told them we'd known you ever since Molly and me took over the inn, and that we admired the way you built up your business. I said that you had every right to call yourself the King of the Canals in this part of the country.'

'And so I have,' said Beckerton, beating his chest.

'They heard nothing bad about you from me, Anthony.'

'What about your wife?'

'Molly never spoke to them,' said Doble, keeping a straight face.

'Where are they staying?'

'Mr Rydall has put them up at The Grange.'

'That's so that he can pour poison about me into their ears. You've got to do the opposite, Peter. Speak well of me. Leeming had the look of a drinking man to me so he's certain to come here again at some point. Build me up, do you hear?'

'You can rely on me.'

'Tell Molly to do the same,' ordered Beckerton. 'And there's something else you can both do for me.'

'What is it?'

'Find out as much as you can about how their investigation is going. I want every detail, however small and unimportant it may seem. I need spies in the enemy camp, Peter. That's you and Molly.'

'We'll do our best.'

'Good,' said Beckerton, slapping him on the shoulder. 'I'll have a pint or two, then I'll get off back to Gloucester.'

Doble looked at the horse and trap. 'Did you drive all the way here?' he asked. 'It must be over twenty miles.'

'That's why I took the train to Stroud and borrowed the trap from a friend to bring me here.' He chuckled. 'Yes, I know that it's shameful for someone who loves canals to use the railways, but I had no choice. Come on,' he said, putting a friendly arm around Doble to guide him towards the inn, 'I'll let you buy me the first pint.'

Even though they were alone, they always took the trouble to dress for dinner. Catherine Rydall was in her bedroom, seated before the dressing table and wondering which item to select from her jewellery box. There was a tap on the door before her husband came in.

'I thought you might have invited Inspector Colbeck and the sergeant to join us,' she said. 'It's our obligation as hosts.'

'I did invite them, Catherine. The offer was politely declined.'

'Oh, I see.'

'All three of them are dining at The Crown.'

'Three?' she repeated. 'Who is the third person?'

'His name is Detective Constable Hinton. He was recruited from Scotland Yard to join in the investigation. Hinton is staying at The Crown. The menu there should suit him. It's resolutely basic.'

'What about the others?'

'I fancy that the sergeant would feel more at home at The Daneway. He'd mix easily with the bargees. The inspector would be hopelessly out of place there. He'd be more comfortable at the King's Arms in Cirencester. Thanks to that French chef of theirs, it offers excellent cuisine.'

'So I'm told,' she said, pointedly.

'I've taken you there more than once.'

'The last time was almost six months ago, Stephen.'

He was shocked. 'I don't believe it.'

'Then you'll have to check your diary.'

'Oh dear, I do apologise. I tell you what,' he said, holding her by the shoulders and planting a gentle kiss on her cheek, 'when this business is finally over, I'll take you there to celebrate. That's a promise.'

'Thank you. I look forward to it.'

He stepped back. 'It may involve a wait, I'm afraid.'

'How long will it be?'

'Inspector Colbeck can't give an exact date, but he guarantees that it will be as soon as possible. Meanwhile, we have to remain patient.' He glanced into the jewellery box. 'Wear that necklace I bought for your birthday. You know how much I like it.'

Catherine smiled at him in the mirror and took the necklace out. After squeezing her shoulders again, he let himself out of the room. His wife glanced down at the box. Earlier that day it had contained the letter from her youngest son. When she thought of how her husband would have reacted if he'd seen it, she trembled so much that the necklace fell from her hands.

They had learnt on their first visit there that top hats and frock coats were very much out of place at The Crown. All three of them had therefore changed into something more in keeping with a country pub. They chose a table in a quiet corner so that they could have their discussion in private. While Leeming and Hinton were drinking beer with their meal, Colbeck opted for a glass of whisky. In his pocket was the letter from Madeleine bearing the news of her latest success as an artist. At a time when they were talking about a major disruption on the railway that affected so many people, it seemed wrong to boast about his wife's achievements, so he kept the information to himself. Instead he turned to Hinton.

'What did the superintendent have to say?' he asked.

'He admired your report,' replied Hinton, 'and noticed the clever way you tried to conceal the fact that we'd made little progress. If we don't have something to show for our efforts very soon, he's threatening to come here in person to lead the investigation.'

'Heaven forbid!' exclaimed Colbeck.

'We *have* made progress,' insisted Leeming. 'I discovered earlier today that Michael Rydall had been seen in the vicinity.'

'Are you sure about that?' asked Hinton.

'He's back, Alan.'

'How do you know?'

'He was spotted in Stroud by a woman who knew him by sight.'

'You're right, Sergeant. That *is* progress.'

'Let's not get over-excited,' warned Colbeck. 'This woman hadn't seen him for over five years so she may have made a mistake. Much as I hope she is right, I'd like some supporting evidence. That's why I've asked the sergeant to go back to Stroud tomorrow to widen his search. You can go with him, Alan.'

'Yes, sir.'

'Don't worry,' said Leeming. 'You won't have to take the reins again. I can drive the trap perfectly well now.'

'I look forward to seeing you in action.'

'What will *you* be doing, Inspector?'

'I'll be attending a church service in Kemble,' said Colbeck.

'Why go all that way?' asked Hinton. 'If you wish to go to church, there's one right here in Frampton Mansell.'

'I'm sorry to be pedantic but St Luke's is actually a chapel of ease.'

'What does that mean?'

'It was built specifically to save people from having to walk two miles to the parish church at Sapperton. That was built centuries ago. According to Mr Rydall, St Luke's has been in existence for less than twenty years.'

'Then why don't you go to Sapperton?' asked Hinton.

'The Reverend Cinderby will be taking the service at Kemble. It will enable me to see him in his natural setting and give me the chance to meet Squire Etheridge, the owner of Kemble Court.'

'He's the one who believes that railways have no right to exist,' said Leeming. 'It's a ridiculous attitude to take. He can't live in the past for ever.'

'My train stopped at Kemble station,' recalled Hinton. 'It's nothing like any of the other stations on the line. Why is that?'

'Squire Etheridge refused to have a proper station built on his land,' said Colbeck, 'even though the GWR paid him an absolute fortune in compensation for building a railway line on his property. Mr Rydall told me that they handed over the exorbitant sum of £7,500.' Hinton and Leeming reacted with amazement. '*And* it was contingent upon the company building a tunnel to ensure that the railway couldn't be seen from Kemble Court.'

'No wonder Mr Rydall is wary of the squire,' said Hinton.

'Wary?' echoed Leeming. 'I'd be hopping mad with him.'

'How did Etheridge get away with it?'

'Property is power,' said Colbeck. 'Mr Rydall told me that Etheridge is viewed by others as a man with amusing eccentricities. Rydall described him as malign and dangerous, and I'd trust his judgement. Etheridge and Cinderby make a formidable team. That's why I'm keen to see them together.'

'Let's come back to Michael Rydall,' suggested Leeming. 'Our problem is that we don't really have a good description of him. Everyone who spoke to me said that he was very handsome, but that's really all that we know.'

'There'll be a resemblance to his father,' said Hinton.

'That's possible.'

'And we've got some idea of his age.'

'It's not enough,' said Colbeck. 'He could walk past all three of us in the street and we wouldn't recognise him. Also, of course, if he *is* responsible for what happened at the Sapperton Tunnel, he might try to disguise himself.'

'That barmaid in Stroud picked him out,' said Leeming, 'so he can't have changed his appearance all that much.'

'Ideally, what we need is a photograph of him, but I can hardly ask Mr Rydall for one. He's probably destroyed every reminder of his youngest son. It's ironic, isn't it?' he mused. 'Though he despises Squire Etheridge, he has something in common with him.'

'What is it?'

'Both of them go to extremes,' said Colbeck. 'Etheridge has hidden the railway out of sight of his home, and Mr Rydall has buried his son in the past. Both men are in flight from reality.'

'Are you going to tell him about Michael being back?'

'Yes,' said Hinton, 'I think that he has a right to know.'

'I'm not sure that he does,' decided Colbeck. 'Besides, it would upset both him and his wife. We don't want to alarm them unnecessarily until we've been able to find Michael and connect him with the derailment. That may take time.'

Although five of them sat around the kitchen table, the room seemed glaringly empty. At the head of the table, the chair was unoccupied, a vivid reminder that Edgar Smayle was no longer there. Everyone was grim, subdued and silent. Reflecting the mood of its master, Will's dog lay curled up in its basket with mournful eyes. Simple fare was served. Instead of eating it, however, the family picked at their food and swallowed it reluctantly.

After looking around at them, Betsy Smayle tried to lift their spirits.

'Cheer up, everyone,' she urged. 'We have to hope for the best.'

'*What* best?' asked Jesse, sourly.

'I get the feeling that the inspector believes Edgar may still be alive.'

'What does *he* know? He's a complete stranger here.'

'I trust him,' said Annie. 'Mother is right. We shouldn't just give up. We should have faith in the detectives and pray for Father's safety.'

'Prayer never works,' moaned Jesse.

'It's all we've got, Grandfather.'

Betsy was about to add a comment when she heard the sound of a walking stick being banged three times on the floor above. She recognised the signal.

'Come on, Annie,' she said, rising wearily to her feet. 'Your grandmother needs to use the chamber pot. Let's see to her.'

Gilbert and Pamela Etheridge sat either end of the long table in their dining room. Placed at intervals, candelabra created pools of flickering light and made the silver cutlery dazzle. After a five-course meal, Pamela waited until a servant cleared away the plates and left the room.

'What are you going to say to him, Gilbert?' she asked.

'I beg your pardon.'

'I'm talking about this detective. If he is bent on seeing you as well as Patrick, you have to decide how to treat him. In your position, I'd simply refuse to speak to him.'

'That's taking incivility too far,' he said.

'Inspector Colbeck has no right to include you in a police investigation.'

'We don't know that that's what he intends.'

'You told me that he hounded Patrick.'

'That was Rydall's fault.'

'That man is beyond contempt,' she said. 'I can't think of anyone less likely to commit a crime than Patrick, especially one as evil and destructive as blocking that tunnel. Can you, Gilbert?'

He was evasive. 'Let's talk about something else.'

'We have to make our feelings clear to the inspector.'

'I agree. Leave it to me.'

'I still think you should snub him, Gilbert.'

'We'll be on consecrated ground, my dear. That fact will help to dictate my behaviour. Now, please, let's leave the subject.'

'Not until I've had my say,' she insisted.

'Oh, very well,' he sighed, reaching for his glass of port.

'This unpleasantness is all down to that hateful man, Stephen Rydall. He haggled with you over the building of that railway line on our land and he fought against you at meetings of the governing body of the college.'

'That's true, Pamela.'

'At every turn, he's tried to thwart you. I detest the man. In fact, I loathe the entire Rydall family.'

'I wouldn't go that far,' he argued. 'There was one member of the brood whom I readily applaud. Unfortunately, he's no longer here. It's a great pity.'

'To whom do you refer?'

'Michael Rydall.'

* * *

Dinner at The Grange had been in the nature of a trial for Catherine Rydall. Her husband had talked obsessively about the crime that had inflicted such damage on the GWR and how no punishment could be severe enough for those responsible for it. Rydall had worked himself up into a lather of vengefulness. Nothing his wife could say was able to calm him down. In any case, she was having difficulty in retaining her composure. Knowing that her youngest son was back in England, she'd concealed the information from him. It was like an angry wasp, buzzing around inside her brain and threatening to sting at any moment.

Nursing a secret was proving to be a curse. It meant that she was deceiving a husband with whom she'd been unswervingly open and loyal in the past. She tried hard to persuade herself that, even if Michael had returned, he would certainly not come back to Gloucestershire. He was more likely to be hundreds of miles away, shunning the family from which he'd been expelled. Yet he could still exact revenge on his father through an intermediary. The letter he'd written to his mother had, after all, been sent to a friend who lived not far away. He'd delivered it to the house when her husband was at work on the estate. From the moment she read it, she felt a sense of betrayal.

It was not only her husband who was being tricked. Inspector Colbeck and his colleagues were also victims. In her possession was information that could either help to exonerate her son or link him to the crime they'd been sent to solve. It horrified her to realise that she was, in effect, impeding the investigation. If it turned out that Michael *was* guilty, she might be arraigned for failing to pass on vital evidence. Her stomach began to churn.

'Are you all right, Catherine?' asked Rydall, solicitously.

'Yes, yes, I feel fine.'

'You seemed to be miles away.'

'I'm tired, that's all. My mind was wandering.'

'Perhaps you should have an early night.'

'I might say the same to you, Stephen.'

'It's good advice,' he said. 'I only wish that I could act on it, but I know that I simply can't. Since the moment when I was summoned to the tunnel, I haven't had a wink of sleep.'

'Why not ask Dr Wyatt to prescribe something for you?'

'Because I feel that it's my duty to stay awake.'

'That's only punishing yourself,' she pointed out.

'I'm driven to find out the truth,' he explained. 'My hope is that Colbeck will soon unmask Anthony Beckerton as the man behind all this, possibly in collaboration with Cinderby, unlikely as that may seem. Neither of them would have been directly involved, of course. They're too cunning for that. They'd have hired someone else to do the actual work of causing mayhem, then luxuriated in the feeling that *I'd* be the major victim.'

'What if it was not the people you mention?' she asked.

'Then it *has* to be someone who once belonged to this family.'

Her stomach churned even more vigorously.

Reclamation work continued throughout the night. Fires still blazed away outside the tunnel to supplement the many lanterns set up there. Cranes had been used to move some of the debris, but there was still much left. Inside the tunnel, teams were still working to clear away the damaged freight. Though most of the wagons would have to be broken up, there were some that could be repaired. All that was needed was the time to do it. When everything was eventually removed from the tunnel, a detailed inspection could be made of the brickwork inside it. No trains would be allowed to run through it until all the repairs had been carried out.

Creeping along the track in the dark, Michael Rydall got close enough to the scene to have some idea of the impact of the derailment. He stood there for a long time. One of the railway policemen on duty then began to walk in his direction. It was time for Michael to flit away into the night.

CHAPTER FOURTEEN

It was a fine, clear morning when Colbeck set off on his journey to Kemble. Following a route recommended by Stephen Rydall, he left the main road to ride down a lane that eventually skirted Coates and gave him a glimpse on his right of the parish church of St Matthew. He kept the horse to a steady canter, marvelling at the fact that he was so close to the source of the Thames, the famous river that travelled all the way to London and beyond before debouching into the North Sea. Almost immediately, as he pressed on at a trot, he had his first sight of the tall spire of All Saints' Church, spearing the sky. To reach the village, he had to go under a railway bridge. As he did so, a train rumbled past over his head, startling his horse. Colbeck soon calmed the animal down.

The village consisted of clusters of small, picturesque, stone-built houses with stone slate roofs. It was a typical farming community with barns wherever he looked. Flocks of sheep grazed contentedly in the warm sunshine. Colbeck needed no direction to the church because several parishioners were already making their way towards it, some clutching prayer books that had been handed down from earlier generations. Some children were clearly reluctant churchgoers, but the adults seemed uniformly eager to attend the service, striding out with a sense of purpose and dragging any protesting infants along.

The ground had been rising ever since he entered the village and Colbeck rode up another incline when he turned into Church Road. Dwellings were, for the most part, larger and more impressive but he paid them no attention. His gaze was fixed on the massive square tower, built in the thirteenth century and topped by a spire of much more recent construction. People were now converging on the church from different directions. Before he dismounted, Colbeck paused to admire the magnificent yew tree in the churchyard, spreading its ancient branches like outstretched arms to welcome the congregation.

Whenever he was at home on a Sunday, he and Madeleine would go to their local church together and join in a service of worship. This time it was different. As well as joining in the praise of the Almighty, he would be looking for signs – however small – that the Reverend Patrick Cinderby and Squire Etheridge were in some way linked to a heinous crime on the Great Western Railway.

* * *

190

'You've really got the hang of this, Sergeant,' said Hinton.

'Yes,' agreed Leeming, driving the trap with comparative ease. 'I may be able to become a cab driver, after all.'

'You'd never leave the Metropolitan Police Force, surely.'

'I have been tempted, Alan.'

'I don't believe it. You were born to be a detective. You have every quality needed for the job.'

'The superintendent doesn't think so. If I do nine things right and one thing wrong, he'll always criticise the mistake. There's never a hint of praise. It's disheartening.'

'I know. I've had the same experience.'

'But it's not only that. It's spending so much time apart from the family. I like to share a bed with my wife,' he complained, 'and enjoy the pleasure of watching my children grow up. I can't do that if I'm stuck in somewhere like the Lake District as I was last year. One case even took us to America.'

'It must be difficult for you,' said Hinton.

'It is, Alan. If I worked as a cab driver, I'd see my family every day and come home safe. I can't guarantee doing that in this job. Most villains resist arrest. I've often had bruises or an occasional black eye.'

'Yes, but there's always the excitement of a good fight. It's one of the reasons I joined the police. I like action.'

'So did I at your age. Wait till you're as old as me. Or wait till you have children of your own.'

'That time is a long way off.'

'I've seen the way you look at Miss Quayle,' said Leeming with a wink. 'And I've seen the way that she looks at you.'

'I can't think of marriage on my pay.'

'*I* did – and it was even lower when I was your age. But let's go back to my point. Children make all the difference. Look at the inspector. He used to be fearless and ready to tackle anybody. Since his daughter was born, he's much more careful. He's still as brave as ever, mind you, but I've seen a definite change in him.' He turned to Hinton. 'What's that old adage about caution?'

'Discretion is the better part of valour.'

'Exactly – I think Inspector Colbeck has taken it to heart.'

Desperate to visit the crash site in order to view progress, Stephen Rydall was duty-bound to follow his normal routine on a Sunday morning. Most people in Frampton Mansell went to St Luke's, a building that seemed curiously at odds with its surroundings since it resembled nothing so much as an Alpine church from Northern Italy. Though it was an easy walk from The Grange, Rydall and his wife never worshipped there, preferring to attend services at St Kenelm's in Sapperton, a larger and much older church and the one in which the couple had been married.

When their carriage drew up outside the church, they were greeted by friends and nodded to respectfully by everyone else. Filing into the building, they took their usual places. Both of them knelt in prayer. While Rydall was asking for a swift resolution to the derailment that had caused such wilful damage, Catherine was praying desperately that Michael was not culpable in any way. She was also asking for guidance in her turmoil. Should she tell her husband the truth and risk causing serious harm to her marriage? Or should she confide only in the detectives and rely on their discretion?

* * *

There was a larger congregation in Kemble, and every member of it had an appointed place. Colbeck was obliged to sit at the rear of the nave, but his height allowed him to have a clear view of the altar. Sunday was the only day of the week when Squire Etheridge got up relatively early and he was allowed privileges. Morning Service was delayed for over ten minutes until he arrived with his wife on his arm. His servants followed in his wake. The newcomers took their seats in pews at the front. Etheridge took advantage of the fact that he was the only person in the congregation permitted to look over his shoulder. When he did so, however, it was not to offer an apology to everyone for his lateness. It was to seek out Colbeck. Once his eyes settled on the detective, Etheridge gave him a long stare before turning his head round again.

The service was taken by the rector, a short, stout man in his fifties with a reedy voice. He was assisted by a curate. Prayers were said, hymns were sung lustily, if not always in tune, and then it was time for the sermon. Having sat quietly in the priest's stall, the Reverend Patrick Cinderby seized his moment. He rose majestically. In his vestments, he was an imposing figure and his voice boomed out with ease to every part of the church. His theme was forgiveness, and Colbeck had to admire the skill with which he'd prepared the sermon. It was clear, well-constructed and delivered without the use of notes. The congregation was spellbound.

At the end of the service, Cinderby lined up with the rector in the porch, and they took it in turns to shake hands with people as the congregation streamed out. Colbeck lingered in the church so that he could have a good look at its many interesting architectural features. He was examining the medieval font when he was accosted by Gilbert Etheridge.

'What are you doing here, Inspector?'

'I always go to church on a Sunday,' replied Colbeck.

'Do you know who I am?'

'Yes, I do. You're Squire Etheridge. You live next door to the church and yet you were unable to arrive in time.'

'That's my prerogative.'

'So I could see.'

'Reverend Cinderby is a fine man. Stop harassing him.'

'I wasn't aware that that was what I was doing.'

'Rydall had the effrontery to name him as a possible suspect for the blocking of that tunnel. That's why he dispatched you to the college. I'm told that you did everything but accuse the principal to his face.'

'My memory of our discussion is rather different.'

'Don't listen to Rydall,' said the old man, wagging a finger. 'He's been conducting a feud with both of us – with Patrick, because of the college and with me, because of my friendship with his son, Michael.'

Colbeck was taken aback. 'You knew Michael?'

'I have the honour to be the president of the Cirencester Cricket Club. My own playing days have long gone, but I have an infallible eye for talent. Michael had it in abundance.' He smirked. 'From the look of surprise on your face, I can see that Rydall forgot to mention anything about his youngest son's cricketing prowess.'

'He's told me very little about Michael.'

'Suffice it to say, he was the best player we've ever had. With bat or ball, he was in a class of his own. I cherish the memory of the century he scored against a team from Worcester. Then, alas, he left the area and hasn't been seen since. It was a grievous loss to us.' He looked Colbeck up and down. 'Are you a cricketer, by any chance?'

'Not any more, I fear. I did play for the university when I was up at Oxford. During the three years in which I was part of the team, we had the satisfaction of beating Cambridge soundly. Work commitments interfered with any sporting activities after that. But let me ask you something about Michael,' he continued. 'At the end of each season, you had a team photograph, presumably.'

'I insisted on it,' said Etheridge, 'and I always made sure that I was in it myself. The walls of the pavilion are covered with photographs and our trophies are also on display. It shows how proud we are of our history.' He tapped Colbeck on the chest. 'Don't pester Patrick again. His appointment as principal was a stroke of genius.'

Turning on his heel, he went briskly out of the church. Colbeck walked down the aisle, admiring the beautiful floral patterns on the kneelers as he did so. Before he could go on to the chancel, he heard footsteps behind him and turned to see Cinderby approaching. The clergyman was wearing the effulgent smile of a man who knows that he's delivered a good sermon and expects congratulation.

'As you saw, Inspector,' he said, 'we are traditionalists here. We have no truck with the ostentation of the Oxford Movement. It smacks too much of Roman Catholicism. Your *alma mater* has a lot to answer for.'

'The blame should fall on John Henry Newman,' said

Colbeck, 'and not on the university itself. But let me say how much I appreciated your sermon. You sent everyone out in a much more forgiving mood.'

'That was my intention.'

'I was interested in your choice of text.'

'Luke, Chapter 17 is a favourite of mine.'

'I'm surprised that you didn't quote the third and fourth verse.'

Cinderby blinked. 'You know it that well?'

'I had only a vague memory of it, so I looked it up in the Bible in my pew. It touches on the very essence of forgiveness.'

'Yes, I suppose that it does.'

'Now, how does it go? "If thy brother trespass against you, rebuke him; and if he repent, forgive him. And if he trespass against thee seven times a day, and seven times in a day turn again to thee, saying, 'I repent; thou should forgive him." I hope I haven't misquoted.'

'Not at all.'

'It's extraordinary how many times that happens, isn't it?'

'What do you mean?'

'The number seven,' said Colbeck, meaningfully. 'It crops up again and again – in the Old Testament and in the New. What is so special about the number, Reverend?'

'Well . . .'

'Seven sheep were slaughtered in the mouth of the Sapperton Tunnel. Is that merely a coincidence – or is someone sending us a message?'

For the first time since they'd met, Cinderby looked extremely uncomfortable.

* * *

The Half Moon Inn was closed but some spirited knocking on the front door eventually brought the landlord into sight. He was bleary-eyed and wearing an old dressing gown. Leeming introduced Hinton and asked if they could speak to one of his barmaids. It transpired that the girl didn't actually live on the premises, but the landlord furnished them with her address and gave them directions how to reach it. A few minutes later, the trap was pulling up in a narrow street with terraced houses on both sides. Sunday was no day of rest for some families. Children were playing in the street, a man was delivering bags of coal from the back of his cart and a woman was standing on a chair to clean her downstairs front window. Loud conversations were taking place between neighbours.

The arrival of strangers aroused general curiosity and some of the children came scampering across to stare at them. Having seen the two of them through her front window, Jenny Duckett came quickly out of the house. The barmaid was a pretty, willowy young woman with a shock of red hair and a face covered in freckles. She was wearing a pinafore over a faded dress with a floral pattern. She said she was pleased to meet Hinton and delighted that information she'd given had been of some use. Because there was so much noise in the street, Leeming asked if they might go inside the house.

Embarrassed to take them into her home, she apologised for the disarray in the front room. They were less worried by the clutter and lack of space than by the acrid smell that was coming from the kitchen. As they settled down in chairs, the door opened and a big, bald-headed, unshaven man in a pair of baggy trousers and a crumpled shirt with no collar came in. He looked suspiciously at Leeming. When his daughter explained who the two visitors were, he relaxed slightly but insisted on being present, leaning against the door jamb with his arms folded.

'Now then, Jenny,' said Leeming, 'have you had time to think over what you told me yesterday?'

'Yes, Sergeant,' she replied.

'And do you still believe that you saw Michael Rydall?'

'I *know* it was him.'

'How close did you get?'

'I was only four or five yards away.'

'And remind us where this was,' said Hinton.

'It was by the railway station here in Stroud.'

'And he was alone, I'm told.'

'That's right, but he might have dropped someone off to catch a train. He drove straight past me as if he was in a hurry.'

'Jenny was there to meet her cousin off the train,' said her father. 'Irene comes over from Stonehouse regular.'

'How would you describe Michael Rydall?' Leeming asked her.

She shrugged. 'I told you, Sergeant. He was very good-looking.'

'Was he tall or short?'

'Oh, he was tall and strapping.'

'What about his complexion – light or dark?'

'He was quite pale, really.'

'What colour was his hair?'

'Dark brown,' she said, 'and he had this lovely moustache.'

'I think it must have been him,' said Hinton. 'She clearly knew him well enough by sight.'

'Let's go through it all again,' said Leeming.

'Before you do that,' Duckett interjected, 'can I ask a question?'

'Please do, sir.'

'If my daughter helps you . . .'

'Yes?'

He grinned. 'Is there any kind of reward?'

Every Sunday, Edgar Smayle led some members of his family to Christ Church, the parish church of Chalford. His wife, daughter and mother usually went with him, but his son was always left behind because people stared at him whenever they heard him trying to speak. On this occasion, nobody went to represent the family. Will was dividing his time between herding the sheep and searching in vain for his father. Supervised by her grandfather, Annie was in charge of lambing. Her mother came out with cups of tea for them.

'One of us should have gone to church,' she said.

'Why?' asked Jesse.

'We could have prayed for Edgar's return.'

'I've been praying for Father every day,' said her daughter.

'It's not the same, Annie. It *means* more in a church.'

'I stopped going there years ago,' said Jesse, grumpily. 'Churches are always as cold as ice. They play havoc with my arthritis. My fingers get so bad, I can't hold anything.'

'Maybe we should all pray together,' suggested Betsy. 'We could do it before a meal, for instance.'

'Waste of time.'

'It's worth trying.'

'No, it isn't,' he said. 'I've been praying for help with my arthritis for over ten years and it's got steadily worse. Explain that, Betsy.'

She heaved a sigh and walked quietly away.

* * *

Before he left the village, Colbeck had a good look at Kemble Court. Occupying land adjoining the church, it was a large, stone manor house, built two centuries earlier and featuring a stone slate roof and gables with verges and finials. It was set well back from the big, iron gates through which Colbeck was staring. He noticed that they were securely locked. Gilbert Etheridge valued his privacy.

After reclaiming his horse, Colbeck rode towards Cirencester, less than five miles away. When he got close to the town, the Royal Agricultural College loomed up ahead. He wondered what its principal would next say about him to Etheridge. There was clearly a close friendship between the two men. He rode on to the heart of town and was astounded by the sight of the Parish Church of St John the Baptist. It had the magnificence and proportions of a cathedral with a huge three-storeyed porch. Of all the so-called 'wool churches' – those financed by wealthy wool merchants – it was the largest and was a fitting memorial to the time, centuries earlier, when the Cotswolds had primacy in the wool trade. Appropriately, the church was adjacent to Dyer Street.

After speaking to a passer-by, Colbeck learnt that the cricket ground was in Cirencester Park, so he turned his horse in that direction. He arrived there as a man was inspecting the grass with a view to cutting it in the near future. Colbeck dismounted and walked across to him. The groundsman was a burly individual of middle years with a full beard and curling hair sprouting from under his hat. He had the most impenetrable local accent that Colbeck had heard so far, but he somehow managed to catch the gist of what was being said.

'I've just been speaking to the club president,' Colbeck began.

'Oh, ar . . .'

'Squire Etheridge told me how successful the club was.'

'That's right, sir.'

'He said I was to be sure to look inside the pavilion at some of the trophies you've won. Is there any chance that you could let me in?'

'Yes, sir – come this way.'

The pavilion was bathed in sunshine. Colbeck noted that the benches on the verandah would afford anyone an excellent view of a match. The groundsman unlocked the door and led the way into the main room. There was a well-stocked bar at one end, but all that interested Colbeck were the trophies and the photographs. The latter were placed in sequence along one wall. He found a photograph from six seasons earlier and saw Etheridge standing in the middle of the eleven players. Colbeck didn't need to read the names neatly written below because he picked out Michael Rydall at once. The resemblance to his father was strong. He was well-built, open-faced and sporting a neatly trimmed moustache. Most players were gazing fixedly at the camera, but Michael was grinning from ear to ear. Colbeck pointed to him.

'This is Michael Rydall, isn't it?'

'Oh, ar,' said the groundsman.

'What sort of player was he?'

'He were the best I've ever seen, sir. He could win games on his own.'

The groundsman went off into rhapsodies about the player's abilities, and Colbeck let him carry on unchecked.

His final question, however, got a very different response.

'What sort of person was Michael?'

'When he weren't playing cricket,' said the other, 'he were nasty. I had a row with him once, and he never let me forget it. Michael had a vicious streak, sir. It were a mistake to fall out with him.'

Having established that the person seen by Jenny Duckett might be Michael Rydall, the two detectives drove up to Stroud railway station. The barmaid had been waiting there when she'd seen Michael go past. Because it was such a surprise after five years or so, she watched which way he'd turned at the end of the street. Leeming and Hinton followed the same route.

'Is there any point in doing this?' asked Hinton.

'We'll see, Alan.'

'But we have no idea where he was going.'

'Yes, we have,' said Leeming. 'He was going to ground. Michael may be back in the area, but he doesn't want anyone to know it. That means he's hiding somewhere with a friend.'

'We've no idea who his friends are.'

'Think of The Grange. If he lived in a place like that, Michael would have got to know people who lived in houses of similar size. In other words, he was part of the county set. He certainly won't be skulking in a tiny little hutch like the one where Jenny Duckett lives.'

Hinton tapped his chest. 'I was born in a house like that.'

'So was I, and I don't mean to criticise it. I'm just pointing out that Michael lived in a different world.'

'Do you think he is still in Stroud itself?'

'I doubt it. Look at the way Jenny saw him racing off. He was anxious not to be seen. My guess is that he's out in the countryside somewhere, and we at least know which road he took.'

'What do we do – knock on the door of every country house?'

'No, Alan, we simply make a note of them for future reference.'

'It could be a complete waste of time.'

'Of course,' said Leeming, affably, 'but, then, so is most of the routine work we do. Every so often, however, we have a stroke of luck. It's Sunday. Let's start praying that we get one today.'

The moment they got back home, Stephen Rydall changed his clothing and set off to see how much progress was being made at the tunnel. Catherine was left alone to brood. Having hoped that the visit to church would ease her conscience and help her make a decision, she was more confused than ever. She was now writhing with guilt. Before it overpowered her, she made herself think about something else by visiting the injured railwaymen. They were both very grateful to her and her husband for allowing them to stay there. Poulter and Treece were facing a long period of convalescence, yet both managed to smile and make light of their problems.

When Leonard Treece's parents arrived, Catherine left them alone with their son and crossed over to Poulter. As she chatted with the driver, however, she kept her ears pricked to catch the conversation around the other bed. Treece's anxious mother did most of the talking, giving him some biscuits she'd made and promising to look after him when he was able to return home. It was a revelation to Catherine. She'd never had such an obviously close relationship with any of her sons. There was more love between them and their respective nannies than with her. Michael was her favourite, but even he had tended to keep her at arm's length. Mrs Treece was a real mother and the most important person in her son's life. It made Catherine feel envious.

She took her leave of the patients and went back into the main house. The demons returned to taunt her immediately. Why was she betraying her husband? How long would she hold back information from him and from the detectives that might well have crucial importance to the investigation? Who was she trying to protect – Michael or herself?

Caleb Andrews had called to see his daughter and to have the pleasure of playing with his granddaughter. He was unusually muted when he arrived.

'Is there any news, Maddy?'

'Not since the letter that Alan Hinton brought yesterday.'

'He must be so pleased to be involved in the case.'

'It's a form of promotion and well-deserved.'

'I just wish that *I* could still be in the Cotswolds with them.'

'You'd only get in the way, Father,' she said. 'Besides, you're supposed to be in retirement. You're entitled to sit at home with your feet up.'

'I'd be bored stiff, Maddy. It would be like a death sentence.

I keep my body and my mind active,' he said, proudly. 'Even at my age, I feel as if I have a lot to offer.'

'And you offer it – as a loving grandfather.'

'That's not enough for me. When I went all that way to see what had actually happened, I came back feeling ashamed. The only way to make amends is to help to catch the person behind the derailment. I have this theory, you see—'

'I'm sure you do,' she said, 'and I'm equally sure that Robert will already have considered and rejected that theory.'

'At least, mention my offer to him.'

'I may not get the chance, Father.'

'He'll write to you again, won't he?'

'That depends on how busy he is. Alan Hinton told me that all three of them are working very long hours.'

'Don't talk to me about long hours, Maddy,' he protested. 'Time after time, I came home from work exhausted.'

'That's why you're entitled to take it easy from now on.'

'My brain simply won't let me do that. Now, listen to me. My theory is that an employee of the GWR is involved. After all, it's the kind of railway company that could make anyone working for it want to cause trouble.' She burst out laughing. 'What's so funny?'

'You are,' she said. 'Two days ago, you were apologising for the way you used to criticise the GWR. Now you're back doing it again.'

'It's because I've seen it in its true light. Let me tell you why the GWR is the worst railway company in Britain. First of all . . .'

* * *

Colbeck felt that his morning had been well spent. He'd attended a church service and watched Cinderby preaching before he later exchanged a few words with him. He'd also met Squire Etheridge and been able to gauge the strength of the friendship between him and Cinderby. Without realising it, Etheridge had done him a favour. In speaking so well of Michael Rydall's abilities on the cricket field, he'd given Colbeck an opportunity to look at a photograph that told him what Michael looked like. An additional treat had been the brief visit to St John the Baptist Church in Cirencester. The church had been mesmerising. Before they left the area, Colbeck was determined to take a closer look at the exterior and interior of the building. He also wanted to explore the abbey ruins at the rear of the church. Meanwhile, there was a crime to solve.

On the ride back to The Grange, therefore, he looked at the suspects one by one, reserving Michael Rydall until the end. His father had bitter memories of him, but Etheridge had spoken of the young cricketer with real affection. If the eyesight of a barmaid at the Half Moon Inn could be trusted, then Michael was within striking distance of the Sapperton Tunnel. Furthermore, the groundsman at the cricket club had made a telling comment. Michael nursed a grudge. If he fell out with someone, he never let that person forget it. Had an estranged son come back to the Cotswolds to get even with his father?

Colbeck was a couple of miles from Frampton Mansell when he saw a horseman in the distance, moving towards him at a gallop. When the rider got closer, he realised that it was Rydall. The latter held up a hand in greeting so Colbeck brought his mount to a halt. He could see from the look on the other man's face that Rydall was desperate to speak to him. Reining in his horse, Rydall took a deep breath before speaking.

'I've had a ransom demand,' he said. 'Edgar Smayle is still alive.'

CHAPTER FIFTEEN

Sunday on the Thames and Severn Canal was, for the most part, just like any other day of the week. There were bargees who'd leave their craft moored while they went off to the nearest church, but they were very much in a minority. Those who had just legged their way through the canal tunnel had no inclination to get down on their knees. All they wanted was a restorative drink. It was the reason why Peter and Molly Doble were kept as busy as ever at the Daneway Inn. As she looked at new customers seating themselves at one of the tables, Molly had a few hasty words with her husband.

'I hope that Beckerton doesn't turn up again,' she said.

'He won't, Molly. He's got what he wanted.'

'You did well to send him on his way. He frightens me.'

'Anthony is not all that bad,' he said, 'and it's important to stay friends with him. I've met people who didn't.'

'So have I. He can be malicious.'

She broke off to serve customers who'd just come into the bar. Doble went outside to take orders from the other newcomers. Husband and wife had little chance of talking to each other after that. It was some time before Doble was able to have a break. As he stretched his back and looked around, he became aware that he was being watched. Somebody was crouching down behind a bush on the side of the towpath. Pretending not to notice the figure, Doble strolled slowly towards the bush as if he was just having some gentle exercise then stopped.

'You can come out, Will,' he said, good-humouredly. 'I won't bite you.'

Will Smayle rose slowly up from his hiding place.

'Hello,' he said, shifting his feet.

'I thought it was you. What are you doing here?'

Will tried to reply but the words refused to come, so he resorted to a few gestures, pointing to The Daneway then over his shoulder. Doble understood.

'Yes, you're right,' he said, tolerantly. 'Your father did come here, but you weren't supposed to know. That means you must have followed him. He told me that I was never to serve you. Some of the bargees can be very cruel, Will. Your father wanted to keep you away from them.'

The young shepherd pointed in the direction of the railway tunnel.

209

'I think I know what you're asking.'

'Father, Father . . .'

'Did I see him that night?' Will nodded. 'No, I didn't, lad. When I heard that terrible noise, I rushed over to the railway tunnel as fast as I could. All I saw was the engine on its side and two men lying on the grass. I rushed to them first to see if they were still alive.'

Will gestured and burbled again.

'It was a long time before I even saw the sheep – what was left of them, anyway. I know what they meant to you and to your father. I hate seeing dead animals, especially when someone's killed them like that. When I pulled Blackie out of the canal, I was really upset.' He put a consoling hand on Will's shoulder. 'I'll keep looking, I promise you that. I'm as eager to catch the person who did all this as you are. We have a lovely part of the country to live in. All of a sudden, the whole place has been poisoned.'

Will nodded again and bunched both fists.

'I feel the same,' said Doble, resolutely. 'If I get my hands on whoever did this, I won't bother with the law. I'll give them what they deserve.'

Eyes lighting up, Will began to punch the air wildly.

Back at The Grange, Colbeck and Rydall were able to discuss the situation at length. They were in Rydall's study, and he had now calmed down slightly. Colbeck examined the blunt demand for money. Turning over the sheet of paper, he sniffed it before handing it back to Rydall.

'Do you think it's genuine, Inspector?'

'Yes and no.'

'It can't be both.'

'I fear that it can,' said Colbeck. 'It's genuine in the sense that it came from someone who wishes to take a lot of money from you – or from the GWR.'

'I'll be happy to pay.'

'Wait a moment, sir. There's no proof given that Smayle is actually still alive. That's where the falsehood might come in. It's highly likely that you're being tricked.'

'How can I find out the truth?'

'Write back and question their honesty. Say that you won't give them a penny until you have clear proof that your shepherd is alive and well.'

'I hope to God that he is,' said Rydall. 'What about the family?'

'Don't say a word to them.'

'But they're on tenterhooks.'

'It would be cruel to raise their expectations then have them dashed. They mustn't hear about the demand until we've established the truth.'

'Have you been in this position before, Inspector?'

'Yes, I have – on a few occasions.'

'What happened?'

'In one case, we were able to rescue the hostage and apprehend the kidnappers; in another, they were demanding money for the release of someone they'd already killed.'

Rydall grimaced. 'That's disgusting.'

'We're dealing with a malign enemy, sir. Whoever is responsible took pleasure from slaughtering those sheep. The driver and fireman also came close to death as a result of the derailment. Remember that, and don't underestimate the person who wrote that letter. This person is utterly ruthless.'

'I'd pay anything to get Smayle released,' said Rydall, seriously. 'I feel that I owe it to the family.'

'This demand is exploiting your emotions, sir. Implicit in it is the knowledge that you're under intense pressure and, in the eyes of the person who wrote to you, it's an ideal time to strike.'

'So, we really are up against someone who *knows* me.'

'We are indeed, sir.'

'They realise how important Smayle is to the farm.'

'A shepherd is emblematic of your whole enterprise. It may be the reason that *he* was chosen and not someone like Mr Walters or one of your many other employees.'

'I begin to see that now.'

'Make contact,' advised Colbeck. 'Do exactly as you are told. But, instead of handing over five thousand pounds, insist on having clear evidence that Smayle is alive and unharmed.'

'What if that evidence is provided?'

'That's where we step in, sir. You'll agree to the arrangements they suggest for exchanging the money for your shepherd, and we'll come out of hiding to make the arrests.'

'How many people might be involved?'

'Two, at least, I suspect – possibly more.'

'Won't they expect you to try and catch them?'

'Of course,' said Colbeck. 'That's why we must proceed with the utmost caution. That letter is trying to scare you into handing over the ransom immediately. Show them that you won't be rushed.'

Rydall sighed with relief. 'I'm so grateful for your advice.'

'Would you like me to help you draft your reply?'

'Yes, please.'

'What about the GWR? Shouldn't the company be involved?'

'The demand was addressed to *me*,' said Rydall, 'and it's the life of my shepherd that's at stake here. I take full responsibility, Inspector.'

'Then we'll proceed on that basis, sir.'

'We must do so at once.'

'Let's get that letter written.'

Rydall indicated his desk. 'There's pen and paper waiting.'

Colbeck got up at once. Sitting at the desk, he reached for a sheet of stationery and paused to consider exactly what he should write. The choice of words was important. If the tone was wrong, the kidnappers would be suspicious, and it was vital to convince them that Rydall was prepared to cooperate. After a few moments, Colbeck reached for a pen. Rydall looked over his shoulder and gave a nod of approval.

'Excellent,' he said. 'It's firm without arousing hostility. They'll know they can't take advantage of me now.'

'Copy it out in your own hand so that they know it was written by you.'

'Then what?'

'We await a reaction.'

After a frugal meal in Stroud, Leeming and Hinton began the journey back to Frampton Mansell. In order to give Leeming a rest, Hinton was driving the trap. He looked back on their morning.

'Did we achieve anything?' he wondered.

'I believe that we did, Alan.'

'What was it?'

'To begin with, we have a much clearer idea of what Michael Rydall looked like.'

'Yes, we do, though we only saw him through Jenny's eyes, and she was obviously dazzled by him. But at least we have something to go on. Michael charmed the other barmaids as well. He clearly had a gift.'

'I wonder how he did it,' said Leeming, wistfully. 'All that I ever get from a barmaid is a wary look. They're always on guard against me.'

'Not when they realise who you are, surely.'

'It doesn't usually get that far. They sidle out of my way.'

'If we ever catch up with Michael,' suggested Hinton with a grin, 'you can ask him his secret.'

'There's one good thing,' said Leeming. 'I feel we're much closer to him after this morning. He's a real person to me now. I can see him in my mind's eye.'

'What's his next step?'

'He'll stay in hiding, Alan. Wouldn't *you* in his position?'

'That depends what his position is, Sergeant. The maddening thing is that we just don't know. On balance, I fancy that Beckerton is the one behind the derailment. Look at the way he treated you and the inspector. I'm wondering if we shouldn't put a tail on him.'

'Mention it to the inspector,' said Leeming. 'If he agrees, then the job will have to fall to you. Beckerton has seen the two of us. He wouldn't know *you* from Adam.'

* * *

Anthony Beckerton was a stickler for keeping up appearances. Having taken his wife to church that morning and saying all of the right things to all of the important people in the congregation, he drifted back to the docks. A barge was about to set off along the Thames and Severn Canal. He sauntered across to the bargee.

'You've got a full load, I see,' observed Beckerton.

'We can cope with it.'

'I'm sure you can. I need to ask you a favour.'

'Just tell me what it is, Mr Beckerton,' said the other, obsequiously.

'When you've fought your way through all those locks, I daresay that you'll stop at The Daneway to wet your whistles.'

'They serve a good pint. It's even better when Molly pulls it.' They both sniggered. 'Yes, we'll certainly be paying a visit to The Daneway.'

'Then you can pass on a message for me.'

'Who's it to – Molly?'

'I'd prefer to give her a message face-to-face.'

'It's for her husband, then, is it?'

'Find a moment when you and Peter are alone.'

'What do I say?'

'Just tell him that I send him my regards. And when you do that, give him a long, hard warning look.'

'Is that all, sir?'

Beckerton smiled. 'It's more than enough, believe me.'

It was only when they were enjoying a preprandial sherry that Squire Etheridge was able to have a proper conversation with

Cinderby. The two men were ensconced in armchairs in the spacious drawing room. Above the mantelpiece was the painting of Kemble Court that its owner had commissioned when he'd first moved into it. Out of force of habit, he kept glancing up at it as if to reassure himself that he lived in such a fine mansion. He looked across at his visitor.

'I must congratulate you on your sermon,' he said. 'It was first class.'

'Thank you,' replied Cinderby.

'Some of it went above the heads of the congregation, of course, but that's more or less inevitable. What they could comprehend had a powerful effect on them. You sent them home with an important lesson.'

'Inspector Colbeck said that he'd enjoyed what I'd said.'

'Did you believe him?'

'At the time, I did,' said Cinderby. 'Now, I'm not so sure.'

'What exactly was he doing there?' asked Etheridge.

'He was obeying Rydall's orders to put me under the microscope and, by extension, to keep an eye on you as well. To be candid, I found his presence unsettling.'

'You didn't seem unsettled, Patrick.'

'Once I began to speak, my nerves disappeared. I forgot that he was there.'

'But the damned fellow *was* there, and I hate interlopers. That's why I challenged him and ordered him to leave you alone.'

'I can fight my own battles, thank you.'

'You may need help in this case,' said Etheridge. 'He's a problem. We both agreed that he needed watching, so I've had someone making discreet enquiries about his movements. Colbeck has been here, there and everywhere.'

'He hasn't been back to the college, thank goodness.'

'He's been to Gloucester for some reason and was later seen at the Daneway Inn. My man lost sight of him after that.'

'What kind of response did you get from him this morning?'

'He was very civil,' replied Etheridge. 'He's cool, and he's astute. I did surprise him at one point, however. When I told him that Michael Rydall had been the best cricketer we'd ever had, he showed a real interest. He asked if there were any photographs of the team in which Michael had played.'

'Why did he want to know that?'

'It was no more than a case of mere curiosity.'

'Michael Rydall vanished about five years ago. I heard that he'd gone abroad.'

'That's what I heard as well, and I daresay that Colbeck would have picked up that rumour, though not from Michael's father, of course. Rydall disowned him. The inspector heard the tale elsewhere. That's why he was fascinated by what I said about Michael.' His brow furrowed in thought. 'There is one explanation, I suppose.'

'What is it?'

'He has a genuine interest in the game,' said Etheridge. 'It turns out that Colbeck got a blue playing cricket for Oxford University.'

'Oh dear!' groaned Cinderby. 'I hate the man even more now.'

Colbeck was waiting outside to greet them when they arrived back at The Grange. Leeming and Hinton were astonished at the news he gave them about the ransom demand. The three of them adjourned to Colbeck's room to discuss the new developments.

Leeming was cautious. 'It could be a trick,' he said.

'We considered that possibility,' said Colbeck, 'and have therefore asked for proof that Smayle is still alive.'

'Why has it taken so long?'

'That's what I was thinking,' said Hinton. 'It's been days since the crash and the disappearance of the shepherd. You'd have expected a demand to come earlier.'

Leeming sniffed. 'I smell a rat.'

'I did the same when I first read the demand,' admitted Colbeck. 'But I've come to the conclusion that whoever sent it has been biding their time. The culprit wanted Mr Rydall – and Smayle's family, of course – to *suffer*. That's why they've been kept waiting.'

'This person could be twisting the knife in the wound, sir,' said Leeming. 'Wanting to raise false hopes before dashing them – *after* the money has been handed over, of course. I think Smayle is dead.'

'What if we're given clear proof that he's alive?'

'Then I'll admit I'm wrong.'

'Alan? What's your opinion?'

'I'm in two minds, sir,' said Hinton, pleased to be consulted. 'I'd *like* to believe that the shepherd has been held as a hostage, but something is holding me back somehow.'

'I'm relying on instinct,' said Leeming.

'My instinct is not as finely tuned as yours, Sergeant. If I had to guess, I think Smayle was killed along with his dog. They're pretending he's been kept alive so that money can be made out

218

of him. After all, he's important to Mr Rydall. That's why the demand is so high. If *I* was abducted, nobody would dream of paying five thousand pounds to secure *my* release.'

'If Mr Rydall stumps up that amount, he'll have the most expensive shepherd in the history of farming.'

'No, he won't, Sergeant,' said Colbeck, 'because we must make sure that the money never changes hands. Let's wait until we get proof that Smayle is alive and unharmed. Mr Rydall can then pretend to agree to pay the demand. That's when Alan will take over.'

Hinton was startled. 'Me, sir?'

'I want you to act as the go-between.'

'Why?'

'The sergeant and I were on the scene from the start. We've both been watched. You won't have attracted the same amount of attention. Also, you're younger and faster than either of us, and those qualities may be needed. Don't worry,' said Colbeck, 'when you put on your disguise, you'll be completely invisible.'

'Where do I get the clothing from, Inspector?'

'It's being donated by one of Mr Rydall's gardeners.'

'*Gardeners?*' said Hinton, aghast.

'There you are, Alan,' said Leeming with a laugh. 'If you're fed up with detective work, you can always get a job looking after the gardens here. It's a healthy, outdoor life, and there's no Superintendent Tallis to bother you.'

'I'm not moving from London for anybody.'

'Talking of the devil,' continued Leeming, 'how can we keep the superintendent from charging over here and getting under our feet?'

'I've sent him a telegraph about the ransom demand,' said Colbeck. 'He'll see that as a sign of progress because he knows that it gives us our chance to catch the kidnappers. In short, we're quite safe for a few days. Tallis won't descend on us just yet.' He saw the consternation on Hinton's face. 'What's the trouble, Alan?'

'It's the gardener's clothing, sir.'

'What about it?'

'Well, it's . . . a rather dirty job. Gardeners look like ragamuffins.'

'You can hardly turn up in a policeman's uniform,' said Leeming. 'They'd realise what you were up to at a glance.'

'What really worries me is the smell,' confessed Hinton. 'They wear the same clothes day in and day out, year in and year out, probably. That means they get filthy and stink to high heaven.'

'We'll ask Mrs Rydall to lend you some of her perfume.'

'Don't tease him,' said Colbeck.

'Or we can stick some lavender bags under your armpits.'

Hinton was embarrassed. 'It's no joke, Sergeant.'

'You'll only have to wear it once,' said Colbeck. 'We were lucky. The gardener who gave us his old clothing has got virtually the same build as you.'

'Did you say *old* clothing, sir?'

'Yes. In fact, he was just about to throw it away. I have it right here. Take it back to The Crown and try it on.' He reached under the bed and brought out a potato sack. 'Here you are.'

Hinton regarded the sack with horror and distaste.

'It's ideal for our purpose,' Colbeck assured him, handing over the sack. 'I understand your objection, but it was too good an offer to refuse. I did thank the gardener,' he went on, smiling. 'He's not exactly a candidate for sainthood, I'm afraid, so his discarded trousers won't have the odour of sanctity.'

It was afternoon when he arrived in Kemble, and he rode straight to the church. After appraising it from outside, he let himself into the building and stood in the nave to take an inventory of its salient features. There was much to be recorded. After searching every nook and cranny, he went out and tried to decide where he'd start first. Sitting on the wall, he opened his notebook and flicked the pages until he came to the one he wanted. It was the scene outside the Sapperton Tunnel.

'Alan Hinton?' he asked in surprise.

'Yes, Father.'

'He's been sent to help Robert?'

'It's a real feather in his cap,' said Madeleine.

'Maybe it will lead to a promotion. He's clever enough to be a sergeant.'

'That may take time. He's still young.'

'Robert was a sergeant when he was only a few years older,' recalled Andrews, 'and he did the job well. That's why he's an inspector now.' His eyes twinkled. 'Does Lydia know what's happened?'

'She arrived when Alan was still here.'

'Was she impressed at his news?'

'Lydia was overjoyed,' said Madeleine. 'That's why I encouraged her to go to Paddington in the same cab so that she could wave him off.'

'I bet he enjoyed that.'

'And so did Lydia.'

He chuckled. 'I'm so pleased for the lad,' he said. 'It's well-deserved. Mind you, I feel sorry for him as well.'

'Why?'

'He has to go back to Gloucestershire on that stupid broad gauge.'

'Father!' she exclaimed.

'We need a unified national system, Maddy.'

'I'm shocked at you.'

'Why does the GWR have to be different to every other railway company? It's sheer madness.'

'You could equally well argue that the GWR gauge is the better one and that everyone else should adopt it.'

His voice was dripping with contempt. 'I'd adopt nothing that Brunel invented. He always had to be the odd man out.'

'You've changed your tune,' she told him. 'When you got back from that visit to the tunnel, you said that you'd come to your senses at last and realised that GWR drivers and firemen deserved respect. They were like comrades of yours.'

He looked blank. 'Did I really say that?'

'More or less.'

'It doesn't sound like me.'

'I've never seen you so apologetic.'

'Well, I don't feel very apologetic today, Maddy. I wouldn't travel on a GWR train if you paid me.'

'Alan spoke very well of the company. He had a comfortable journey in both directions.'

'That's more than I did,' said Andrews, pugnaciously. 'Whatever possessed me to entrust my life to the GWR? I was on the edge of my seat throughout both journeys. I tell you, I was scared.' She held up a hand to silence him. 'What, are you shutting me up?'

'Someone has to.'

'I'm just offering an opinion.'

'You're like a pendulum, Father,' she said, forcefully. 'First, you swing one way and now you've swung in the opposite direction. When you got back from seeing that tunnel, you had tears in your eyes. Today, you've forgotten all about the two men on the footplate who barely escaped with their lives.'

'No, I still have some sympathy for them.'

'If they worked for the London and North Western Railway, you'd be extremely sorry.'

'That's different. *Our* drivers and firemen are very special.'

'You can be so annoying sometimes.'

'Calm down, Maddy.'

'Remember what those two men went through,' she said, throbbing with anger, 'and stop carping about the GWR. Otherwise, I'll send you back for a *second* look at the carnage outside the tunnel. They were human beings, Father. Doesn't that matter to you? Alan Hinton has probably *seen* their injuries. They've been in agony and they'll be off work for a long time.

Imagine what that will mean to them. They're suffering,' she went on, 'yet all *you* can do is to complain about GWR's broad gauge. It's shameful!'

Andrews backed away at once. It was time to shut up.

When Colbeck had described his trip to Kemble and his visit to the Cirencester Cricket Club, it was Leeming and Hinton's turn to deliver a report. Leeming told the inspector that there was little doubt about Michael Rydall's being seen in Stroud. Wherever he had been, he was now back in the Cotswolds.

'Now do you think that you should inform his father?' asked Hinton.

'I hesitate to do so,' replied Colbeck. 'The very mention of his name is enough to make Mr Rydall foam at the mouth. Besides, all we can tell him is that someone caught a fleeting glance of his son. We need more than that.'

'I'll keep on searching,' volunteered Leeming.

'You do that, Sergeant.'

'I wondered if I should tail Beckerton,' said Hinton. 'You both seemed to think that he's involved somehow. Do you want him followed?'

'It's something I considered, Alan,' said Colbeck, 'but the interest has shifted to the ransom note now. If Beckerton or an associate of his sent it, we have to find a way to lure them out into the light. I need thinking time,' he went on. 'You go back to The Crown and try on the gardener's clothing.'

'Put a peg on your nose first,' warned Leeming.

'I'll certainly leave the window open,' said Hinton, picking up the potato sack and holding it at arm's length. 'Excuse me.'

He let himself out and trudged disconsolately across the courtyard. Leeming recognised the look on the inspector's face and knew that he wished to be alone.

'If you'll excuse me,' he said, moving to the door, 'I need to keep my notebook up to date. The superintendent will want to read it in due course. And we know he's a stickler for detail.'

'That's true.'

Leeming went out and left Colbeck alone to reflect on the new evidence that had been unearthed. He was soon interrupted. When there was a tap on his door, he assumed that the sergeant had come back for some reason. He unlocked the door and was surprised to see Catherine Rydall standing there.

'I wondered if I might speak to you, Inspector,' she said.

'Yes, of course, Mrs Rydall. Do come in.'

She entered the room quickly as if anxious not to be seen. Colbeck closed the door again. Catherine stood there rather self-consciously. He waited for her to speak but she remained silent. It was as if she'd forgotten what brought her there. Eventually, some words seeped out.

'My husband told me about the ransom demand,' she said.

'It's a promising sign.'

'Does it prove that Edgar Smayle is still alive?'

'We hope so.'

'Why else should they make contact?'

'They want money. That's why the shepherd was kidnapped. He's being used as a bargaining device – whether he's alive or dead.'

'Oh, I see.'

There was another long silence. Colbeck eventually broke it.

'May I mention your youngest son, Mrs Rydall?'

Her cheek muscles tightened. 'If you wish . . .'

'Your husband refuses to talk about Michael.'

'I know that, and it distresses me. Before I say anything more,' she went on, nervously, 'I need your promise that whatever I tell you will go no further than this room.'

'I give you my word, Mrs Rydall.'

'Thank you.'

There was another long, uneasy pause. It was clear to Colbeck that she'd been keeping her eye on his room to see when he'd be alone. Approaching him had required a huge effort on her part. Catherine was so unaccustomed to doing something behind her husband's back that she was almost trembling with guilt.

'What did you wish to ask me, Inspector?' she said.

'Is it true that Michael was an outstanding cricketer?'

She was caught off balance. 'Who told you that?'

'I attended a service at All Saints', Kemble this morning and spoke to Squire Etheridge. He has the greatest admiration for your son.'

'He doesn't speak quite so well about the rest of the family,' she said sharply. 'However, it's true. Michael loved cricket. I watched him play once and he was the best player on the field.'

'I saw a photograph of him.'

'Where?'

'It's hanging in the pavilion at the cricket club. Because there are so many people in the photograph – including Squire Etheridge – the faces are necessarily small. But I pride myself that I picked him out.'

'He takes after my husband.'

'So I discovered.'

'Why did you take such an interest in him, Inspector?'

'We have to consider *all* possibilities, Mrs Rydall, however remote.'

'Michael is not even in this country.'

'Are you *certain* of that?'

'Well . . .'

'I think you know that your son is back.'

'My husband and I do not regard him as part of our family any more.'

'That's Mr Rydall's position,' he said, 'but I suspect that you have reservations about it. It's the reason you wanted to speak to me in private. There's something on your mind, isn't there?' She lowered her head. 'What is it, Mrs Rydall?'

'He's still my son,' she whispered, 'whatever he's done.'

'You're still in touch with him, aren't you?'

She looked up at him. 'My husband must never know.'

'I won't betray your confidence.'

'Thank you, Inspector.'

'Do you happen to have a recent photograph of him, Mrs Rydall?'

The question troubled her, and she took a long time to answer it.

'Yes, I do.'

'Might I see it, please?'

'You can't think that Michael is in any way connected with this horrific crime, can you?' she asked, defensively. 'It's just not in his nature.'

'You know him far better than I do.'

'He's accepted . . . what happened between him and the family, and he realises that he behaved badly.'

'I'd still appreciate the sight of that photograph.'

She swallowed hard, and he could see the pain and indecision etched into her features. It was over a minute before she spoke.

'Very well, Inspector,' she murmured. 'I'll get it for you.'

CHAPTER SIXTEEN

Alan Hinton carried the potato sack back to The Crown as if it contained a dangerous animal. In the privacy of his room, he took out the coat, hat, trousers and an old shirt. The gardener had also included a pair of mud-encrusted boots that looked a little too large for the detective. In spite of his initial fears, the clothing was not quite as noisome as he'd thought. The armpits of the shirt had been discoloured by sweat and the coat had lost the leather patches sewn onto its elbows, but both items were at least wearable. The trousers were another matter. When he struggled into them, Hinton discovered that both knees had been worn so thin as to be almost transparent. Gardening had taken a cruel toll of the garment.

He still felt uncomfortable about the role assigned to him. Having selected Colbeck as his model, he'd always taken pains to look smart and fashionable. While he couldn't afford the trappings of a dandy, he could strive to ape the inspector's appearance. In the tattered clothing, he'd look like a vagrant. Hinton was glad that Lydia Quayle couldn't see him because he always tried to look at his best in her company. As he changed back into his own clothes, he chided himself for being so sensitive, and he realised that he ought be delighted that he'd been chosen to act as a go-between. It was a gift. However briefly, he'd be at the very centre of the action he craved.

After putting on the shirt and coat to complement the trousers, he learnt that the boots were unexpectedly snug. All that remained was the battered hat, ingrained with filth but having a strange rustic charm about it. When he looked in the little mirror on the wall, he was amazed at the transformation. Hinton had become scruffy, anonymous and unthreatening. It was the perfect disguise.

Stephen Rydall's prime concern was the ransom demand. A prompt response had been ordered. He therefore copied out the reply that Colbeck had drafted for him and took it to the isolated spot that had been designated. As he set his letter down on a small rock, he knew that he was being watched and that, as soon as he'd gone, the letter would be retrieved. Colbeck had warned him not to linger in the hope of catching sight of the person who'd taken it. Rydall had to appear as if he was complying with the directions he'd been given.

He was very much aware of the suffering of the Smayle family. While he'd agreed with Colbeck that they should not be told about the ransom demand, he felt that they deserved some comfort. He therefore rode on over to their cottage. Will and Annie were out with the sheep, but Betsy was there, toiling in the kitchen, and so were Jesse and Mildred. All three of them fell silent out of respect for Rydall and because they feared that he'd brought bad news. After a brief exchange of greetings, he looked around their faces.

'No,' he said, holding up both palms. 'I'm not the bearer of sad tidings.'

'That's a relief,' muttered Jesse.

'At the same time, however, I have no good news to report. Nevertheless, I believe that we can still hope.'

'What does the inspector say, sir?' asked Betsy.

'His advice is to watch and pray.'

'We've all done a lot of praying, Mr Rydall.'

'I daresay that you have,' he said. 'How are the children coping?'

'Annie believes that her father is still alive, but Will worries us. He hardly says a word. We just don't know what goes on inside that head of his, sir, but it's not very nice. You can see it in his eyes. They're smouldering.'

'Will is like the rest of us,' said Jesse. 'He feels so helpless. We all want to *do* something, but we don't know what it is. Meanwhile, Will is doing Edgar's job as well as his own. He never seems to sleep.'

'The lad is not afraid of hard work,' said Rydall. 'I've always known that.'

231

'What he really wants is revenge.'

'You must talk him out of that. Brooding on revenge will get us nowhere. I've brought detectives from London to solve this crime. Leave it to them. We don't want Will getting in their way.'

On the point of leaving, he put a hand in his pocket and left some coins on the table before he went out.

Will Smayle used his knife to carve a crude outline of a heart on the trunk of a tree. It had no romantic significance, however. In his fevered mind, it belonged to the man who'd somehow abducted his father then killed his beloved sheepdog. No sympathy would be shown to him. Walking a few yards away, Will stared at his handiwork on the tree and let his rage slowly build. His breath was eventually coming in short bursts, his temples began to pound and his whole body seemed to be alight. As his fury reached its height, he pulled the knife from its sheaf and flung it with all the force he could muster at the tree.

It embedded itself in the very centre of the heart.

Catherine Rydall was away for such a long time that Colbeck feared that she'd changed her mind about showing him the photograph. It was possible that her husband had returned, but that was unlikely because Colbeck knew that Rydall had planned to visit the Smayle family before going back to inspect the work of reclamation at the tunnel. He might not return until evening. Catherine's delay was worrying. She was clearly a woman in great distress, and Colbeck felt guilty that his request to see the photograph had only intensified that feeling.

Eventually, however, she did return. When he opened the door, she stepped swiftly into the room before anyone else saw her. Her discomfort was palpable.

'I can't let you have it,' she warned.

'I wouldn't ask you to do so, Mrs Rydall. It's your property, and you've every right to keep it. I would just like to see it, please.'

She opened her reticule and took out the photograph. After looking into his eyes to confirm that he could be trusted, she handed it over. Colbeck studied it with interest. It had been taken outdoors on a sunny day. There was a farmhouse in the background. The passage of time had been unkind to Michael Rydall. In the photograph at the cricket pavilion, he'd looked young, buoyant and carefree. The much more recent photograph showed him to have aged, put on weight and started to lose some hair. But the real surprise was that he was holding a baby in his arms. Yet there was no smile of a doting father. He wore the anxious look of a man with doubts about what the future might hold for him and his child.

'That's my granddaughter,' said Catherine.

'How old is she?'

'When the photograph was taken, she was no more than a few weeks old.'

'What's her name, Mrs Rydall?'

'Michael has named her after me.'

Her eyes moistened, and she fought hard to hold back tears. Colbeck felt sorry for her. Like any grandmother, she'd be desperate to see, hold and love the newborn child, but she was unable even to acknowledge its existence. The strain on her was almost unbearable. He handed the photograph back.

'Thank you, Mrs Rydall,' he said. 'I won't need to see it again.'

'I destroyed the letter that came with it,' she admitted, 'but I couldn't part with the photograph.'

'I understand.'

'Do you have children, Inspector?'

'I have a young daughter.'

'Then you'll have some idea of how I feel.'

After taking a last look at the photograph, she slipped it back into her reticule. She was on the verge of saying something but changed her mind at the last moment. She thanked him for being so discreet and left the room. He was interested that Michael had named his daughter after his mother. Understandably, it was a gesture that meant a great deal to Catherine. Yet she was unable to share it with her husband. Colbeck had the utmost sympathy for her.

One of the first things that the Reverend Patrick Cinderby did when he was appointed as principal of the college was to institute a short service in the chapel on a Sunday evening. It was both a way of remaining visible to the students and of assisting their moral development. As a rule, he was articulate, assured and audible, but he let his mind wander that evening. While he sang the hymns with his usual determination to be heard above the congregation, he was still wondering why Colbeck had turned up to watch him at All Saints', Kemble. Were he and Squire Etheridge still considered to be possible suspects? If so, what evidence did the inspector have to justify his interest in the two of them?

Cinderby's fear was that his staff and students might catch wind of the fact that their principal was under police investigation. It could undermine his authority. Yet it was already being mocked. As they launched into the final hymn, he became aware that some students at the back of the chapel were already showing their disrespect. One was grinning, another was adopting the same distinctive, upright stance as the principal and the third was pulling faces to amuse the others. It only served to toughen Cinderby's resolve to seek out a better class of student. The trio at the rear were teenage sons of local farmers, lively, extrovert characters who enjoyed the practical side of agriculture while having little enthusiasm for studying theory. Cinderby wanted students with intellectual rigour, conscientious young men who would go on to achieve great things in the world of agriculture, thereby advertising the college that had educated them to such a level. He could then bask in reflected glory.

Whenever Dr Wyatt or other visitors came, the injured railwaymen made the effort to keep smiling and claim they felt much better than they really did. Left alone, however, they were afflicted by a mixture of pain, doubt and boredom. They had two major concerns. The first was that they'd never get back to full fitness again. There'd always be physical scars of the crash as well as hideous memories. Their deeper anxiety was financial. Rydall had promised to tackle the GWR about giving them some sort of compensation to tide them over, but there was no certainty that it would be forthcoming. That worried Poulter and Treece. The steady wage that each brought in would disappear. Only when they fully recovered could they return to work.

They were moaning to each other about future difficulties when Leeming came into the room. Both patients immediately brightened. They plied him with questions about the investigation, then lapsed into a series of anecdotes about disasters on the railway. Leeming replied with tales of the dreadful mistakes he'd made when he was pounding the beat in uniform. They roared with laughter. Having cheered them up, the sergeant let himself out. Colbeck was coming down the corridor.

'I was just about to knock on your door, Victor,' he said. 'I see that you've been visiting our patients.'

'Yes. I know what it's like to be stuck in bed with my arm in a splint. You feel cut off from the world. I spent hours praying for a visitor to come.'

'I'm sure that you did. It must be the same for Poulter and Treece.' He indicated the exit door. 'Let's step outside, shall we?'

They came out into the fresh air and strolled across the lawn.

'On a day like this,' said Leeming, looking around, '*I* wouldn't mind being a gardener.'

'That's Hinton's job. He'll look the part when he's properly dressed. In fact, that's what I wanted to discuss with you. Do you think he's up to it?'

'I'm certain that he is, sir. He's as keen as mustard.'

'It's his enthusiasm that I'm worrying about. He needs to have icy control.'

'Alan won't let us down. Nothing scares him. Don't forget that he was ready to keep watch on Beckerton for us, and we know what a dangerous task that might be.'

'It's dangerous,' said Colbeck, 'but it's also unnecessary. The kidnappers have shown themselves at last. If Beckerton is giving them orders, we'll catch him in due course.'

'What if it's Michael Rydall instead?'

'Then I'll be shocked as well as surprised.'

'We know that he's in or near Stroud.'

'We also know that he seems to be keeping his head down.'

'That suggests he's up to something.'

'Not to me,' said Colbeck. 'It suggests that he doesn't want his father to know that he's back in this country again.'

'Mr Rydall is such a strange man. Whatever *my* sons do – and they can be little terrors sometimes – I could never cut either of them right out of my life. Estelle would kill me if I tried.'

'That's because you have a strong-willed wife, Victor. I don't think that Mrs Rydall would challenge her husband in the way that Estelle would tackle you. It's . . . not in her nature.'

Colbeck said nothing more about her. Having given his word to Catherine, he was not going to betray her by revealing the long conversation the two of them had had earlier. It was a private matter between them.

Leeming was puzzled. 'I keep thinking about that demand,' he said. 'Five thousand pounds is a huge amount of money to me. Is Mr Rydall able to find that much at short notice?'

'He assures me that he is. Since the banks are closed today, he can't withdraw any cash until tomorrow. In any case,' said Colbeck, 'he won't actually lose it. We can intervene when the hostage is handed over – if Smayle is still alive, that is.'

'Is five thousand pounds the going rate for a shepherd?'

'It is, in this case.'

'I wonder how much *I'd* be worth in the same situation.'

Colbeck grinned. 'Make sure that you're never *in* that situation,' he advised. 'As for Mr Rydall's money, our job is to make sure that he doesn't lose a farthing of it.'

After leaving the Smayle family, Rydall had made his way back to the western portal of the tunnel. Work was continuing apace, and many more wagons had been dragged out. Rydall spoke to the foreman in charge of the navvies and congratulated him on the rate of progress. Much, however, still remained to be cleared, and the tunnel would not be opened again until repairs had been made to the damaged brickwork inside it. The cost of it all would be prohibitive, but it was vital to restore the track to full use so that the normal timetable could be resumed as soon as possible.

Rydall stayed long enough to feel optimistic for the first time, then he mounted his horse again and rode off. Instead of going back to The Grange, however, he headed for the Daneway Inn. His visit to the Smayle family had triggered a thought that was worrying him. He hoped that Peter Doble might be able to help him.

When the landlord saw him coming, he broke away from the bargees with whom he'd been chatting and walked over to the newcomer.

'Good evening to you, Mr Rydall.'

'And the same to you,' said the other, dismounting and tethering his horse.

'It's not often we see you here, sir.'

'I needed a word with you – a *private* word.'

'In that case,' said Doble, 'let's step inside.'

He led the way inside the inn and behind the bar. Molly was serving some customers, and she gave Rydall a deferential smile as he passed. Doble took his visitor into the room at the back. It was small, cluttered, and they had to duck under a low beam. Rydall found the whiff of beer too strong.

'Is there anything we can offer you?' asked Doble.

'This is not a social visit.'

'I see.'

'I've been to see the Smayle family.'

'How are they, sir?'

'As you can imagine,' said Rydall, 'they're suffering. Smayle's wife is having to carry the rest of them and is tortured by the fact that she doesn't know if her husband is still alive. The children – Annie and Will – are looking after the flock and doing wonders.'

'Will Smayle popped up here.'

'Really? I thought his father deliberately kept him away.'

'He did, sir. As we all know, the lad's not right in the head. There's no telling what might happen if he had too much beer inside him. Also, Edgar didn't want his son laughed at. My customers are good people at heart, but they'd certainly make fun of the way Will tries to talk.'

'Why did he come here?'

'I wish I knew,' said Doble. 'He was hiding behind a bush so that he could spy on us. When I spotted him, I tried to find out what brought him here, but his tongue got more twisted than ever. Will knew his father used to come to The Daneway a lot. I reckon he followed Edgar from time to time.'

'What did you say to him?'

'I spoke kindly, then sent him on his way. I feel sorry for the lad – and for the rest of the family, of course.'

'That's what I wanted to talk about,' said Rydall. 'I know that Edgar caused a spot of bother here from time to time and that you refused to serve him.'

'He was always very sorry afterwards, sir. That's why me and Molly let him use The Daneway again after a few weeks.'

'Did you ever see anything of Edgar's wife?'

'Betsy? No, sir, she never came anywhere near us.'

'What about their life at home?'

'It was grim. He always said that Betsy had far too much to do, looking after them all.'

'I'm asking about how they got on as husband and wife,' said Rydall. 'When I called at the cottage earlier, I was reminded of rumours I'd once heard.'

Doble's eyelids narrowed. 'What sort of rumours?'

'There was talk of him . . . beating his wife.'

'Well, those rumours never reached us, sir. Was there anything in them?'

'At the time,' admitted Rydall, 'I dismissed them. When I looked at Betsy earlier, however, I began to wonder. All the stuffing seemed to have been knocked out of her. That's partly because of the awful situation that the family is in, of course, but I sensed there was another reason as well. You probably knew Edgar as well as anybody. Did you ever suspect that—?'

'No, I didn't,' said Doble, cutting him off. 'If I had, then he wouldn't have been allowed anywhere near The Daneway. No, Edgar wouldn't have raised a fist to his wife. It just wasn't in his nature. He had lots of other faults, but that certainly wasn't one of them.'

'Thank you, Doble. It's reassuring to hear you say that.'

'Molly would say the same, sir. Now and again, my wife bumps into Betsy at the market. She's never heard a word of complaint about Edgar – and you know how women like to grumble about their husbands.'

They traded a wry grin.

Betsy Smayle was never allowed to rest for long. There was always far too much to do. When she saw that they needed fresh water, Betsy went off dutifully with the bucket. She walked to a nearby well and, after tying a rope to the bucket, she lowered it down until she heard a splash. It was hard, slow work, but she persevered. When she tried to lift the full bucket out of the well, however, pain shot through her right arm and forced her to let go. Betsy was still rubbing her arm when her daughter came into view. Annie realised what had happened.

'Leave it to me, Mother,' she said, rushing forward to lift the bucket out of the well and put it on the ground. 'You have to wait until your arm is better.' She undid the rope and picked up the bucket with ease. 'Come on. I can manage it.'

'Thank you, Annie.'

After kissing her daughter in gratitude, Betsy followed her back to the cottage. The stabbing pain in her arm continued to trouble her.

'He looked such a disagreeable person,' said Pamela Etheridge, dismissively.

'That's not true at all,' argued her husband. 'He's highly educated and was unfailingly polite when he spoke to me. The wonder is that he's wasting his obvious talents by working for the Metropolitan Police Force.'

'Did you say that to his face?'

'I was too busy warning him to leave Patrick alone.'

'Why should you need to do that?'

'Inspector Colbeck is a confounded nuisance.'

They were sitting alone in the luxurious drawing room at Kemble Court. No sign of the railway was visible from the property, but they could hear occasional hissing of steam and the distant rattle of wheels.

'Is he a nuisance to Patrick or to you?' she asked.

'To both of us, really,' he replied. 'If he speaks out of turn to the local newspapers, Colbeck could damage the reputation of the college, and that means that Patrick, as the principal, and I, as a member of the governing body, would be seen in a bad light.'

'That's intolerable.'

'It's the reason I was so blunt with him.'

'Stephen Rydall is to blame for setting the inspector onto you.'

'Too true,' he said, ruefully. 'I mean to confront him.'

'Well, you can't do it at a meeting of the governing body because he resigned. How he ever became a member of it in the first place is beyond me.'

'He's well-respected in certain quarters, I fear. And farming is in his blood, so he seemed like an obvious choice. I had no idea that he'd be so contentious. The way that he tried to block Patrick's appointment was unpardonable.'

'Thank heaven that he failed!' she said, tossing her head. 'Our dear nephew, Darley, would have stood no chance of a professorship without your friendship with the principal.'

'Yes, it would have been dashed inconvenient.'

'All is well, thank God.'

'We're not quite out of the woods yet,' he cautioned. 'There are still major financial difficulties at the college. We managed to improve the situation but were forced to sell the farm to do so. Patrick has worked hard to create more stability. It's the reason we're both afraid of any adverse publicity,' he went on. 'If people knew that a detective inspector from Scotland Yard had questioned Patrick with regard to a heinous crime, it would damage us. Investors are unlikely to come forward if there's even a shadow of suspicion over the college.'

'I thought you told the inspector to go away.'

'I did,' he said, 'but it seemed to have little effect. The trouble is that Colbeck doesn't respect his betters. We may have to deliver the same message in a different way.'

Having strolled around the grounds together, Colbeck and Leeming made their way back to The Grange. They were just passing a stand of trees when a shot rang out. Both of them ducked instinctively. When the echo died away, they looked around cautiously, trying to work out the exact direction from which the shot had been fired. Feeling that it was safe to move, they walked over to a tree and saw the hole where the bullet had penetrated the bark.

'Someone doesn't like us being here,' said Leeming.

'Yes,' agreed Colbeck. 'It's a timely warning. From now on, we must go armed.'

When they gathered around the table that evening, the Smayle family were unusually silent. Annie helped her mother put the food on the table while Jesse and Mildred sat there waiting.

'Where's Will?' asked Mildred.

'We don't know,' replied Betsy.

'He should be here.'

'Yes,' said Jesse. 'We're hungry.'

'We'll start without him,' said Betsy.

'His place is at the table.'

'Will knows that.'

'Shall I go and fetch him?' volunteered Jesse.

'No,' said Annie, 'leave him be.'

'Where is he?'

'Will is still searching for Father.'

'Then he'll be walking around in circles. He has no chance at all of finding him. Someone must make that clear to him.'

'I've tried, Grandad,' said Annie, 'but he just won't give up. Let him do what he feels that he has to. He'll come back eventually.'

* * *

With his dog scurrying along beside him, Will Smayle walked purposefully along a trail that ran through the woodland. Though he'd already searched it three times, he was determined to take another look. Convinced that his father was on the estate somewhere, he pushed himself on relentlessly. The knife was no longer his only weapon. Will was now carrying a shotgun.

The burden of responsibility that Stephen Rydall had been carrying for days finally got the better of him. Having eaten his meal that evening, he dropped quietly asleep with a cup of coffee untouched in front of him. Catherine was alarmed. She didn't know whether she should let him sleep on or gently wake him up. As it happened, no decision was necessary because he suddenly came awake and sat up. Realising what had happened, he was embarrassed enough to mumble an apology.

'You don't need to apologise, Stephen,' she said. 'You've been working too hard. It was bound to tell on you in the end.'

'I must remain alert,' he declared.

'What you must do is to get some proper rest.'

'I can't even think of it in a crisis like this.'

'Stop driving yourself,' she pleaded.

'I can't let people down, Catherine.'

'Then this is only the first time you'll fall asleep like that.'

His wife was right, and he had to accept it. He looked across at her with an amalgam of love and remorse. Since the derailment, he'd been so preoccupied that he'd paid her almost no attention. Though it was patently wrong of him, he was simply unable to show her due consideration. Other things took priority. After holding his head in his hands for a few moments, he looked up at her.

'Am I such an ogre?' he asked.

'Don't be ridiculous.'

'Why do people hate me so readily?'

'Nobody hates you, Stephen.'

'Oh, yes, they do. That crash at the mouth of the tunnel was proof of it. Somebody wanted to hurt the GWR and punish me for my connection with it. There's no getting away from it. I inspire hatred.'

'I refuse to believe it. You're a kind man, and you do so much for other people. What's happened may be nothing whatsoever to do with you, Stephen. It could be the work of a rival railway company, bent on damaging the GWR.'

'It's a personal attack,' he insisted. 'There's something about me that arouses enmity. Anthony Beckerton is at least honest about his dislike of me. Is this all *his* doing? Or is it the work of Squire Etheridge and that infernal principal of the Royal Agricultural College? I've locked horns with both of them at meetings of the governing body. Don't be fooled by Etheridge's social position or by the bands that Cinderby wears as a clergyman. They're quite merciless. They have a pact to get back at me.'

'You're imagining it.'

'Am I imagining the sight of that ruined locomotive and those shattered wagons? Am I imagining the fact that the driver and fireman of that train are now trying to recover from injuries that will haunt them for life? Those are the bare facts,

Catherine. Solely because of me,' he said, banging the table, 'people have *suffered*. I have to take responsibility.'

'No – you must pass it on to Inspector Colbeck and his detectives. That's what they're here for. Stand back and let them take over.'

'My conscience won't let me do that.'

'You can't take all the blame, Stephen.'

'Yes, I can. The fact is that I make enemies. I've mentioned some of them, but there are several others. They're all driven by an urge to wound me badly.' His voice darkened. 'And there's someone else with the best reason of all to wreak his revenge—'

'That's enough,' she said, rising to her feet. 'I'll hear no more of this.'

'What if it's *him*, Catherine?'

'I think I'll have an early night. You should do the same.'

'How can I sleep when I'm in this mood?' He got up and took her by the shoulders. 'I'm sorry to put you through this, Catherine. It's *my* ordeal and I must face it on my own. In fact—'

A tap on the door made him break off and step back from her. A servant entered and handed him a letter.

'This has just been delivered, sir.'

'By whom?'

'We don't know, Mr Rydall. It was slipped under the front door.'

'I see.' He gave a nod. 'Thank you.'

The servant went out immediately. Rydall tore open the letter. Catherine was tense and nervous, frightened at the state her husband was in. She watched as he read the missive and saw his jaw drop open.

'What is it?' she asked. 'Who sent it, Stephen?'

'*They* did,' he replied.

CHAPTER SEVENTEEN

Now armed with pistols, Colbeck and Leeming were much more circumspect as they left The Grange to walk to The Crown. They kept looking in all directions. Neither of them had the impression that they were being watched. It was reassuring. When they settled down with Hinton at a table in the inn, they told him about the shot fired at them.

Hinton was alarmed. 'One of you could have been hit.'

'Whoever fired that gun missed us deliberately,' said Colbeck. 'They just wanted to issue a warning. In one way, I was pleased.'

'*Pleased*, sir?'

'Yes, Alan.'

'In your place, I'd have been worried.'

'It's the person with the gun who is worried,' explained Colbeck. 'It was a clear sign that we're making more progress than we dared to believe. Someone is anxious to scare us off.'

'That's why we're carrying weapons,' said Leeming, patting his coat.

'Were they issued by the superintendent?' asked Hinton in surprise.

'No, but there are times when a pistol may be needed.'

'I don't have one.'

'I don't think you'll need it, Alan. We're the ones in the line of fire.'

'Besides,' added Colbeck, 'nobody will realise who you are. You'll be mistaken for one of Mr Rydall's gardeners.'

The barmaid took orders for their drinks, then went off behind the bar. Hinton had some information to pass on.

'I took your advice, Inspector,' he said.

'Which particular piece of advice?' asked Colbeck. 'I seem to remember giving you rather too much of it.'

'You told me to pick up the local gossip.'

'That's always a useful thing to do.'

'I heard two people in here discussing a stranger.'

'Were they talking about you?'

'No,' said Hinton. 'They hadn't actually seen this man themselves, but they'd heard reports of him hanging about the area.'

'What sort of reports?' asked Leeming.

'Well, it seems that he's always lurking close to churches. He was seen here and in Sapperton, apparently, and one of the men heard a rumour that he'd turned up in Coates, wherever

250

that is. For some reason, he always has this notebook with him.'

'Is he an artist of sorts?' asked Colbeck.

'Nobody knows, sir. If someone shows an interest in churches, you'd expect him to be religious. That's not the case here.'

'Oh?'

'All the reports say the same thing. This man was quite sinister. He just stood there and stared at those churches. People were glad when he moved on.'

Leeming slapped his knee. 'I think I know who he is.'

'Who?'

'It's the gongoozler, of course.'

'We're being serious,' said Colbeck.

'So am I,' declared Leeming. 'The landlord at the Daneway Inn told me about him. This peculiar man was spotted at the mouth of the tunnel. He stood there for ages, gazing at the brickwork. Then he began to draw something. It *has* to be him, sir,' he went on. 'It's what gongoozlers do. They come and go for no particular reason. They stare at something for hours on end before disappearing. That's who you heard those men talking about, Alan – the gongoozler.'

Colbeck's curiosity was aroused. Local people had been uniformly pleasant to them since they'd arrived. If a stranger had managed to upset them, there had to be something very odd about him. Then he remembered the seven dead sheep at the mouth of the tunnel. Their slaughter, too, could be construed as having a sinister aspect. It also had religious affiliations.

'Frampton Mansell, Sapperton and Coates,' he mused. 'I wonder where he'll go next.'

* * *

Dressed almost entirely in black, the man was pale, plump, middle-aged and of medium height. Having stabled his horse and left his luggage in the room he'd just booked, he came out of the front door of the King's Arms and looked across the marketplace at the soaring magnificence of the Parish Church of St John the Baptist. Pure delight coursed through his veins.

'Wonderful!' he said.

Before they could even think about food, Colbeck was interrupted. A servant arrived from The Grange with an urgent message. Mr Rydall needed to speak to the inspector as soon as possible. Abandoning the others, Colbeck followed the messenger out. The man had no idea why his employer was so eager to speak to the inspector, but he did confide that his master was in an excitable state.

Arriving at the house, Colbeck was shown into the drawing room and left alone with Rydall. The latter was on his feet at once.

'He's alive,' he cried. 'Edgar Smayle is still alive.'

'How do you know, sir?'

'This was sent to me earlier.'

'What is it?'

'It's the proof that I demanded,' said Rydall, 'and it's written in Edgar's own hand.' He thrust the letter at Colbeck. 'See for yourself.'

Taking it from him, Colbeck read the letter. It was short, spidery and ungrammatical. Its message was chilling. Smayle was begging his employer to pay the ransom so that he could be released. Otherwise, he said, his captors would kill him.

'Are you sure that Smayle wrote this?' asked Colbeck.

'Without a doubt – I'd know his hand anywhere.'

'Has the demand been repeated?'

'Yes,' said Rydall, holding up another sheet of paper. 'This was the covering letter that came with Edgar's plea. They want the money tomorrow evening. If not, they'll have no compunction about slitting Edgar's throat.'

Colbeck took the letter and read it carefully before handing it back.

'How amenable is your bank manager?' he asked.

'In a crisis like this, he'll be *very* amenable, believe me.'

'They've stipulated the time but not the place. That shows how careful they are. They're not giving us any chance to reconnoitre the area beforehand.'

'Yet they're very specific about the exact hour.'

'It's another example of their caution, sir. It will be twilight. Once they've got their hands on the money, they can vanish into the shadows.'

'Smayle is still alive. That's the real bonus.'

'Is it?'

'Yes,' said Rydall, smiling. 'When I first read his letter, I wanted to take it straight to his family.'

'I think that it's just as well that you didn't, Mr Rydall.'

'Why not?'

'Think how devastated they'd be if it turned out to be a hoax.'

'But it's not, Inspector. This is definitely Edgar's handwriting, and it's exactly how he strings words together.'

'Then why wasn't it sent to you earlier?'

Rydall was taken aback. 'I don't follow.'

'When the original demand was made, why didn't they include this plea to prove that the hostage was still alive?'

'Well . . . I suppose that they didn't think it necessary.'

'They hoped that you'd accept their word that they'd spared his life. But you saw the wisdom of challenging them. You asked for proof.'

'And that's what I've got. They made Edgar write to me.'

'When?' asked Colbeck.

'Earlier today, of course,' said Rydall. 'It's proof positive.'

'The only thing it proves is that Smayle was forced to write it. There's no date on his letter. My fear is that your shepherd penned this days ago. That's why it would be foolish to tell the family that he's alive. The person or persons we're up against will have no qualms about leading you astray. In fact,' he went on, 'they'd take a perverse delight from it.'

Rydall was deflated. 'But I thought . . .'

'You thought what you were meant to think, sir. I may be wrong, of course. I sincerely hope that I am, but my feeling is that they compelled Smayle to write this then kept it as an insurance policy.'

'They *killed* him?'

'Once he'd done what they asked, he was of no further use to them.'

'But he was going to be exchanged for the money.'

'Can you really *trust* their promise, sir?'

'When you put it like that . . .'

Rydall was wounded by the realisation that he'd been naive. What he thought was cast-iron evidence of his shepherd's survival might actually be a cruel trick. Hoping for the best, he'd wanted to hear the cries of joy from the Smayle family when he told them the good news. Fearing the worst, however, Colbeck had been more realistic. He'd saved Rydall from possible humiliation.

'What must I do, Inspector?' he asked.

'Follow their instructions.'

'What about you?'

'There's a full day before the ransom is handed over,' said Colbeck. 'That gives us plenty of time to continue the search for evidence. Your first task tomorrow is to visit your bank manager. In short, do as you're told.'

By the time Will finally returned to the cottage, the rest of the family had long since finished their meal. Jesse scolded him for staying out so long, but Will ignored the criticism. Betsy went to the larder to fetch the plate of food she'd kept for him. Morose and silent, Will munched his way through it. As soon as he'd finished, he went outside to feed his dog.

Annie followed him. 'Where have you been, Will?'

'I went everywhere.'

'You don't need to,' she said.

'Yes, I do.'

'If they took Blackie, they'll have taken Father as well.'

'He's out there, Annie,' insisted her brother.

'Then why haven't we seen any trace of him?'

'It's because we haven't searched in the right place.'

His voice was rising, and his eyes were flashing. Words tumbled out so fast that even Annie had a problem understanding every one of them. She did her best to calm him down, then tried to make him concentrate.

'Your place is here, Will.'

'Don't give me orders.'

'You can't just wander off when the urge takes you. It leaves me on my own, and it's not fair. We've got to show Mr Rydall that we can cope. Don't you understand? If Father *doesn't* come back,' she stressed, 'we could be turned out. The only way to stay in the cottage is to prove that we can manage. Grandad can't do very much, but we're both young and strong. Between us, we can do most of what needs to be done.' She shook his arm. 'Are you listening?'

'Yes.'

'Then say something.'

'Father comes first.'

'He may already be dead, Will.'

'No!' he yelled, grabbing her by the arms and shaking her. 'Don't you dare say that, Annie! He's alive, and he's out there somewhere. I've got to find him. It's what any son would do.'

When Colbeck arrived back at the inn, more customers had arrived and there was less chance of privacy. He therefore decided to say nothing about his visit to The Grange, postponing a discussion of it until later. Meanwhile, keeping his voice low, he spoke to Hinton.

'Tell me more about this man who stares at churches,' he said.

'The gongoozler,' added Leeming.

'No, I don't think you could call him that, Victor. When you first told me what a gongoozler was, you said he was an idle and inquisitive person. The man that Alan described is far from idle. He has a clear purpose.'

'I wish I knew what it was,' admitted Hinton. 'All I know about him is what I told you. He was creepy. Something about him unnerved people. When he went to Coates, it seems, he spent a long time reading the inscriptions on the gravestones. What kind of man would do that?'

'A stonemason?' said Leeming with a grin.

'I was being serious.'

'Keep your ears pricked, Alan,' suggested Colbeck. 'Go across to The Bell in Sapperton tomorrow morning and see if the landlord knows anything about this stranger. Sergeant Leeming will join you so that you can call on other pubs in the area to see if they've had reports of odd behaviour from a stranger. Ah,' he went on, pleased to see the barmaid approaching with the meal that he'd ordered earlier, 'that's what I was waiting for.' She put the plate on the table in front of him. 'Thank you very much.'

Business was brisk that evening at the Daneway Inn. Several barges were moored nearby, and there was a certain amount of local trade. Peter and Molly Doble were popular figures who knew how to treat their customers well. The disadvantage was that they often had so much to do that they had little chance to talk to each other. Molly had to choose her moment to pounce on her husband.

'Hold on a moment,' she said as he tried to walk past. 'There's something I want to ask you.'

'What is it?'

'There was a man who talked to you earlier.'

'I've talked to lots of men,' he said with a laugh.

'This one was different, Peter. He was a big, thickset bargee with a black beard. I didn't like the way he was looming over you.'

'Forget him, Molly.'

'Do you know who he was?'

'I do now.'

'What did he want?'

'He was just passing on a message from Beckerton.'

'What sort of a message?'

'There's only one kind that he ever sends. That man was told to pass on Beckerton's regards. It was just another way of warning me to do exactly what he told me to do. Beckerton never lets you off the leash,' complained Doble. 'Every so often, he gives you a sharp tug. That's what I had earlier.'

'I was afraid it was something like that.'

'No harm was done, Molly. It's just something we have to put up with.'

'I know,' she sighed.

'We have to keep Beckerton sweet.'

After Colbeck's visit, Rydall's mood had changed. Instead of being excited by the possibility that his shepherd was still alive, he'd become gloomy and fearful. He sat in the corner of the drawing room with the brandy decanter beside him. As she watched him pour another glass, his wife was apprehensive.

'You've already had two glasses, Stephen.'

'I may well have two more.'

'What did the inspector say to you?'

'It doesn't matter.'

'If it's made you reach for brandy, it obviously does matter.'

'I don't want to go into details, Catherine,' he said. 'Colbeck made me think again – that's all I'm prepared to say.' He looked over at her. 'I thought you wanted an early night.'

'I feel that my place is here with you.'

'I'm not good company at the moment.'

'I'll stay if you wish. We don't have to say anything to each other.'

'I think I'd rather be alone, my dear.'

'Oh, I see.' She got to her feet. 'Goodnight, Stephen.'

'Goodnight.'

After hovering for a few seconds, she left the room. Rydall took a long sip of his drink and ran a hand through his hair. He felt foolish at being so thrilled by the letter from his shepherd. Now that he'd had time to consider it, he could see that Colbeck might well have been right. Rydall could have been handing over a large amount of money for someone who was already dead. It was a frightening thought.

He was so depressed that he found little solace in the prospect of saving the ransom when those who'd demanded it were arrested. It was the stage beyond that which worried him the most. He would have to tell the family that Smayle had been killed. Colbeck had volunteered to speak to them on his behalf, but Rydall knew that it was his obligation. They would blame him. For the rest of their lives, they'd hold him responsible for the murder, and he couldn't, in all honesty, escape that charge. But for him, the disaster would never have taken place. Rydall had provoked enough burning hatred in one of his enemies to make the person lust for revenge. The crime had been tailored to cause him the utmost pain. It had to be someone who knew how much the railway meant to him and understood just how much he depended on the services of Edgar Smayle.

One name kept coming back to him, and it made him shiver.

Michael Rydall.

The discussion was held in Colbeck's room. Because of its lack of space, it was not ideal, but they scorned comfort. Hinton sat on the single bed, Leeming perched precariously on a three-legged stool and Colbeck occupied the only chair. When they heard the news about the letter from the kidnappers, the detectives reacted in different ways. Hinton took the message at face value and thought that the hostage would be handed over unharmed. Given his greater experience, Leeming supported the view that the shepherd had been disposed of as soon as he'd written the letter.

'Each side is offering something that doesn't exist,' he observed. 'They're after the ransom for a man who is already dead and we're waving money in their faces that we're not going to give them.'

'That's an admirable description of the situation,' said Colbeck.

'So, what will they do?' asked Hinton.

'They'll have someone who *looks* like Smayle but who can't be seen properly in the fading light. The moment the money is handed over, the so-called hostage will take to his heels.'

'That's what he'll *try* to do, Alan,' said Leeming, 'but you'll be on hand to catch him. Don't forget to wear the gardener's clothing.'

'Where will *you* both be?'

'Oh, we won't be far away.'

'They'll think that they've frightened us off,' said Colbeck. 'That was the purpose of the shot they fired. It was to keep us away. Nothing will do that.'

'Don't worry, Alan. We'll be there.'

'To tell you the truth,' said Hinton, 'I'm not afraid. The very thought of it makes me tingle with excitement. I'm just so grateful that you're putting your trust in me.'

'You deserve it.'

'I second that,' said Colbeck.

Hinton smiled. 'Thank you.'

'I know someone who'd say exactly the same.'

'It's not the superintendent, surely.'

'I had another name in mind.'

'And who is that?' asked Hinton.

'Miss Lydia Quayle.'

Lydia sat at the dining table at the end of a delicious meal. Madeleine and her father were equally pleased with the quality of the cooking. Lydia, however, was perplexed. Whenever she'd dined at the house before, Andrews was often there, and he was always lively and loquacious. That evening, by contrast, he'd been subdued and virtually silent, avoiding her gaze whenever she looked in his direction. She began to wonder if he was unwell. Then, unexpectedly, Andrews felt the urge to initiate a conversation.

'What did you think of Alan Hinton's promotion?'

'In my opinion,' said Lydia, 'it was long overdue. He's given outstanding service to the Metropolitan Police Force. Strictly speaking, it's not exactly a promotion, but it will be seen as such at Scotland Yard. Every detective constable there would love to be assigned to one of Robert's cases.'

'Yes,' said Madeleine, 'especially one as challenging as this.'

'With luck, you may get another letter tomorrow.'

'I hope so, Lydia.'

'Robert is so considerate. If at all possible, he always lets you know exactly what he's been up to.'

'Our postal system is a boon to us.'

'I'd appreciate a letter from him myself,' said Andrews.

'I make a point of passing on any news that I get, Father.'

'It's not the same as being told direct, Maddy.'

'It's the way that it has to be,' said Madeleine with a slight edge, 'so perhaps we should get off the subject of this investigation.' She got up from the table. 'Why don't we adjourn to the drawing room? It's more comfortable in there.'

'I'll join you in a while,' said Andrews, rising to his feet and taking a watch from his waistcoat pocket. 'It's time for my goodnight kiss from the loveliest granddaughter in the world. Excuse me.'

The old man went out with a broad smile on his face, and the two women walked through to the drawing room. They settled down on the sofa.

'What's wrong with your father this evening?' asked Lydia.

'We had an argument earlier today,' confessed Madeleine, 'and I had to be unduly firm with him.'

'In that case, the argument was about the GWR.'

'I'm afraid that it was, Lydia. He lambasted the company unjustly.'

'Yet he actually travelled on one of their trains.'

'He did, and he apologised for being so hostile towards the GWR. Today was a different story. He forgot all the nice things he'd said and unleashed another attack. I just couldn't stand it, Lydia, and I said so. As a result, he's been behaving himself.'

'At least, you're still on speaking terms,' said Lydia. 'That's more than I was with *my* father. I still feel guilty about it. When he was murdered, I realised that we hadn't had a proper conversation for years.'

'You'd made a new life for yourself.'

'I was driven to do so, Madeleine.'

'Are you happy with it?'

'As long as you're part of it, I'm *very* happy. Being friends with you and Robert has been my salvation. You've taken me into your family.'

'Helena loves you as much as we do. You're her favourite aunt.'

Lydia beamed. 'She's such a joy, Madeleine.'

'She's a little magician. No matter how grumpy a mood my father is in, Helena can shake him out of it. You wait until he comes downstairs again. He'll be sweetness itself.'

'What will happen if I mention the GWR?'

'Don't you dare,' said Madeleine, laughing.

After their discussion at The Grange, Hinton took his leave and walked back to The Crown, excited by the thought of what the following day would hold. Accompanied by Leeming, he would begin by visiting pubs in the vicinity to see if any of them could provide information about the mysterious stranger. If possible, the detectives would track and overhaul the man. Hinton's day would end when he donned his disguise for a confrontation with the people who claimed to be holding Edgar Smayle. The notion was exhilarating.

Back at The Grange, meanwhile, Victor Leeming was about to return to his own room when he remembered someone. He turned to Colbeck.

'We've rather lost sight of Michael Rydall,' he said.

'*I* haven't.'

'Do you still think he may be implicated somehow?'

'No,' said Colbeck. 'I don't.'

'Why is that?'

'Having got to know Michael's parents, I've seen how their opinion of their youngest son differs. Rydall effectively exiled him against his wife's wishes. All that she could do was to obey her husband. In private, I believe, she grieved over her loss – what mother wouldn't do that?'

'Women are more sentimental, I suppose,' said Leeming.

'There's a lot more than sentimentality involved. The bond between mother and son is enormously strong,' said Colbeck. 'Mrs Rydall brought him into the world and cherished him as the youngest of her three children. Those feelings never disappear. Now, look at it from Michael's point of view.'

'He hated his father for throwing him out of the family.'

'But he didn't hate his mother. I'm absolutely sure that he was always much closer to her than he was to his father,' said Colbeck, thinking of the photograph of Michael she'd shown him. 'Mrs Rydall is the reason I don't believe that her youngest son is behind the blocking of that tunnel. It might assuage his desire for revenge against his father,' he argued, 'but Michael would know that it would inflict misery upon his mother as well. For her sake, I'm certain, he'd stay his hand.'

'Does that mean we stop searching for Michael?'

'No, it doesn't, Victor. We just change the nature of the search.'

Leeming frowned. 'I don't understand.'

'We've been looking for a culprit,' explained Colbeck, 'whereas Michael is, in fact, someone who might help us to *find* that culprit. He must know things that could be very useful to us. Bear in mind that Rydall has only told us what he wants us to hear. From the very start, I had the feeling that he was keeping some information back. Michael might be more forthcoming. After all, he lived here for the bulk of his life. He's familiar with this area and with the people who inhabit it.'

'How do we find him?'

'We may not need to, Victor.'

'What do you mean?'

'I've got a strange feeling that he may decide to find us.'

Michael Rydall studied the newspaper article by the light of an oil lamp. It gave full details of the derailment and the resulting damage. The reporter had also mentioned the inspector sent from Scotland Yard to lead the investigation. Robert Colbeck was described in glowing terms. Rydall had read the article many times. It had prompted him to visit the site to see the scale of the destruction with his own eyes. He put the newspaper aside.

Taking out a pencil, he put a circle around Colbeck's name.

CHAPTER EIGHTEEN

Left alone in his room, Colbeck was able to reflect on the day's events. What struck him most was the difference between a typical Sunday in London and the one that was coming to an end in Gloucestershire. He and Madeleine would have attended church, met with friends and, if the weather was fine, found time to take their daughter to the nearest park. Colbeck's father-in-law would have joined them for dinner, and Lydia Quayle might also have been a guest at their table. The simple rhythms of family life were a great tonic for him, and it was a source of abiding regret that his work deprived him of them so often.

Sunday in the Cotswolds had been starkly different,

yet it had yielded results. The investigation had suddenly speeded up. By way of a warning, Colbeck and Leeming had been shot at by an unseen gunman. Later on, the inspector had been shown a second communication from those who'd abducted Edgar Smayle. Rydall had been delighted at what he thought was indisputable proof that his shepherd was still alive, and Colbeck had felt guilty at having to puncture his optimism.

The ransom demand had been repeated, and a date set for the exchange of hostage and money. Given the significance of the event, Colbeck should have been concentrating on it, but his mind kept wandering elsewhere. He kept thinking about the gossip that Hinton had picked up about a strange man lurking around churches. Ordinarily, he would have dismissed such reports, but not in this case. If someone had been seen behaving in such a peculiar way by so many people, he needed to be found and questioned. Evidently, the man was following a route that he'd carefully planned.

Had it begun at the mouth of the Sapperton Tunnel?

After enjoying a hearty meal at the King's Arms, the man lingered in the dining room until he had drunk the last of his bottle of wine. He returned to his room and leafed through his sketchbook, relishing the amount of architectural detail that he'd accumulated. The drawing he spent most time on was the one he had made of the railway disaster, and he was on the verge of excitement as he looked at the figures he'd drawn struggling to clear up the wreckage. He smiled as he remembered the sheer pleasure he'd felt while commemorating the event in his sketchbook.

Though it was getting late, he had no thoughts of retiring to bed. He deliberately stayed awake until midnight and heard the chimes from the clock in the parish church opposite. Letting himself out of the hotel, he came into the market square and looked to his right along Dyer Street. Buildings were silhouetted against the night sky like so many giant ghosts hovering over the town. The combination of dark and silence was exhilarating. He was in his element.

Gliding along like a phantom, he explored the streets and alleyways, listening to the vibrations of the Cotswold stone, imbibing its history and hearing its secrets. At the end of his walk, he found himself in the graveyard and stopped beside a marble headstone that leant over at a slight angle. The man put one arm lovingly around it and used the other hand to feel his way along the inscription chiselled into the stone. To his delight, he discovered that he was communing with a woman who had died over a century earlier and whose epitaph he could read with his fingers. As he hugged the headstone closer, he vowed to find it again in daylight so that he could open his sketchbook and put the woman into his collection.

When she heard where her husband was going that morning and why he had to do so, Catherine Rydall was apprehensive.

'Take the inspector with you,' she urged.

'He did offer to act as my bodyguard,' he replied, 'but he's far more use staying here and continuing his search for evidence.'

'You're not going alone, surely.'

'I'm not that stupid, Catherine. All being well, I'll be carrying a large amount of money. That's why I'm taking Walters with me. He'll be armed.'

'That's a relief!' she said, a hand to her throat.

Rydall gave her a token kiss and let himself out of the house. Sidney Walters was waiting outside for him in a trap. The two of them set off. Since his bank was in Gloucester, he'd decided that they'd ride to Stroud before catching the train to the county town. On the first leg of the journey, he was able to tell his farm manager the latest news. When he heard about the second ransom demand, Walters was angry.

'They'd have had to beat Edgar Smayle to a pulp before he'd write that letter,' he said. 'If and when you get him back, he'll be in no state to work.'

'Inspector Colbeck thinks he might already be dead.'

'But you saw what he said in that letter.'

'When was it written? That's the question.'

'Oh,' said Walters, as he began to understand. 'What cunning devils!'

'We can't expect mercy of any kind from them.'

'Have you told the inspector that I'm on hand if needed?'

'He knows that.'

'Edgar was a good friend. I'd like to be involved.'

'I'd rather leave it to Colbeck and his men.'

The bushes to their left suddenly thinned out and gave them a glimpse of the scene below. Railway policemen were still on duty as the navvies continued their work. There was a gaping pit in the earth where the locomotive had come to rest. It would need to be filled and sprinkled with fresh grass seed before it could return to its former appearance. Meanwhile, it was an open wound.

Walters switched his gaze away and changed the subject.

'Are you expecting the bank to cooperate?' he asked.

'I'll demand that they do, Sidney.'

'It's a lot of money to take out without warning.'

'I'll get it,' said Rydall, determinedly. 'I have to.'

Leeming and Hinton were also sharing a trap, but they'd driven in the opposite direction. Obeying orders from Colbeck, they'd gone the short distance to Sapperton so that they could call in at The Bell. It was not yet open, but when the landlord's wife saw them coming she came out. She gave them a friendly greeting. They alighted from the trap to go across to her.

'I wonder if you could help us,' said Leeming.

'As long as you're not asking us to serve you outside opening hours,' she replied with a wink. 'If you did that, we'd have to report you to the police.'

'We *are* the police,' said Hinton.

She laughed. 'I was only joking.'

'We've heard stories about a stranger who's been in the area,' said Leeming. 'He's been seen close to the church in Frampton Mansell and Sapperton was also mentioned.'

'That's right. He was here a few days ago.'

'What can you tell us about him?'

'I can only pass on what I heard in the bar,' she said. 'This man turned up and walked around the church before taking out a notebook and drawing something in it. When people asked him what he was doing, he ignored them. Worst of all, he didn't come in here for a drink. I mean, it was a very hot day and his throat must have been as dry as a bone. But,' she went on, spreading her arms in a gesture of surprise, 'he ignored The Bell altogether.'

'More fool him,' said Leeming.

'Can you describe this man?' asked Hinton.

'No,' she said, 'but my regulars could. They reckon that he was sort of middle-aged and dressed all in black. He had this white face and podgy cheeks.'

'Can you remember any other details?'

'He was a proper gentleman and not short of money. They knew that because of the way he dressed and the fine horse he rode. He didn't stay long,' she said. 'Once he'd done what he'd come for, he disappeared.'

'So he didn't cause any trouble,' concluded Leeming.

'He caused a lot, Sergeant. He upset everyone who saw him. There was something . . . not quite right about him. Maggie Hodson, who cleans the church, told me that he made her shudder.'

'If he turned down the chance of a pint here,' said Leeming, 'he must have been mad as well as odd.' She giggled. 'Thank you very much. What you've told us has been very helpful.'

'Has he done something wrong?'

'That's what we're trying to find out,' said Hinton.

After trading farewells with her, they drove off.

Riding on horseback, Colbeck had gone well beyond them to the Parish Church of St Matthew in Coates, noting how disproportionately large it was compared to the village it served. He'd ridden past it the previous day on his way to Kemble but had had no chance to admire it or its idyllic setting. When he tried the door, he found that the church was locked, but his journey was not in vain. The rectory was nearby.

Built at the start of the century, it was a big, solid, impressive house with a central block of two storeys and three bays. It was constructed of the coursed rubble stone that Colbeck had noticed wherever he went. In response to his knock, a servant opened the door. When the visitor started to explain who he was, the study door opened, and a man came scuttling out to clasp Colbeck's hands between his own.

'Come on in, come on in, Inspector,' he said, effusively. 'I'm so glad to meet you.'

'Thank you.'

'My name is Martin Bradshaw, and I'm the rector here.'

He conducted Colbeck into his study, and they sat down. The rector was behind a desk that was laden with piles of magazines and papers. Pride of place went to a large Bible.

'May I offer you some refreshment?' asked the rector.

'No, thank you,' said Colbeck. 'I've not long had breakfast.'

'You're staying at The Grange, I believe.' He laughed at his visitor's patent surprise. 'Word travels quickly around here, Inspector. We were shocked to hear about the derailment at the tunnel but reassured that you were summoned. In fact, you were mentioned in our prayers yesterday.'

Colbeck was startled. 'Really?'

'Not by name, of course. We simply prayed for the success of the investigation you're leading.'

'That's very heartening.'

'Most people think that you're an anonymous detective from Scotland Yard, but I know better. With a name like Bradshaw, I'm bound to take an avid interest in railways and in your triumphs related to them.'

'Those triumphs, as you call them, relied very heavily on Bradshaw's Railway Guides.'

'But *they* didn't solve crimes. *You* did that – and brilliantly.'

'Thank you – I'm flattered.'

'Well-deserved praise is not flattery.'

The Reverend Martin Bradshaw was a sinewy man in his fifties with an almost permanent smile. Though his hair was starting to whiten, he exuded energy and passion. Colbeck only had to run his eye along the well-stocked shelves behind the rector to realise that he was in the presence of a scholar. New books nestled beside old tomes. Several titles were in Greek or Latin.

'How can I help you?' asked Bradshaw.

'I'm ashamed to say that I've come as a result of some tittle-tattle,' admitted Colbeck. 'There are rumours that a strange individual was seen hanging around churches in Frampton Mansell and Sapperton. Apparently, the man had a notebook with him and drew things in it. Someone claimed that he turned up here in Coates.'

'Indeed, he did,' said Bradshaw.

'You saw him?'

'I didn't, but the churchwarden did. And you're right about this fellow being strange. He was offhand to the point of being rude. His major interest seemed to be in our anthropophagus.'

'I beg your pardon,' said Colbeck.

'It's a carving of a mythical cannibal who is in the act of swallowing his latest victim. I always find it difficult to describe,' said Bradshaw, rising to his feet, 'so I'll let you meet him in person. Come on, Inspector. It's time you made your acquaintance with our Wild Man of Coates.'

The bank manager was sympathetic to Rydall's request, but he harboured doubts. Unlike his client, he was not at all sure that the money would never actually be paid over. Caution was his watchword. He did his best to persuade Rydall that taking out so much money in cash was unwise.

'And what am I supposed to do?' asked Rydall. 'Suffer the consequences?'

'From what you've told me,' said the other, 'you don't know what those consequences will be. Even if your shepherd is still alive—'

'Enough of this,' snapped Rydall, tiring of his prevarication. 'If you value me as a client, you'll do as I say. I have two questions for you.'

'What's the first one?'

'Whose money is it?'

'Well, it's yours, naturally.'

'I'm glad that we agree on that. You've been talking as if I'm trying to steal some of your own capital from the bank.'

'I'm sorry to give you that impression, Mr Rydall.'

'My second question is this. How soon can you give me what I ask for?'

The bank manager got up. 'I'll see to it at once, sir.'

Less than five minutes later, Rydall was leaving the bank with five thousand pounds in cash inside the valise he'd brought. Walters was waiting for him outside the building.

'Did you get what you asked for, Mr Rydall? he said.

'Yes, I did – eventually.'

'Was the manager reluctant?'

'It was like getting blood from a stone. However,' said Rydall, patting the valise, 'I got it in the end. I look forward to seeing the look on his face when I deposit it back in the bank in due course.'

They walked in the direction of the railway station. It was only when they were standing on the platform awaiting their train that Walters remembered something.

'By the way,' he said, 'I saw someone you know only too well.'

'Who was that?'

'Anthony Beckerton.'

Rydall gulped. 'Where did you see him?'

'He just happened to walk past.'

'Did he speak to you?'

'No,' said Walters, 'he just grinned and went on his way.'

Standing beside the rector, Colbeck gazed up at the carving on the south-west angle of the church. It was a grisly sight. The cannibal was consuming a human being as if he were famished. Some long-forgotten lines popped into Colbeck's mind and came straight out of his mouth.

'*And of the Cannibals that each other eat,*
The Anthropophagi, and men whose heads
Do grow beneath their shoulders.'

'We are two of a kind,' said the rector. 'When I first set eyes on that carving, I, too, quoted those lines from *Othello*. It's remarkable, isn't it? Shakespeare has a way of embedding himself in the memory.'

'It's such a strange thing to find on a church.'

'All kinds of theories have been put forward as to how it got there. Some people see it as a kind of warning. Others fancy that it's a symbol of the bestial ignorance that Christian missionaries have sought to address. My own theory is that it may well have been the work of a whimsical stonemason who wished to leave his mark on the building.'

'I've seen such inappropriate carvings elsewhere,' said Colbeck. 'An earlier case took me to North Cerney where the church has a manticore beneath the window on the south wall.'

'I know it well. It's a creature with the body and tail of a lion and the head and shoulders of a man. Who put it there and why?'

'It's a fascinating church in many ways – as, indeed, is St Matthew's.'

'I'll be happy to unlock the door and show you around, Inspector.'

'Thank you,' said Colbeck, 'but I'll postpone that pleasure until another time. If this carving is what attracted that strange visitor the most, then I've learnt something important about him.'

'Do you think he quoted *Othello* when he first saw it?'

'That's highly unlikely.'

'Then why was he so fascinated by it?'

'I think he has a perverse interest in religion. Your church is an inspiration to those who wish to follow the precepts of Christianity and lead a good life. The man that I'm looking for has no interest in a good life. He is rumoured to have spent a long time among your gravestones.'

'And what do you deduce from that?'

'His primary interest is in death.'

Lambing was still taking up much of their time. Annie and Will Smayle had tried to compensate for their father's absence by finding someone to help them. He was the teenage son of a labourer and had never worked with sheep before. As a result, he kept making mistakes.

'He means well,' said Annie to her brother, 'but he's no shepherd. He kept picking up newborn lambs. That made the ewes distressed. I told him to hold the lambs down low where their mothers could see them.'

Will gave her a non-committal nod.

They were taking a rest and munching the bread and cheese their mother had given them. Annie was worried that her brother had said virtually nothing to her for hours. He'd just worked away as if sleepwalking. She probed for answers.

'Where did you go last night?'

'Nowhere,' he mumbled.

'Don't lie to me. I saw you leave the cottage.'

'It's nothing to do with you.'

'Yes, it is. I fear for you, Will. You need your sleep.'

'No, I don't.'

'We're working harder than ever now. It's telling on you.'

'I'm fine.'

'No, you're not.'

Biting into his cheese, he turned away from her as if to signal the end of the conversation. Annie was persistent. She kept asking where he'd been. When he refused to answer, she threatened to tell their mother.

'Don't do that,' he implored.

'Then tell me where you go.'

'I'm looking for Father.'

'If you can't find him in daylight,' she said, 'you have no chance at all in the dark. You need a rest.'

'I must keep searching, Annie. It's my duty.'

Stephen Rydall was glad when the train came to take them away from Gloucester. Having collected the money he wanted he'd left the bank with a sense of achievement. That feeling disappeared when Walters told him about seeing someone they knew. As the train chugged along, he broke his silence.

'When did you see Beckerton?' he asked.

'It was while you were in the bank,' said Walters.

'Was it soon after I went in or minutes later?'

'What difference does it make?'

'Just tell me, Sidney – it could be important.'

'As it happens, it was almost immediately after you went in there.'

Rydall winced. 'I was afraid you'd say that.'

'Why are you getting so upset about it?' asked Walters. 'It was pure coincidence that Beckerton walked past.'

'I don't think it was.'

'What else could it be?'

'He was waiting for me.'

'How on earth could he know you'd go to the bank this morning?'

'It was because he ordered me to do so,' said Rydall. 'He knows where I bank because I've met him inside that building on more than one occasion. Yesterday evening, I had the ransom demand for the second time. Today was the first chance I'd have of getting the money. Beckerton knew that so he waited and watched until he saw me turn up in Gloucester.'

'I'm still not convinced.'

'Why else would he be there?'

'Perhaps he'd been to the bank himself. You just told me that he has an account there. Beckerton might have done some shopping then walked in the direction of the docks. That was the way he was heading.'

'It fits, Sidney. Don't you understand?'

'Beckerton is a crook,' argued Walters, 'but he's not stupid. If he wanted to check that you'd visit the bank, he wouldn't dream of walking past it the way he did. He'd watch from a concealed position – or he'd have somebody doing that for him.'

It was a sensible comment, and it silenced Rydall. His farm manager could be right. Beckerton's appearance outside the bank could have been coincidental. The man did, after all, live and work in Gloucester. When seen by Walters, he was walking towards the docks where his office was located. There was nothing out of the ordinary in that. Yet the anxiety still remained at the back of Rydall's mind. He wondered if Beckerton had been there to gloat. It would be highly characteristic of the man.

Rydall looked forward to passing on the information to Colbeck.

To get to the village of Rodmarton, they had to go past a row of large barns. The air was filled with pungent country smells. Victor Leeming, who was driving the trap, pulled a face.

'I'd hate to put up with this stink every day.'

'London's stench is just as bad.'

'Yes, but you get used to that.'

'You could get used to this just as easily,' said Hinton. 'There are places in the East End that smell far worse. Living in the country is much healthier than living in a big city.'

'As long as you hold your breath, it is.'

The trap pulled up outside the Parish Church of St Peter, a Norman building that had stood there for centuries and survived recurring assaults from wind, rain and snow. They noticed how the stone had been blackened by age and pitted by hostile weather. Since there was no inn visible, they assumed that the village was too small to sustain one. There was therefore no friendly landlord who would be a fund of local gossip. In the event, they didn't need one because a man came hobbling towards them.

'Good morning, gentlemen,' he said. 'Have you come to see the church?'

'We've come to ask about it,' replied Leeming.

'Then you're talking to the right person. I'm Adam Cheeseman, one of the wardens.'

Getting out of the trap, they introduced themselves and explained why they were there. Seeing a chance to boast to his friends about his encounter with the detectives, Cheeseman was eager to help them. He was a tall, cadaverous man in his sixties with a slight hump.

'Yes, he did come here, as it happens.'

'What sort of man was he?' asked Hinton.

'Quite frankly,' said Cheeseman, 'he had the look of a gentleman but the manners of a pig. When I tried to engage him in conversation, he more or less brushed me aside. Nobody in this village knows the history of this church as well as I do. I could have instructed him.'

'How did he speak?'

'Oh, he was well-educated. Of that there's no question. But he looked at me as if I belonged to a lower form of the animal world.'

'That's hardly a Christian attitude.'

'Yet he shows such an interest in churches,' said Leeming.

'Oh,' said Cheeseman. 'Has he been elsewhere?'

'He's certainly been to Frampton Mansell and Sapperton, and there was talk of him being in Coates as well. This is the fourth church we know of. Did he have a notebook with him?'

'Yes, he did.'

'Did he make many drawings of the church?'

'Not really,' said the other. 'He spent most of his time looking at the gravestones and running his fingers against the names engraved on them. You expect children to behave badly on consecrated ground. They don't know any better. But he was a fully grown man. When I saw what he was doing, I had to chastise him. We must respect the dead in every way, I insisted. Those gravestones are there for a purpose. He was trespassing on their privacy.'

'How did he respond?'

'He didn't take my criticism kindly.'

'Was he angry or offensive?'

'No, nothing like that,' replied Cheeseman. 'He was really upset at being spoken to like that. I'd obviously hurt his feelings.'

'Can you remember what he actually said?'

'I'll never forget it. He drew himself up to his full height and told me that nobody respected the dead as much as he did. He'd devoted his life to them. Then he hauled himself into the saddle and rode off.'

From the moment he'd left The Grange, Colbeck had had the vague feeling that he was being followed. Whenever he looked back, however, there was nobody there. If he was being trailed, he decided, his shadow was someone who knew how to keep well back and use the trees as cover. Colbeck bided his time. After leaving the church, he rode in the direction of the Tunnel Inn. When he rounded a bend, he suddenly kicked his horse into a gallop and sped along the track until he came to a stand of elms. They provided an ideal hiding place. It was not long before he heard the approach of cantering hooves. A chestnut mare soon went past with a slim rider in the saddle. Colbeck waited.

Minutes later, he heard the horse coming back towards him. Having discovered that he'd been shaken off, the man was retracing his steps. When the mare got within thirty yards of him, Colbeck rode out from the trees and confronted the rider with his loaded pistol.

'Stay there!' he demanded.

The man pulled his mount to a stop. He was open-faced, well-dressed and still in his twenties. Colbeck trotted over to him.

'Why were you following me?' he asked.

'I wasn't following anybody.'

'You know full well who I am and are aware that I have the power to arrest you. We can either have this conversation right here, or you'll spend the night behind bars and be taken before a magistrate tomorrow.'

'I was doing nothing wrong,' whined the young man.

'You were obeying orders. Who gave them?'

'I can't tell you, Inspector.'

'Was it Anthony Beckerton?'

'I've never heard of the man.'

'That eliminates one name but leaves two more.'

'Look,' said the other, fearfully, 'I meant no harm. If you let me go, I promise I won't follow you again.'

Colbeck holstered his pistol. 'You won't get the chance. This is the second day in a row when somebody was keeping me under surveillance. On the previous occasion, a shot was fired. What's your name?'

'Jacob, sir . . . it's Jacob Overy.'

'And where are you from?'

'I live near Kemble.'

'Then that answers my question, doesn't it? You were hired by Squire Etheridge to spy on me. What were your orders?'

'Well . . .'

'I want the truth, Jacob, or I'll have to arrest and handcuff you.'

'Oh, please don't do that, Inspector,' cried the other. 'What would my family think?'

'They'd think the same as me, I daresay. They'll wonder why an educated young man like you has to stoop to this kind of employment. Now, let's not waste any more time. I want the full details of how long you've been following me and what you reported to your paymaster.' He pulled back his coat to reveal the handcuffs attached beneath it. 'I'm listening, Jacob Overy.'

Catherine Rydall looked fondly at the photograph of her son and wished that more of the baby's face was visible. She was still uncertain if she'd acted wisely when she'd trusted Colbeck. He had certainly not breathed a word of the photograph to her husband or confirmed that their son was back in England. She decided that the inspector was worthy of her trust. The sound of the wheels of a trap rasping over the gravel in the courtyard took her to the window. When she saw that her husband had returned, she hid the photograph away at once. Then she went downstairs.

She arrived in the hallway as Rydall was coming into the house.

'Well?' she enquired.

'I managed to get the money.'

'What did the bank manager say?'

'He tried to talk me out of taking such a risk.'

'I've been on edge ever since you left,' she confessed. 'I was afraid that someone would steal the money from you.'

'I was well-protected by Sidney Walters.' He patted the valise. 'The money is safe and sound. I've never had this amount in my hands before.'

'Lock it away, Stephen.'

'That's exactly what I'm going to do.'

'Oh, I'm so worried about handing that money over.'

'So am I, Catherine.'

'I fear for your safety.'

'I won't actually give it to them myself. The inspector wants one of his men to take on the office so that I won't be in any danger. But I'm glad that we went to Gloucester.'

'Why is that?'

'I believe I may have identified the person who arranged that derailment.'

'Who is it?'

'I'll tell you when I'm quite certain, my dear, and that will only happen when I've talked to the inspector. My spirits have suddenly lifted,' he declared. 'I believe that this nightmare will soon be over.'

Embracing his wife, he held her tight for minutes.

Gilbert Etheridge had woken much earlier than usual. After sitting up in bed and producing a deafening yawn, he rang the bell for attention. Almost immediately, a servant came into the room.

'What's the weather like?' asked Etheridge.

'It's very sunny, sir.'

'What's the news?'

'You have a visitor,' said the man.

'Who is it?'

'It's an Inspector Colbeck.'

CHAPTER NINETEEN

Over the years, Molly Doble had built up a lot of friendships with canal folk. One of the closest was Bridget Culshaw, a middle-aged mountain of a woman who dressed in men's clothes, wore a flat cap and smoked a pipe. She lived on a gaily painted narrowboat with her husband, a short, wiry, bearded man who patiently endured the many jokes that were made about the disparity between his slight frame and that of his corpulent wife. Puffing on her pipe, Bridget was sitting on a stool on the deck of her barge when Molly walked over to her.

'It's good to see you again, Bridget,' she said, hugging her.

'Thanks, Molly. How is business?'

'It keeps us on our toes.'

'I wish I could say the same, but we've had a lean time of late.'

'You work mostly for Beckerton, don't you?'

'Not any more,' said Bridget. 'We fell out with him. That's to say I got fed up with the way he teased my husband unbearably and kept making lewd suggestions to me. I love a bit of banter, but he took it too far.'

'Say no more. I've had the same trouble from him.'

'There's something evil in that man.'

'I feel sorry for his wife,' said Molly. 'He must be hell to live with.'

'Yes,' agreed her friend. 'Mind you, people say the same about me.' She gave a throaty cackle, and her whole body shook. 'But I'm glad of a word with you,' she went on. 'When we moored here early this morning, I saw something very strange.'

'What was it?'

Bridget pointed a finger. 'There was somebody crouched in those bushes over there and it wasn't for the obvious reason. He was keeping watch on The Daneway and, to tell you the truth, I didn't like the look of him.'

'Describe him.'

'He was a big, sturdy lad in a shepherd's smock, and he had this sort of wild look in his eye. When he realised I'd spotted him, he sneaked away.'

'It was Will Smayle.'

'Who?'

'His father looks after the sheep on Mr Rydall's estate,' said Molly. 'The son works with him. It's about all that Will's fit for, really. When God doled out brains, the lad didn't get his full share – but he's no problem.'

'So, what was he doing this morning?'

'He's been searching for his father. Edgar Smayle disappeared some days ago with his sheepdog, Blackie. The dog was found in the canal with his head smashed in. Peter hauled it out.'

'So, what happened to the father?'

'Nobody knows,' said Molly with a shrug, 'but Will seems to think that he'll find him if he hangs around here. Peter has caught him spying on us before as well. He thinks that Will might have followed his father to The Daneway in the past.'

'He looked old enough to drink. Why didn't he come *with* his father?'

'Will is not allowed to touch alcohol.'

'Why not? I started drinking when I was twelve, and I've never looked back.' Molly's laugh was drowned out by the sound of Bridget's ear-splitting cackle. 'Anyway,' she continued, 'I'm glad I told you, and I'm glad the lad is no danger to you.'

'No danger, just a nuisance.'

'Tell Peter to frighten him off.'

'That would be cruel, Bridget. We feel sorry for him and for his family. They're going through a terrible time. Because of what's happened, there's a chance they may soon be evicted.'

Having done her usual chores, Betsy Smayle was in the kitchen gathering together the ingredients for the next meal. Mildred watched her and offered the occasional suggestion. Jesse had gone out to help with the lambing, but he was unable to do much more than bark orders at the youth who'd been brought in to help. Annie and Will were still hard at work.

Back in the cottage, the two women heard a tin cup drop on

the bare floorboard above and saw something seeping through the ceiling.

'Oh, no,' groaned Mildred. 'She's knocked her tea over yet again.'

'I'll see to it,' said Betsy, grabbing a dishcloth and heading for the stairs. 'I'm coming, Mother!'

'Tell her to be more careful,' advised Mildred.

'She can't help it.'

'Yes, she can.'

Mildred settled back in her chair, but her daughter-in-law's scream of horror made her leap straight out of it. She struggled up the stairs as fast as her old legs would allow and went into the back bedroom. Seated on the bed, Betsy was in tears. Her mother lay dead beside her.

Mildred was philosophical. 'That's one less mouth to feed.'

Gilbert Etheridge was infuriated that Colbeck had dared to call on him and outraged that his butler had let the inspector into the house. In the hope that his visitor might get tired of waiting, he took almost forty minutes before he was ready to come downstairs. To his chagrin, he found Colbeck seated in the drawing room as if he were an honoured guest.

'What are you doing here?' demanded Etheridge.

'For quite some time,' said Colbeck, 'I've been looking at your cricket team.' He indicated the framed photographs on the wall. 'Judging by the smile you have on your face in each one, you're very proud of them.'

'Please state your business, then leave.'

'I want to talk to you about Jacob Overy.'

'Who?'

'Jacob is the young man you ordered to follow me.'

'I'm sorry but I've never heard of him.'

'That's strange,' said Colbeck, rising to his feet and crossing to one of the photographs. 'He's a member of your beloved cricket team.' He pointed to a figure in the front row. 'Look, here he is, standing right next to you. Jacob has a sportsman's build – just like Michael Rydall.'

Etheridge was guarded. 'Did this young man *say* that I'd hired him to follow you?'

'No, he didn't.'

'Then your accusation is false.'

'He didn't name you because he was afraid of repercussions.'

'I need detain you no longer,' said Etheridge, standing aside and gesturing towards the door. 'Goodbye, Inspector.'

'I've no intention of leaving, sir.'

'Are you going to repeat your slanderous allegation?'

'Once was perfectly adequate, I think.'

'Beware, Inspector,' warned the other, 'I have an excellent lawyer.'

'Then I'd be pleased to meet him,' said Colbeck with a smile. 'Before I joined the Metropolitan Police Force, I worked as a barrister. I always took a special delight in making provincial lawyers look like the country bumpkins they usually were. Yours, I am sure,' he added, 'may not come into that category, but he'd nevertheless be foolish to lock horns in court with me.'

Etheridge was visibly shaken by the resolute way in which Colbeck spoke. He could see that his visitor would not be dismissed quite so easily.

'What do you want, Inspector?' he asked.

'I want an explanation, sir.'

Etheridge flicked a hand. 'I never give explanations.'

'Then you and I will adjourn to the police station in Cirencester. If I make the arrest there, it will get maximum publicity in the local newspaper. They may even send a photographer along.'

'Arrest!' howled the other. 'You have no grounds.'

'I believe that I have,' said Colbeck. 'In having me followed by Jacob Overy, you were interfering in a police investigation. That's the kindest interpretation I can place on your actions. Anyone else would believe that you needed to keep an eye on me because you had something to hide.'

'Damn you, man!'

'Your bluster is wasted on me, Squire Etheridge.'

'I want you to leave my house at once.'

'Then you must put your coat on and come with me,' threatened Colbeck. 'Even this excellent lawyer of yours would have to concede that I have evidence enough to arrest you.'

Etheridge's face went red with exasperation. Not trusting himself to speak, he walked up and down the whole length of the room. When he confronted Colbeck again, his manner had softened.

'You've been misled, Inspector.'

'I know. Please don't try to mislead me any more.'

'That young man was not really following you.'

'Then what was he doing?' asked Colbeck.

'Unauthorised by me, he was reacting to a casual remark I made.'

'Ah, so you have at last remembered that you *do* know Jacob Overy.'

'He was one of a number of players who were there at the time,' said Etheridge. 'Two days ago, I hosted a drinks party at the cricket pavilion to discuss some important fixtures we have coming up. Not surprisingly, the blocking of the Sapperton Tunnel came into the conversation.'

'I can't honestly see its relevance to the game of cricket.'

'Someone mentioned that a famous detective from Scotland Yard was in charge of the case. I remember saying – and bear in mind that I'd had a few drinks at this point – that I'd dearly love to know what happened at every stage of the investigation. Overy must have heard me and taken my words at face value.'

Colbeck's eyebrow lifted. 'Do you really expect me to believe that?'

'Has Overy said anything different?'

'He was clearly ordered by you to say as little as possible.'

'I deny that.'

Colbeck held his eye long enough to convey the message that Etheridge was still under suspicion of involvement, however indirectly, in the train crash. When the older man took a step backwards, Colbeck knew that he'd made his point effectively.

'What sort of cricketer, is he?'

'Who?'

'Jacob Overy.'

'He's a good batsman.'

'Is he on a par with Michael Rydall?'

'No,' said Etheridge, relaxing for the first time. 'Nobody could compare with Rydall. He was peerless.'

Michael Rydall's disguise was so complete that he felt able to move around in public without fear of recognition. He and his companion rode side by side on horseback until they came to the cutting near the western portal of the tunnel. Rydall watched the activity below for a couple of minutes before turning to his friend and issuing instructions.

'It won't take you long to get there,' he said. 'Just do what I told you and come straight back. I'll wait for you here.'

Edward Tallis was restive. Sunday had been a continuous trial for him. Persistent toothache had plagued him during morning service in church, and he got back to his lodging to discover that he'd run out of cigars. When he stormed into the office that morning, therefore, he was in desperate need of some good news to brighten his day and ease the throbbing in his bad tooth. At least, he was able to grab a cigar from its box and it was alight within seconds of his arrival. He scanned the documents on his desk and noticed that there was nothing from Colbeck – no letter, no telegraph, no source of information whatsoever. Tallis accepted that Alan Hinton was needed in the Cotswolds and couldn't easily be spared to go all the way back to Scotland Yard again with a full report of the state of the investigation. But the superintendent had counted on receiving information of some sort. Exhaling a veritable cloud of tobacco, he announced his ultimatum to the empty room.

'If I don't hear from you by tomorrow morning, Colbeck,' he vowed, 'I'll be coming to find out exactly what's going on.'

Colbeck had taken great pleasure from his visit to Kemble Court. He'd seen inside the house, admired the many landscape paintings in the drawing room and discountenanced the squire. Having been followed for two days, he decided that it was his turn to become a shadow. When he rode away from the house, therefore, he stopped behind a barn and waited. Within minutes, someone came through the huge iron gates of Kemble Court in a hurry. The man was so eager to kick his horse into a canter, that he saw nothing else but the road in front of him. Colbeck was able to emerge from cover and follow from a safe distance.

He already had a good idea of the rider's destination. It was clear to him that Etheridge was working hand in glove with the Reverend Patrick Cinderby. Understandably, the squire wanted to warn his friend immediately. The servant therefore rode post haste to the Royal Agricultural College. Colbeck waited until he saw the man gallop through the entrance gates, then he reined his own horse in. On the way back to The Grange, he amused himself by imagining the look on Cinderby's face when he read the message from his friend.

Since they were searching for a man with a passion for ecclesiastical architecture, they assumed that he would certainly visit the best example of it in the area. Victor Leeming and Alan Hinton therefore headed for Cirencester. As the trap rattled along at a steady pace, they saw the steeple of the Parish

Church of St John the Baptist some while before they reached it. They entered a pleasant, picturesque town that consisted largely of houses and streets built in medieval times. Both of them marvelled at the church and its magnificent porch.

'He'd have spent ages here,' said Leeming. 'There's so much for him to draw.'

'Shall we try to find a churchwarden?' asked Hinton.

'There's something else we should do first, Alan.'

'What's that?'

'Let's see if he stayed here. We know that he's a man of means so he'll probably choose one of the best hotels.' He nodded towards the King's Arms. 'That might be a good place to start.'

Having parked the trap, they went into the hotel. The manager, a short, squat individual of middle years, was standing behind a counter with his hands clasped together. When he saw what he hoped were new guests, he opened the ledger in front of him.

'Good day to you, gentlemen,' he said. 'How may I help you?'

'We need some information,' said Leeming.

He explained who they were and described the man in whom they were interested. Leeming wondered if he'd reached Cirencester yet. Almost immediately, the manager raised a hand to silence him.

'The gentleman stayed here last night, sir,' he said.

'Is he still here?'

'No, he left this morning.'

'What was his name?' asked Hinton.

The manager consulted his ledger. 'Mr Francis Gregory.'

'What sort of a man was he?'

'He was rather unusual,' replied the other. 'He paid for a bed, yet he hardly slept in it. The porter saw him slip out of the front door at midnight, and he didn't come back until hours later.'

'We've been told that he's not very talkative,' said Leeming.

'That's true. He hardly said a word and kept himself to himself. To be honest, he had a rather lordly attitude as if he was doing us a favour by staying here. We were glad to see the back of him.'

'Did he say what he was doing here?'

'No,' said the manager, 'but it was easy to find out.'

'How?'

'Well, he had a large sketchbook and some much smaller ones. We know this because they were piled up on the table when one of the servants took him an extra pillow he demanded. What he did, you see, was to draw pictures in the notebooks then transfer them to the big sketchbook when he had the time.' He treated them to a sly smile. 'You're going to ask me how I happen to know this, aren't you?'

'That servant of yours saw him doing it,' guessed Hinton.

'No, she was in and out of his room in seconds.'

'So what's the explanation?'

'Most of the smaller books had no drawings at all in them. That's what I reckon, anyway. When he'd filled one of them – and copied all he needed into the big sketchbook – he threw it away.'

Leeming was excited. 'Is that what he did here?'

'Yes, sir.'

'And do you still have it?'

'We do. Mr Gregory has a gift. His drawings are very clever. They bring churches alive. I've only had time to glance through at a few pages, but I could see that he was a real artist.'

'Where is the notebook now?'

'We threw it away, sir,' said the manager, 'but don't worry. It will still be in the shed with all the other rubbish. We won't burn it until later on. If you wait here a moment, I'll fetch it for you.'

When the man disappeared, Leeming turned to Hinton.

'If we'd got here a few hours ago, we might have caught him.'

'I'm beginning to wonder what use that would be, Sergeant.'

'You heard the inspector. This man must be questioned.'

'But all he's done is to make some drawings of churches.'

'Yes,' conceded Leeming, 'but remember what people said about him being weird. Look at the way he treated that churchwarden in Rodmarton. We know for certain that he was in the area when the crash occurred. That may have been deliberate. Those seven dead sheep that were slaughtered are telling.'

'Are they?'

'I think so. There's a strange link with the Bible somehow. Francis Gregory may yet be the man we're after.'

'I'm not sure about that.'

'Think it through, Alan.'

'That's what I'm trying to do.'

'We'll soon find out if I'm right.'

Leeming had seen the manager coming back with a notebook in his hands. When he took it from him, he flipped through the pages and saw drawings of church after church. He then came to a very different illustration. Across two pages, the crash site outside the mouth of the Sapperton Tunnel had been sketched in detail. The locomotive and shattered wagons were all there and so were tiny figures trying to clear up the wreckage. Leeming showed it to Hinton.

'Do you *still* think it's a waste of time searching for him?'

Mildred Smayle went out to tell the others what had happened. It was impossible to decide from the tone of her voice what her feelings really were.

'Betsy's mother is dead,' she announced. 'It's a tragedy.'

They responded in their own ways. Jesse Smayle hid his delight under a few gruff words of sorrow, Annie collapsed into tears and had to be comforted by her surviving grandmother, and Will seemed completely unaffected. It was not an important death for him, so it never touched his emotions. His mind was still fixed immovably on his missing father.

When Colbeck returned at a trot to The Grange, he saw that Rydall was watching from the window. The latter came out at once and followed him to the stables.

'I need to speak to you, Inspector,' he said.

'Has something happened?'

'I believe so.'

'Then I'm at your disposal.'

Dismounting from the horse, he handed the reins to a stable lad, then followed Rydall into the house. When they'd settled down in the study, Rydall told him what had happened outside the bank in Gloucester.

'Beckerton gave himself away,' he urged.

'That's not how I see it, Mr Rydall,' said Colbeck.

'It's tantamount to a confession.'

'Having met him, I don't believe that Beckerton would confess to anything. If you caught him standing over a dead body with a bloodstained knife in his hand, he'd have a plausible excuse.'

'He was there to make sure that I took out the money.'

'Then why didn't he wait until *you* came out of the bank?'

'He didn't need to do that,' said Rydall. 'When he saw Walters standing there, he knew that I'd be inside the building.'

'But he had no idea what business you'd be transacting. I presume that you or Mr Walters go to the bank on a regular basis to deposit money or to take advice from the manager. Seeing you there today was not unusual for Beckerton. You just told me that you'd met him inside the building occasionally.'

'Yes – and I always got the same fiendish grin that he gave to Walters.'

'I can see how you came to your conclusion,' said Colbeck, 'but I'm still sceptical. The man is far too clever to give himself away so blatantly.'

'He was crowing over me, Inspector.'

'I thought it was Mr Walters who actually saw him.'

'Beckerton knew that I'd be inside that bank. That second ransom demand was like a gun to the head,' said Rydall. 'He knew that it would force me to go to Gloucester this morning so he made sure that he could stroll past the bank at the right moment. It wasn't an act of stupidity on his part. What he was saying was, in effect, that he was culpable but that I'd never be able to prove it.'

'If he *is* guilty, sir, there will be irrefutable proof.'

'Does his behaviour this morning mean nothing to you?'

'It's irrelevant.'

'He was flaunting his invincibility,' said Rydall with gathering vexation. 'I've told you before how the police have failed to prosecute him successfully for crimes they know he committed – crimes, in some cases, that involve hired thugs of his. Beckerton has a whole gang of them on his payroll.' He paused to catch his breath. 'I must say, Inspector, that I'm very disappointed. I expected you of all people to agree with my assessment of what happened this morning.'

'Did Mr Walters agree with it?'

'That's neither here nor there.'

'Oh, yes, it is. Did he?' Rydall shook his head. 'He must know Beckerton almost as well as you do yet he didn't reach the conclusion that you did. First, let me assure you of one thing – nobody is invincible. Our system of justice has punished scheming rogues like Beckerton time and again and it will go on doing so. If he's guilty, he will be punished.'

'He's managed to escape justice for his crimes until now.'

'It won't happen in this instance.'

'Then why are you disregarding evidence against him?'

'It's because I'd rather tell you about evidence against someone else,' said Colbeck. 'While you were in Gloucester, I was making enquiries about two other suspects. One has already been named by you.'

'Who was that?'

'Squire Etheridge of Kemble Court.'

He told Rydall how he'd been followed and how he'd

cornered the young man on his tail. He then described the way that, after his visitor had left, the squire had promptly dispatched a letter to the Royal College of Agriculture, unaware that Colbeck would trail the messenger.

'In other words,' he said, 'I learnt something important about two suspects whom you told me were in league with each other. Since they went to such lengths to monitor the investigation, suspicion of them must increase. If *they* are involved in some way then Beckerton is innocent. Don't you agree?'

'I suppose that I must,' said Rydall with reluctance.

'Beckerton, Cinderby and Etheridge remain the most likely villains, though not, I would contend, as a kind of triple alliance. And there's someone else to add to that trio.'

'Who is it?'

'I don't as yet have his name,' admitted Colbeck, 'but his behaviour in this part of the Cotswolds has been somewhat bizarre. He's managed to upset people in a number of churches, so I've ordered my officers to run him to earth.'

'I'm glad to hear it.'

'Perhaps you'll now understand why I wasn't so ready to embrace your belief that the man we're after is Anthony Beckerton.'

'Yes, yes,' said Rydall. 'I was perhaps too hasty.'

'You may still be right, of course,' said Colbeck, 'but there's one thing on which you may rely. Whoever it is, we'll catch him.'

After securing what they felt was a vital piece of evidence, Leeming and Hinton treated themselves to some refreshment in Cirencester. As they ate their food, however, their excitement began to dwindle slightly.

'We still don't know where he is at the moment,' said Hinton.

'We will, Alan.'

'How?'

'Well, we know he's not far away. This county is bristling with churches. He'll work his way through more of his little notebooks before he's finished.'

'Do we keep on looking for him?'

'No,' said Leeming. 'We must get back to The Grange this afternoon to tell the inspector what we've found. Besides, the money has to be handed over today.'

'Where will you and the inspector be when that happens?'

'We'll be keeping a fatherly eye on you, Alan.'

Hinton chewed another mouthful of pie and brooded for a while.

'You said something very odd at that hotel.'

'Did I?'

'Yes,' replied Hinton. 'You mentioned that seven sheep had been slaughtered just before the crash. What have they got to do with the Bible?'

'Seven is a number that comes up time and again in the Good Book.'

'Is it?'

'Don't you go to church?'

'Well, yes, but I don't really have much time to study the Bible.'

'The inspector wonders if what we saw outside that tunnel is some eerie religious message.'

'What kind of message?'

'I don't know,' confessed Leeming, 'but when we finally catch up with Francis Gregory, we'll be able to ask him, won't we?'

Colbeck could see that Rydall was chastened. Having believed that Beckerton had brazenly admitted his guilt in the knowledge that it could never be proved, the man was forced to accept that he'd been too quick to condemn the haulier. The revelation about the new suspect had taken him by surprise.

'I owe you an apology, Inspector,' he said.

'It's wholly unnecessary, sir. Your frustration is understandable. By the end of the day, hopefully, we will have unmasked the culprit and his associates. I promise you that we will then be embarrassed by all the needless speculation in which we indulged.'

'I'm sorry I pounced on you when you returned.'

'My superintendent does that all the time, Mr Rydall. Over the years, I've become immune to it.'

'I promise not to do it again.'

After exchanging a few more comments with him, Colbeck took his leave. He went back to his room to give himself time to weigh the evidence he'd gathered that morning. When he got there, however, a letter was waiting for him. As soon as he read it, he forgot about everything else.

The letter was unsigned. It contained an offer of help with regard to the investigation and asked for a meeting with Colbeck at the earliest opportunity. The appointed place was only ten minutes' ride away. His initial reaction was that he might be lured into an ambush. Having read the missive a few times, however, he was won over by the educated calligraphy and by the evident sincerity in what was more of an appeal than an invitation.

Since he'd asked the stable lad to leave his horse saddled, Colbeck was able to mount up immediately. He trotted out of the courtyard and followed the route dictated in the letter. His loaded pistol was in its holster. When he finally reached the suggested meeting place, he could see why it had been chosen. It was in a clearing in a wooded area. He could easily be seen by someone concealed nearby who would want to be certain that he'd come alone. Colbeck dismounted and waited patiently.

It was minutes before there was a rustling noise among the trees. A tall, impeccably dressed young man stepped into view. He appraised Colbeck.

'Thank you for coming, Inspector,' he said.

'May I know who summoned me?'

'It's perhaps better if you do not. My name would not be entirely welcome in the Rydall household. I need to remain anonymous.'

'In that case,' said Colbeck, 'I'd rather talk to the person who dictated that letter. You, I am sure, actually wrote it because he'd be afraid that his hand would be recognised at The Grange.' He raised his voice. 'You can come out, Michael. If you have something to say, I'll be glad to hear it.'

After a few moments, Michael Rydall came into view. He looked nothing whatsoever like the figure in the photographs Colbeck had seen.

'Is that really you?'

'Yes, Inspector,' said Michael. 'In view of the situation, you'll appreciate why I prefer to travel incognito. This is a good friend of mine,' he went on, turning to his companion. 'That's all you need to be told about him.'

'I accept that.'

'How did you know that I'd be here?'

'It had to be someone close to the family, and you were once an integral part of it. Also, I knew that you were back in the Cotswolds. Someone recognised you outside Stroud railway station.'

'That was a bad lapse on my part,' said Michael. 'I've moved about in disguise ever since.'

'I called on Squire Etheridge this morning. He has photographs of the cricket team on his wall. You were in one of them.'

'Those days are gone, I'm afraid.'

'Your prowess on the field is still remembered.'

'Michael was a natural cricketer,' said the friend. 'I loved watching him play. He won game after game for the team – but Squire Etheridge always tried to claim the credit.'

'I can well believe it.'

'Why were you so certain that I'd be here?' asked Michael.

Colbeck smiled. 'I've been expecting you.'

'Apart from my cricketing exploits, you know nothing whatsoever about me. My father won't even let my name be mentioned in the house.'

'Your mother is not so heartless. She's kept in touch with you.'

Michael was worried. 'Did she tell you that?'

'Have no fear,' said Colbeck. 'I haven't told anybody

else. Your mother showed me the photograph you sent her. However,' he went on, 'you brought me here to talk about your father. You're well aware of what happened at the tunnel a few days ago, and you know the profound impact it must have had on your father. He views it as a direct assault on him.'

'Then he may be wrong,' said Michael.

Before they left Cirencester, they had a closer look at the little notebook and discovered that some pages were devoted to gravestones, their epitaphs carefully copied as if they were cherished members of Gregory's family. More arresting were drawings of a dead lamb, a half-eaten rabbit caught in a snare, a sparrowhawk pecking at the remains of a smaller bird and the anthropophagus at St Matthew's Church in Coates.

'Francis Gregory seems to revel in death,' said Hinton.

'Then he'll be disappointed by the derailment.'

'What do you mean?'

'Nobody was killed.'

'The driver and fireman had serious injuries.'

'Gregory wanted more than that.'

'But we don't know for certain that he caused the crash.'

'Why else was he able to make a drawing of it so soon afterwards?' asked Leeming. 'In the immediate aftermath, he probably kept out of the way for fear of being seen, then he crept back and got to work with his pencil.'

'There's something to bear in mind.'

'What is it?'

'According to the inspector,' said Hinton, 'more than one

person is involved. If and when the ransom is handed over, there'll be lookouts posted to make sure Mr Rydall does as he's told.'

'So?'

'Gregory works alone, Sergeant.'

'Ah, I see what you mean.'

'He hates company of any sort, even when he's in a church. Who'd want to work with a man like that?'

As the day progressed, Catherine Rydall became ever more anxious. Fearing for the safety of her husband, she was also worried about the amount of money he was prepared to hand over. Whoever had demanded it would be determined to get every penny. They would show no mercy.

When she saw the opportunity, she taxed her husband.

'Leave everything to the inspector,' she begged.

'I have to be *seen*, my dear. That was stipulated.'

'I can't bear to think what might happen.'

'Be brave, Catherine. That's what I'm striving to be.'

'I'd hoped an arrest would have been made by now.'

'It's not for want of trying,' he said. 'After my visit to the bank, I was certain that Anthony Beckerton was the man we wanted, but the inspector told me of evidence that pointed to Squire Etheridge and Cinderby. A new suspect has also come to light, and he sounds even more threatening. It may well be that none of these people is guilty and that I'm the victim of some nameless villain bent on inflicting pain on me and damage on the GWR.'

'The uncertainty is gnawing away at me, Stephen.'

'And me, my dear. There is, however, one consolation.'

'I don't see it.'

'After devoting serious thought to the matter,' he told her, 'I'm convinced that there's someone we can eliminate altogether.'

'Who is it?'

Rydall had to make a conscious effort to spit the name out.

'Michael.'

CHAPTER TWENTY

They had moved from the clearing to an even more secluded spot so that they could talk freely. Michael's friend was acting as a lookout. The two men were therefore left alone. They took some time to study each other. Colbeck was surprised to find Michael taller and fleshier than he'd imagined. There was a profound seriousness about him which seemed unlikely in someone so relatively young. For his part, Michael was amazed at how suave and well-spoken Colbeck was. Cool and watchful, he seemed to possess wisdom beyond his years. But the inspector's most important quality was his apparent trustworthiness. Michael was encouraged to confide in him.

'You're still in the dark, aren't you?' he said.

'Let's say that we've only been able to shed a limited amount of light.'

'My father's told you that *he's* the one suffering.'

'There's no doubt about that,' said Colbeck. 'This business has been a continuous torture for Mr Rydall. He blames himself for being responsible for this tragedy.'

'Yet *he* didn't derail that goods train.'

'Indirectly, he believes, he did. By unknowingly provoking an enemy of his, Mr Rydall is convinced that he set off a chain of events.'

'Is that what *you* believe?'

'No, it's too narrow and restrictive a view.'

'Yet I fancy that you've been working on that basis,' observed Michael. 'That's why you've had little success so far. You haven't made a single arrest.'

'We have suspects in mind.'

'They'll be ones that my father suggested. That's typical of him, I'm afraid. He's obsessed with the idea that a blocked railway tunnel is a direct warning to him.'

'Do you have an alternative suggestion?'

'I might do.'

'Please share it with me,' said Colbeck. 'I'm not too proud to take advice when it comes from someone with your experience.'

'I'd like to point you in a different direction.'

'Go on.'

'I don't believe that my father was the target of this crime, Inspector.'

'Then who was?'

'Edgar Smayle.'

Sidney Walters responded to the summons immediately. The death of an old woman whom he'd barely known had no personal significance for him, but he understood the impact it must have on the family at a time when they were already suffering. He drove at once to the Smayle cottage. Alone with her mother-in-law in the kitchen, Betsy was weeping copiously. When she saw him approach, she used the edge of her pinafore to dry her eyes.

'It's good of you to come so quick, Mr Walters,' she said.

'When she brought the news,' he explained, 'Annie told me how distressed you were. Please accept my condolences.'

'Thank you.'

'It's a shame,' said Mildred. 'She was such a nice woman.'

'We don't know much about funerals,' apologised Betsy, 'and that's why I sent for you. We need to be told what to do. Mother's gone and . . . there may be someone else to bury soon.'

Reference to her husband made the tears trickle down her face again. When she tried to apologise, Walters told her that her reaction was a perfectly normal one and that she was entitled to express her grief.

'What we don't know,' said Mildred, taking over, 'is how much it's going to cost. Betsy's mother had a little put by but . . . it won't be enough.'

'Don't worry about the cost,' said Walters.

'We want to do everything proper.'

'Yes, of course you do, and I understand that. Naturally, you're worried about the arrangements. You'll need a visit from the vicar first. Would you like me to get in touch with him?'

'Would you?' asked Betsy, almost pleading.

'It will be no trouble at all.'

'Mother would have been seventy-three later this year. She's led a terrible, hard life, sir. The wonder is she stayed alive so long.'

'Leave everything to us,' said Walters, 'and don't worry about the cost. I'm sure that Mr Rydall will be able to make a contribution to the expenses.'

'That's so kind of him,' said Betsy, overwhelmed.

Mildred was practical. 'How much is a contribution?' she muttered to herself.

Colbeck was an attentive listener. Understanding Michael's situation, he appreciated why the latter chose his words carefully. Michael said nothing about his present situation or why he'd moved back to England. That was irrelevant. It was his earlier life as a member of the Rydall family on which he concentrated.

'I wanted to be different,' he said. 'My brothers thought only of owning their own farms. They knew what they'd be doing at every stage of their lives. I found that stifling and not a little scary. I wanted more experience of life.'

'Didn't you like farming?' asked Colbeck.

'I loved it, Inspector. From the time I was knee high, I was out in the fields, watching what was being done until I reached an age when I could do it myself. I worked beside the labourers during the harvests and that's something my brothers wouldn't deign to do.'

'It must have kept you fit for playing cricket.'

'That was one bonus. There were others.'

'How did you get on with Squire Etheridge?'

'I did what the rest of the team did,' said Michael with a hollow laugh, 'and endured him. In fairness, he paid for our pavilion and for the maintenance of the ground. But he can be very crotchety and liked to remind everybody that he was the club president.'

'Yes, I've noticed that.'

'He insisted on having his own way.'

'He still does that,' said Colbeck. 'Tell me about Edgar Smayle.'

'He is a genius with sheep. I used to watch him for hours when I was younger. He had two dogs in those days. All he had to do was to whistle and they obeyed his command at once. Do you know what a sheepdog trial is?'

'No, I don't.'

'It's an idea that's been around for some time, but it never took root. Then someone came up with a plan. Three shepherds devised a competition. Smayle was one of them. They took it in turns to manoeuvre a small flock of sheep into a pen. Each competitor was timed to see who was quickest.'

'I take it that Smayle won the competition,' said Colbeck.

'He did. I was there. His dogs rounded up the flock in seconds, well ahead of the others. Not content with winning, however, Smayle had to taunt the other shepherds. Then he went off to The Daneway that night and drank far too much by way of celebration.'

'Yes, we were told he was too fond of his beer.'

'When he was in that state, he didn't care what he said or to whom he said it. Smayle was aggressive, Inspector. He loved to cause trouble.'

'That was a dangerous thing to do in a place where there were so many bargees. As a rule, they're powerful men.'

'Smayle always had Blackie, one of his dogs, with him. Anyone who dared to take on Smayle had to take on a snarling sheepdog as well.'

'I thought you said that he had *two* dogs.'

'He did,' said Michael, 'but shortly after that competition, one of them was shot dead. That was a warning.'

'Who sent it – a rival shepherd or one of the bargees?'

'It could have been anyone. He'd made so many enemies.'

'What happened?'

'Smayle ignored the warning. You've seen the result.'

The Reverend Cinderby had always prided himself on his self-control. When the message arrived from Kemble Court, however, he was grateful that he was alone because he was visibly upset by the letter. It took him minutes to recover. After cancelling an appointment with a member of staff, he left the college at speed and drove his trap towards Kemble. The notion that Colbeck had threatened Etheridge with arrest – and, by implication, Cinderby himself with the same fate – was more than alarming. It had thrown him into a panic. His whole future as the principal of an agricultural college had suddenly been cast into doubt.

He arrived at his destination to find that someone had

considerately left the gates open for him. Cinderby also learnt that he was not the only person who'd been summoned. Jacob Overy was just leaving. Head down and body drooping, he shuffled past the newcomer without even seeing him. Overy looked like an animal that had just been given a severe beating and was slinking away with its tail between its legs.

Cinderby was admitted to the house and shown straight into the drawing room. Etheridge was pacing up and down with a face corrugated by anxiety. When his friend appeared, Etheridge went swiftly across to him.

'Thank heaven you've come!'

'Who was that I just saw leaving?'

'That was the imbecile who landed us in this mess. His name is Jacob Overy, and I asked him to keep close watch on Colbeck. Unfortunately, he got *too* close and gave himself away.'

'The phrase you used in my hearing was "discreet enquiries". Couldn't you find someone a little more reliable?'

'He did his job well at first.'

'What use is that?' shouted Cinderby.

'Don't raise your voice with me, Patrick.'

'Then don't give me cause. *You* were the one who hired this fellow.'

'I also gave him specific instructions,' said Etheridge. 'I told him that, if he *was* caught, he must on no account bring my name into it. To his credit, Overy obeyed that order.'

'Then why did Colbeck turn up on your doorstep?'

'He did much more than that. When I came downstairs, he was lolling in a chair as if he was a guest here. Worst of all, he'd been looking at the photographs of the cricket team.'

'Why was that such a problem?'

'Jacob Overy was in them,' said Etheridge. 'There was I, swearing that I'd never heard of him and he'd seen Overy standing right next to me in one of the photographs. It was embarrassing. We've underestimated Colbeck.'

'Was *my* name mentioned at all?'

'I did my best to keep you out of it.'

'Thank you.'

'But if he'd arrested me, I'm sure that he'd have come after you next. He knows how closely we work together. Colbeck was all for taking me to the police station and inviting a photographer from the local paper to come along.'

'That would be disastrous!'

'It certainly wouldn't do either of us any good, and we'd have to face searching questions from the governing body. We're desperate for good publicity to rope in new benefactors. News of our arrest would be the complete opposite. In fact—'

'You don't have to spell it out,' said Cinderby, wiping his brow with a handkerchief. 'The consequences would be unimaginable. Oh, why on earth did this interfering busybody from Scotland Yard have to descend on us?'

'You know the answer to that. It's Stephen Rydall's revenge.'

'It could ruin everything.'

'What about our nephew's professorship? That will vanish like a puff of smoke. I've more or less promised it to him.'

'We must think of our own salvation first.'

'I agree.'

'The question is this – what do we do?'

Etheridge grimaced. 'I was hoping that you'd tell *me* that.'

He walked to the whisky decanter and poured two glasses.

Bridget Culshaw was seated at one of the tables outside the Daneway Inn. She swallowed the last of her beer in one gulp and gave a smile of contentment.

'I needed that,' she said before belching. 'It's my turn at legging.'

'That's man's work, surely,' opined Molly Doble.

'My legs are much stronger than my husband's, so I'll take my turn. My son and me will soon get the barge through the tunnel. All I have to do is to lie on my back and suffer.' She laughed. 'It's a bit like having a baby.'

'I wouldn't know, Bridget. We never had children.'

'Didn't you want them?'

'Of course,' said Molly, sadly, 'but it . . . just didn't happen.'

'Oh, I'm sorry.'

'We learnt to live with it, and we did employ a girl a few years ago who became like one of the family. Besides, me and Peter always say that our customers are our children. They're a blooming nuisance during the day, mind, but at last we don't have to read bedtime stories to them.'

'There is that, Moll,' said her friend. 'By the way, everyone's talking about that accident on the railway line. Is it true that some sheep were killed?'

'Yes, it's a real shame. They were looked after by Edgar Smayle and his son. That's Will, the lad you spotted earlier.'

'Why should some harmless sheep be killed?'

'It doesn't make sense to me.'

'Nor me – it's so cruel. I know that we kill lambs and so on, but that's to put food on the table. It's normal. Penning them up like that so that a train smashes into them – well, what sort of person could do that?'

'I don't know, Bridget. It sickens me to think of it.'

'What must that lad, Will, make of it?'

'Peter says that he's still in a daze. Will's known those sheep since they were born. In fact, I think he's happiest when he's out in the fields with them. All of a sudden, he loses his father and part of the flock. They're terrible blows for someone like him. They've sent him clean out of his mind.'

Taking advantage of a break in lambing, Will went off into the woods with the shotgun and the knife. After selecting a tree as a target, he first hurled the knife at it with vicious force, then fired two pellets after it. His attack had not finished there. Holding the weapon by the barrel, he ran forward and swung it madly in the air as if battering an invisible enemy. The assault continued until he finally ran out of breath. Falling to his knees, he began to weep.

Colbeck had found the meeting with Michael Rydall both interesting and instructive. It showed that he cared enough about his family to come forward with a suggestion. He'd been subdued to the point almost of solemnity. The experience of emigration to Canada had apparently transformed him. He'd come back with a sense of responsibility he'd never had before.

Since he'd been persuaded to look at the case from a slightly different angle, Colbeck felt that it was only right to confide in him. He told Michael about the forthcoming exchange of the ransom during which he and his men hoped to unmask whoever had caused the derailment. In addition, he passed on the evidence that had been gathered against the suspects named by Michael's father. They'd then parted.

When he arrived back at The Grange, he found Leeming waiting outside the stables for him. Having left Hinton at The Crown, the sergeant was on his own, waving the little notebook in the air.

'You won't believe what we discovered, sir,' he said.

'I've made a rather startling discovery myself, as it happens.'

'That man's name is Francis Gregory and he's—'

'Tell me in the privacy of my room,' said Colbeck, interrupting. 'I'll just hand my horse to the stable lad then I'll be glad to hear your news.'

They soon adjourned to the annexe, and Leeming was able to pour out his tale excitedly. At the end of his recitation, he handed the notebook to Colbeck. The latter went through it methodically page by page. He stopped at the drawing of the carving he'd seen at the church in Coates.

'That's the anthropophagus,' he said.

'What's that?'

'It's a sort of gongoozler who eats people,' teased Colbeck. 'Seriously, it's a cannibal and a hungry one at that.'

The final set of drawings incorporated features of the parish church in Cirencester. They included the flowery epitaph on a gravestone marking the burial place of a woman who died many years ago.

'Why did he want to draw that?' asked Leeming.

'Let's ask him.'

'But we have no idea where he is.'

'Yes, we do,' said Colbeck. 'If you look at the order in which he's visited various churches, you'll see where he's likely to go next. Let me show you.'

He took out the map from his valise and unfolded it. Laying it on the table, he pointed out the places where Gregory had gone and in which direction he was obviously heading.

'We've picked up his scent, Victor. Let's go after him.'

'Do we have the time?'

'Yes, we've got hours before twilight sets in.'

'What about this discovery you said you'd made?'

'I'll tell you all about it on the way.'

There'd been other places of worship to visit in Cirencester, and Francis Gregory had inspected them all, whatever their denomination. Whenever an interesting feature attracted his attention, it was recorded in his notebook. That afternoon, he was picking his way through yet another churchyard, examining the epitaphs and absent-mindedly picking the moss off the gravestones. He felt completely at home among the long since departed and rested on a tomb in the middle of them as if visiting the house of dear friends. Many more names were listed in his notebook and inscriptions were copied out in full. Gregory was enthralled.

With Leeming seated beside him, Colbeck drove the trap away

from The Grange. The first thing he told his companion was about the way that he'd been followed.

'That never happened to us,' said Leeming. 'I know it for certain because Alan Hinton kept looking over his shoulder.'

'I didn't have the luxury of a lookout, so I relied on instinct. A young man named Jacob Overy was on my tail. He'd been working for Etheridge, so I rode off to Kemble again and gave the squire a nasty shock.'

He went on to explain how he hid outside so that he could follow a messenger sent from Kemble Court to the Royal College of Agriculture. Leeming felt that they now had grounds to arrest both Etheridge and Cinderby, but Colbeck recommended patience. Even if they were guilty, neither of the men would be directly involved in the exchange of ransom and hostage due to take place that evening.

'They'd keep their hands clean,' said Colbeck, 'and leave the dirty work to others. It's through the men they've hired that we'd have to trace them.'

'I'd love to put handcuffs on a clergyman,' said Leeming.

'That might be viewed as a form of sacrilege, Victor.'

'I'd still enjoy it.'

Colbeck told him about the offer he'd received from Michael Rydall and the long discussion they had as a result. Leeming was astonished. Having identified him as a potential suspect, he saw how foolish he'd been in making a judgement without garnering sufficient information beforehand.

'You *spoke* to Michael Rydall?' he said in wonderment.

'Actually, I listened most of the time.'

'What do you think his parents would say if they knew he was living in the Cotswolds again?'

Colbeck was tactful. 'In my opinion,' he said, 'they'd react in very different ways.'

Catherine Rydall was alone in the bedroom. She studied the photograph she'd received from her son as if it were a precious object. It was the only sight she'd had of him in over five years. Notwithstanding the differences in his appearance, she was delighted to be able to look at him once more. The sound of hoof beats in the courtyard signalled her husband's return. She hid the photograph away in her jewellery box before going downstairs.

When she went outside, Catherine saw her husband dismounting and handing the reins to a stable lad. As he came over to her, Rydall's face was shadowed with concern.

'I've just spoken to Sidney Walters,' he said. 'He tells me that old Mrs Ackerley has died.'

'Who?'

'She's Edgar Smayle's mother-in-law.'

'Oh, no,' she said with a sigh. 'That family already has far too much to endure. It's cruel.'

'Walters thinks that worrying about the fate of her son-in-law might have contributed to her death. The poor woman was bedridden. You can imagine how helpless she must have felt as bad news kept coming into the house.' He sucked his teeth. 'First of all, Smayle disappears, then his dog is found dead and now Mrs Ackerley has gone.'

'It makes you wonder what's going to happen to them next.'

'I daren't think, Catherine.'

'How are they all bearing up?'

'According to Walters, it's rocked them. They're worried stiff about the cost of the funeral.'

'You've helped families in that position before, Stephen.'

'It looks as if I may have to do so again.'

'Mrs Smayle must feel beleaguered,' she said. 'The death of a mother is such a loss. I know that from experience.'

'It might help if you called on the family, Catherine – just to pay your respects. Pass on my condolences as well.'

'Yes, of course. It's important that they know we're thinking of them. I'll take a basket of food for them. Leave it to me, Stephen. You've got too many other things on your mind at the moment.' She grasped his arm. 'How are you feeling?'

'To be quite honest,' he confessed, 'I'm scared rigid.'

St Mary's Church had been at the heart of a small community devastated by the plague in the fourteenth century. As a result, the village of Ampney St Mary had been moved some distance away. Guarded by a noble old cedar, the church remained as a relic of former times. It was built for the most part in the early twelfth century and had a relatively plain appearance. St Mary's was best known for its wall paintings, much eroded in some places.

One painting, however, was sufficiently clear for Francis Gregory to copy it. Between the door and the east window of the south wall was a mural based on the commandment 'Keep Holy the Sabbath Day'. To show that labour on a Sunday injured Christ, there was an image of him with blood coming from his wounds. Lying beside him were the implements of manual labour that had inflicted them. Gregory liked the sense of pain and betrayal in the scene. He was so eager to transfer the mural to his notebook that he didn't hear the approach of a horse and trap.

He was still working away when the two of them entered.

'Mr Gregory, I believe,' said Colbeck.

The man swung round angrily. 'Who the devil are you?' he demanded.

'We are detectives from Scotland Yard and were assigned to investigate the train crash at the mouth of the Sapperton Tunnel.' He held up the notebook discarded at the King's Arms Hotel. 'It's the one so faithfully reproduced in this notebook of yours.'

'Where on earth did you get that?'

'We found it in Cirencester where you abandoned it,' said Leeming. 'It's identical to the one you hold in your hand.'

'That's the way I work,' said the other, testily. 'I make a sketch in miniature of something that appeals to my taste then enlarge and embellish it in a full-sized sketchbook. But why are you bothering *me*?'

'In view of what we found in your notebook,' said Colbeck, 'we think that you may have had some connection with the train crash.'

'My only connection is that I preserved it on paper.'

'And you seem to have taken a perverted delight in doing so.'

'There's nothing perverted in confronting the truth. I'm an artist by trade. Death and destruction are my themes.

Look here, for instance,' he said, standing back so that they could see the mural, 'Christ's wounds are streaming blood. It's a dire warning to those who flout the Sabbath. They *caused* those wounds.'

'Why do you always paint people or animals that are wounded or killed?'

'It's because I wish to tell the truth about life. It's a downward path that we all have to walk along. What lies at the bottom is what you'll find in most of the sketches I made – the inevitability of death.'

'You've collected all those epitaphs,' Leeming pointed out.

'I was welcoming new friends to my little world.'

'Why did every one of those "new friends" have to be women?'

Gregory smirked. 'You're surely old enough to realise that,' he said. 'There are many biblical precedents. Look how many wives King David had.'

'Before he became king,' Colbeck pointed out, 'David was a shepherd. We were brought here to search for another shepherd, one who was abducted in the night and whose sheep were slaughtered by a goods train.'

'*You* were in the area at the time,' said Leeming, accusingly.

'I'm glad that I was,' retorted the artist. 'I seized the moment and drew my picture when the blood from those sheep was still staining the rails.'

'You have a twisted mind, Mr Gregory.'

'Since when has that been an offence that merits arrest? By your standards, all artists have twisted minds because they see the world as it really is and portray it as such. That's all that *I* do – though not with the clarity of the Old Masters.'

'Do you know what I think?'

'It doesn't matter, Sergeant,' said Colbeck, putting a hand on his shoulder. 'I've seen enough to realise that we've been misled. Mr Gregory is not the man we're after. I'll speak with him no further because he's far too ill-mannered to deserve an apology. It's time to leave him be.'

'One moment,' said Gregory, stepping in their way. 'There's something I'd like to know. How did you find me?'

Colbeck held up the notebook. 'This was my guide.'

'There's no mention of Ampney St Mary in there.'

'Perhaps not, but I knew that you'd stayed in Cirencester. Someone with your fascination for churches would surely visit Fairford. It's reputed to have the finest stained-glass windows in England. The chances were,' explained Colbeck, 'that you'd be somewhere on this road. After we'd been to Ampney St Crucis and Ampney St Peter, therefore, we came here.'

'Then you must take advantage of the fact,' said Gregory. 'There's a striking, primitive lintel above the north doorway. The design shows the Lion of Righteousness triumphing over the agents of evil, who are aided by a griffin. Study it, if you please.'

'Why?' asked Leeming.

'You might find it instructive.'

'I'm not sure about that.'

'As an artist,' said Gregory with a grand gesture, 'I confess that I incline more towards the agents of evil, but you are clearly Lions of Righteousness.' He raised his hat in mockery. 'Good day to you, gentlemen.'

* * *

328

It was either a feast or a famine at the Daneway Inn. Most of the time, it was swarming with customers, but there were occasional gaps when hardly any of them were there. Peter and Molly Doble were taking advantage of a rare moment when the place was almost deserted. It was an opportunity when they could sit down, get one of their employees to serve them for a change and actually have a proper conversation. Doble had taken inventory of their stock and wanted to talk about the next order for the brewery. Molly introduced a comical note.

'Did you know that Bridget was going to leg it today?'

Doble grinned. 'Are you serious?'

'She's mentioned it before, but I always thought she was a joking. But no, Bridget was serious. She's going to lie on her back and power the barge with her son. Can you imagine it?'

'Yes, I can – all too clearly.'

'I don't think I'd have the strength to do it.'

'Bridget is as strong as an ox,' he said, laughing, 'and it must be quite a sight to see her on her back with her legs in the air.'

She prodded him hard. 'Don't be unkind.'

'Well, you've seen the woman, Molly. She's huge and it's no wonder. When it comes to drinking beer, she can hold her own with any man.' He nibbled at a hunk of bread. 'What else did she have to say?'

'They've lost their contract with Beckerton.'

'Oh?'

'Bridget says that they got fed up with the way that he kept making fun of her husband. Also, of course, he kept pestering her.'

'He does that to every woman. Beckerton can't help himself.'

'He picked the wrong person this time. Knowing Bridget, I bet she gave him a real mouthful in return. If it wasn't for the fact that he's important to us, I'd do the same.'

'Just keep out of his way, Molly.'

'That's easier said than done.'

'We're supposed to be enjoying a quiet rest,' he said, 'so let's forget our problems. That means we don't say another word about Anthony Beckerton.'

There were three of them, burly men with hard faces and uncompromising stares. Beckerton met them at Gloucester station and handed out their tickets. Looking from one to the other, he issued his command.

'You all know what to do,' he said, menacingly. 'I want no mistakes. If you fail, don't bother to come back to me.'

As she went up the stairs alone, Annie Smayle steeled herself. She had finally plucked up the courage to pay her respects to a woman who'd played an important part in her life. When Annie was a child, she knew Mrs Ackerley as a kind, loving, lively countrywoman who'd always had time for her granddaughter. Over the years, she had slowed down then gradually decayed into a bedridden old crone. When Annie entered the room, the smell of death was already in the air, even though the window had been left open. A bedsheet had been drawn up over her grandmother's face. It took Annie minutes before she felt able to draw it back and gaze down at the corpse. The sight was too much for her. Drawing the sheet back into position, she kissed her fingers, then transferred the kiss to the old woman's forehead. It was the briefest of farewells.

Coming back downstairs, she went straight into her mother's arms, and they held each other until the tears finally dried up. Annie tried to change the subject.

'I'm worried about Will,' she said.

'We've been worried about him since he was born,' said Mildred, acidly.

'He went off with the shotgun. I heard him fire it.'

'If there's any animal worrying the sheep,' Betsy reminded her, 'he's entitled to kill it. That's why your father taught him how to shoot. Will has also brought pigeons, rabbits and other game for the pot.'

'He's not after animals this time,' said Annie. 'He wants to kill the man who took our father away. We must stop him. Will is out of control.'

Patrolling the margins of the estate, he kept his eyes peeled. Every so often, he pretended that someone had tried to creep up behind him. Turning in a flash, Will used the barrel of the shotgun to jab into his assailant's stomach, then he knocked him to the ground and kicked him unmercifully. Anyone watching would have found his behaviour mystifying, but it brought Will a sensation of the utmost pleasure. He continued the process at regular intervals.

Before they left St Mary's Church, they looked at the carving on the lintel. The lion was trampling on what looked like two serpents though Colbeck thought that it might be a single serpent with two heads. Good had triumphed over evil.

On the drive back, Leeming voiced his disappointment.

'That was a complete waste of time.'

'No, it wasn't.'

'I thought he might be the person we're after.'

'So did I,' said Colbeck, 'and that's why it was so important to track him down. In doing that, we eliminated a suspect. The meeting with Gregory did something else for me.'

'What was it?'

'He persuaded me that I'd been wrong to assume that there was a religious import in the fact that seven sheep were killed. His eccentric behaviour at a series of churches suggested a demented man who'd created a parody of a biblical scene outside that tunnel. I now believe,' admitted Colbeck, 'that I was easily misled. If I'd had sense, I'd have postponed my judgement until I'd talked to Michael Rydall.'

'How does he come into it?'

'He told me about that contest between the three shepherds. With the help of their sheepdogs, they had to manoeuvre a small flock into a pen. Each of the shepherds was timed. Because of the way he controlled his dogs, Smayle won it easily. All of the sheep were penned straight away. Neither of the others managed to get the whole flock in there together. In each case, a couple went astray.'

'I'm sorry,' said Leeming, 'but I'm lost.'

'It's not easy to herd sheep, Victor. Even experienced shepherds make mistakes. During that competition,' Colbeck emphasised, 'Smayle was operating in daylight with two sheepdogs. When he was forced to take those animals to the mouth of the tunnel, it was dark, and he only had Blackie to help him.'

'I think I understand what you're saying now. Picking out seven sheep would have been difficult.'

'Exactly,' said Colbeck. 'All that was needed was a small selection to act as a symbol of what Smayle did for a living. It was pure chance that they numbered seven. There could equally well have been six or eight. In fact,' he added, 'we have to remember that those ewes might have been close to producing their lambs. That would have made *fourteen* animals in all, and I can't recall that number featuring in the Bible.'

'Your meeting with Michael Rydall was very useful.'

'It opened my eyes in many ways.'

'That's all to our advantage, sir. Did you tell him the ransom was due to be handed over this evening?'

'Of course I did,' said Colbeck.

'Was that wise, sir?'

'Michael was honest with me. It was only fair that I was honest with him. After all, it's the Rydall family that is stretched on the rack. He still feels part of it.'

Poring over the map, Michael Rydall felt a flood of memories surging back from his childhood. He was looking at places where he and his brothers had played hide-and-seek endlessly among the bushes and trees. He'd come to know the area intimately. Even after a long absence, he recognised the location of every hill, hollow and meandering stream. Taking out a pencil, he started to draw a series of tiny circles on the map.

* * *

They met in the drawing room at The Grange. The last to arrive was Alan Hinton. He ambled across the lawn in his borrowed garb and pretended to examine some flowers about to come into bud. He then went around the stables to the rear of the house and let himself in. Nobody watching would ever have connected him with the detectives. Colbeck and Leeming were sitting there with Rydall when the counterfeit gardener entered the room. Hinton felt embarrassed.

'I can't sit down in one of those nice chairs like this,' he said.

'Then you'll just have to stand,' said Leeming. 'It may not be for long.'

'I didn't see anybody watching the house.'

'That's good to know,' said Colbeck. 'But it won't be long before they make contact. Light has already faded badly.' He picked up a leather pouch from the table. 'Have a feel of this, Alan.'

'What is it, sir?' asked Hinton, taking the pouch from him.

'You're holding five thousand pounds in cash.'

'Good heavens!'

Leeming laughed at his obvious alarm. 'You'd never make a burglar,' he said. 'As soon as you stole some money, you'd give the game away.'

'I've never held this amount of money before.'

'If you remain working at Scotland Yard,' warned Colbeck, 'you'll never do so again. Our wages are on a far more modest scale.'

'But there are rewards,' said Leeming. 'Working with the superintendent is one of them. It's impossible to put a price on that honour.'

'What about you, sir?' asked Colbeck, turning to Rydall. 'You're the important person in the transaction. How do *you* feel?'

'I'm nervous,' said the other. 'I'm also worried that nobody will come.'

'Yes, they will.'

'How do you know?'

'They've set everything up in readiness, and they don't want to wait any longer for their money.'

'I wish I could believe that Smayle is still alive.'

'We all feel that way, sir.'

'Earlier today, his mother-in-law died. The family is already in mourning.' Rydall was startled by a knock on the door. 'Come in.'

A servant entered the room and held out a letter.

'This has just come, Mr Rydall,' he said, handing it over.

'Did you see who delivered it?' asked Colbeck.

'I'm afraid not, sir.'

'Thank you,' said Rydall. 'That will be all.'

The servant withdrew. Rydall was hesitant. Instead of opening the letter, he stared at it as if it were about to explode in his hand.

Colbeck intervened. 'Would you like me to look at it for you, sir?'

'No, no, it bears my name.' Making the effort, he opened the letter and read the message before passing it to Colbeck. 'The handover point is near Ash Hill. That's not far from here.'

'You're told to go immediately,' noted Colbeck, reading

the instructions. 'They'll be watching to make sure that you're not taking us with you.' He took out his map and unfolded it on the table. 'Perhaps you'll be kind enough to point out exactly where Ash Hill is and how we could reach it without being seen.'

'I'll do my best, Inspector.'

'When that's done, you and Hinton can set off.'

'Keep a tight hand on that money, Alan,' said Leeming, patting him on the back. 'Pretend that it's all yours.'

They'd chosen the site because they could hide in a copse and make a quick escape if it was necessary. Anyone approaching from Frampton Mansell would have to come across an open area where they'd be in full view. Dark shadows were striping the ground and pulling a shroud over the trees. They conversed in gestures so that their voices didn't carry. Two of them were dressed in black and wearing masks. The third was a big man in a shepherd's gown liberally stained with blood. His hands were tied together in front of him, but he looked, in any case, as if he was too weak to offer any kind of resistance. His head was on his chest and his face invisible beneath the battered hat.

A trap eventually came into sight, driven by Rydall. When it got within thirty yards of the copse, it stopped.

'Do you have the money?' demanded a rough voice.

'Do *you* have Edgar Smayle?' replied Rydall.

'I ask the questions.'

'Then the answer is that I do,' said Rydall, nudging Hinton.

The latter alighted from the trap, opened the pouch and took out the bundles of banknotes. He held them up for inspection. The man came out of his hiding place and walked a dozen paces before stopping.

'Let me count it,' he snarled.

'I've still not seen my shepherd,' argued Rydall. 'Until I do, there'll be no exchange. I've done as I was told. Fulfil *your* side of the bargain.'

The man held up an arm and the bulky figure in the shepherd's smock was pushed into sight. He staggered forward as if in pain until he reached his captor. Rydall was at once relieved and disturbed, glad that Smayle seemed to be alive but worried about the obvious distress he was in. Grabbing him by the scruff of his neck, the man shook him so that he lifted his head. Rydall saw that he was gagged and that his face was a mixture of blood and bruises.

'What have they done to you, Edgar?' he called out.

'You've seen the shepherd,' said the man. 'Bring me the money.'

After a moment's consideration, Rydall nodded to Hinton who began to walk steadily towards the two men. The pouch suddenly felt much heavier than it really was, but he didn't break his stride. When he got within five yards of them, he took out the banknotes again and held them up for inspection.

'Put it on the grass,' ordered the man.

Hinton looked over his shoulder for a signal from Rydall. When he got another affirmative nod, he stuffed the money back into the pouch and placed it on the ground.

'Right,' said the man, pushing the captive forward. 'I've got what *I* wanted. Mr Rydall can have this piece of sheep dung back in return.'

He eased the prisoner forward towards Hinton. All of a sudden, the shepherd came to life. Tossing away the rope binding his wrists, he gave Hinton such a violent push that he hit the ground and rolled over on his back. The pouch, meanwhile, had been scooped up by the other man. The two accomplices raced into the trees. All that Rydall could do was to watch in despair as his five thousand pounds disappeared from sight.

Colbeck had been cautious. When he saw the location of the exchange on the map, he guessed that the copse would be brought into play as cover. He and Leeming had therefore ridden in a wide semicircle so that they approached the place from the opposite direction. They were in time to see three figures mounting the horses tethered in readiness. The detectives swooped on them immediately. Leeming tackled the biggest of them by diving at him and knocking him from the saddle. When Colbeck tried to arrest another of them, he was beaten off and the man kicked his horse away. Before he could go in pursuit, Colbeck saw another rider coming out of the gloom and giving chase.

Leeming was still on the ground, trading punches with the big man and slowly getting the upper hand until he was attacked from behind by the other rider who'd dismounted and started to belabour him. Colbeck responded by grabbing the assailant by the shoulders and pulling hard. To his amazement, he heard a loud female scream. Overpowering the woman, he tore off the mask and realised that he was holding Molly Doble from the Daneway Inn.

* * *

Her husband's attempt at escape, meanwhile, was about to be foiled. Though he was galloping hell for leather, he couldn't outrun the man in pursuit who was younger, fitter and astride a far swifter horse. When they reached an open patch of land, the second rider drew level, then flung himself at Doble, knocking him from the saddle. Both of them landed heavily on the ground, but they ignored the pain and began to punch, grapple, twist, turn and kick. Doble was also spitting and biting. As a last resort, he got his hands on his attacker's neck and squeezed with all his might. The intense pressure slowly began to tell. Then his assailant had a surge of energy and pushed hard. Before he could resist, Doble was rolled over onto his back, kneed in the groin and hit with such a powerful relay of punches that he was unable to defend himself. His attacker kept hitting him with both fists until the landlord was unconscious.

Followed by Hinton, Stephen Rydall struggled through the copse and came out of the trees to find Leeming standing over the man he'd just handcuffed. Colbeck was holding Molly Doble firmly by the arm.

Rydall was bewildered. 'What happened?' he asked.

'We've caught two of them, sir,' explained Colbeck. 'The sergeant arrested the man who was posing as your missing shepherd. He was Doble's brother. And I was able to overpower someone I think you'll recognise.'

He pushed the woman forward so that she was clearly visible.

'Molly Doble!' gasped Rydall.

'We enjoyed doing it,' she said, defiantly.

'What do you mean?'

'Edgar Smayle was an animal. He beat his wife and pestered other women. He deserved to die.'

'I can't believe that you were involved.'

'She was *my* daughter as much as Peter's. We swore we'd get even.'

'Who are you talking about?' said Colbeck.

'And where is your husband?' asked Leeming.

She laughed derisively. 'Peter got away with five thousand pounds,' she said. 'You'll never find him.'

'We don't need to,' said Colbeck, looking over her shoulder. 'It seems as if someone has saved us the trouble of searching.'

They turned to see two figures approaching. One was sitting high in the saddle as he towed the other horse along. Slumped across it, like the carcase of a dead animal, was a man's body.

Colbeck smiled. 'I fancy that you'll get your money back, after all, Mr Rydall.'

Rydall gaped. 'Who, in God's name, *is* that?'

He soon had the answer. When the horses came to a halt, the young man dismounted and took off his hat. Though he was still in disguise, his voice confirmed his identity at once.

'Hello, Father,' said Michael. 'I'm back.'

Sweeping into his office at Scotland Yard early next morning, Tallis was delighted to find a telegraph awaiting him. His delight was short-lived. When he read the message from Colbeck, he saw that it consisted of five words.

Culprits caught. Case almost closed.

'*Almost!*' he exclaimed. 'What the hell do you mean by "almost", man? I want the full story in minute detail. I demand to know *everything*.'

After lighting a soothing cigar, he read the telegraph again then scrunched it up and threw it towards the wastepaper basket. He missed.

Colbeck was not there when Michael Rydall was reunited with his mother, and he had no wish to be. Whatever happened was their business. He just hoped that some sort of reconciliation had taken place. On the following morning, he went first to Stroud telegraph station to send news to the superintendent, then drove Leeming back in the direction of the Daneway Inn.

'You must seize your opportunity, Victor.'

'I'm not sure that I want to now,' said the other, uneasily.

'Ever since we got here, you've been entranced by the canal. You learnt all the technical terms, and you couldn't wait to explain to me what a gongoozler was. You also told me how the bargees leg it through the tunnel. This is your chance to do it yourself.'

'I'm having second thoughts.'

'Would you rather *I* did it?'

'No, no, it's not your responsibility, sir.'

'Then the task falls to you, Victor.'

'I'll get soaked to the skin.'

'You'll do what the bargees do and pull the tarpaulin over you when necessary. I'll be aboard as well to urge you on. Let me be serious,' he added. 'We're not going into that tunnel for our own benefit. It's for the sake of the Smayle family. Whatever discomfort *you* may suffer, it's nothing compared to the agony with which they're forced to cope.'

'That's true, sir,' said Leeming, 'and I'm ashamed that I tried to wriggle out of it. Mr Rydall has a far more difficult job. He has to explain to the family that Edgar Smayle was murdered.'

'But I doubt if he tells them why.'

Peter Doble had been uncooperative under questioning, but his wife could not hold back the truth. Molly told them that Smayle had not only caused them endless trouble at the inn, he'd seduced a young woman they'd taken under their wing and employed as a barmaid. She'd become the daughter they'd never had. Once he'd established a hold over her, the shepherd had ruthlessly exploited her innocence. It was only a matter of time before she became pregnant. The shame was too much for her, and she ran away. They later heard that she'd drowned herself in the canal.

'And that's where Smayle ended up as well,' said Colbeck. 'Doble and his wife brooded for years on how to get their revenge. Smayle was always pestering Molly so she eventually pretended to respond to his interest in her. Telling him that her husband was away, she agreed to a midnight rendezvous.'

'She's a handsome woman, much more so than his wife.'

'When he got there, Smayle realised he'd been duped. Peter Doble was waiting with a gun in his hand. He was supported by his brother, Harry, who later daubed his face with what looked like blood and tried to pass himself off as Smayle.'

'But it wasn't enough for them to drown him,' recalled

Leeming. 'They wanted to destroy something of his that was dear to his heart – his sheep.'

'He was literally forced to take them to slaughter.'

'In a sense,' decided Colbeck, 'winning that sheepdog trial was his death warrant. He boasted about it endlessly at The Daneway. So they erected that pen outside the tunnel and forced Smayle to show off his skills. Once the sheep were safely in the pen, they killed Blackie and tossed him in the canal.'

'What about that letter Smayle wrote?'

'They convinced him they'd let him stay alive if he made that appeal to Rydall. Once he'd scrawled his message, they killed him, then took him into the tunnel in a barge.'

'Nobody would ever have thought of looking there.'

'It's what *we* are going to do, Victor.'

'They came so close to getting away with it,' said Leeming. 'While we were busy chasing the wrong suspects, they were rubbing their hands with glee.'

'As it was, Doble almost escaped. But for the bravery of his son, Rydall would have lost a large amount of money.'

'Yes, Michael is the real hero of the hour.'

'I'm so glad that I told him about the handover of the ransom,' said Colbeck. 'He'd have had no idea where it would take place, but he had the sense to realise that we'd be there somehow. So he lurked outside The Grange until we left and followed us at a safe distance.'

'Going back to the tunnel,' said Leeming, still puzzled. 'I can see why those sheep were penned on the line as a way of tormenting Smayle. But why did the goods train have to be derailed?'

'The Dobles are canal people. Railways are their sworn enemies because they've substantially reduced traffic on the canals. They saw a chance to get their revenge on Smayle and inconvenience the GWR at the same time.'

'Inconvenience?' echoed Leeming. 'They did far more than that, sir.'

'They certainly did,' said Colbeck. 'And they'll be made to pay the ultimate price for their crimes.'

Alighting from the train, Alan Hinton ran across the concourse at Paddington and summoned a cab. It took him straight to the house in John Islip Street. When she saw who her visitor was, Madeleine Colbeck was overjoyed.

'This is only a flying visit,' he warned. 'I have to deliver a full report of the investigation to Superintendent Tallis. I just thought you'd like to know that the case is solved and that the inspector will be home later today.'

'That's wonderful!' she cried.

'Perhaps you could pass on news of our success to Lydia.'

'I'll send her a message immediately, Alan.'

The bargee was waiting for them when they finally arrived. After introducing his son, who'd be propelling the vessel with Leeming, he gave both detectives their instructions. Colbeck was given an iron rake for hauling things up from the bed of the canal. Leeming was shown the wings, flat pieces of board rigged for the purpose of legging. They were there to allow him and the bargee's son to extend their reach. The bargee himself acted as steersman. When the two men were lying on their backs in readiness, they set off.

As they entered the tunnel, Leeming felt as if they were descending into hell. When his feet made contact with the roof of the tunnel, he realised how difficult a task he'd taken on. It was punishing work. When his foot slipped, the boat baulked a little.

'Keep 'er straight!' yelled the bargee.

'You're doing well, Victor,' said Colbeck, encouragingly.

'I don't think so,' grumbled Leeming.

He shifted his position and felt marginally more comfortable. What he hadn't foreseen was the effort involved. It was really testing. Disappointingly, they were moving very slowly, hardly fast enough to cause a ripple. But at least he was keeping pace with the bargee's son. The further they went into the tunnel, the more intense became the dark. Leeming began to fear that he'd never see daylight again. Ignoring the discomfort, however, he kept his legs moving. At the start, the roof of the tunnel had been brick-lined, but it eventually became bare rock, jagged in some places. It was one more hazard with which to contend.

Colbeck's sharp ears first picked up a low, continuous, murmuring sound. He had no idea what it was until it gradually became louder and louder. The rush of water was soon unmistakable.

'Easy a minute, boys!' ordered the steersman.

Leeming seized gratefully on the chance of a brief respite and rested his aching legs. When the bargee's son dragged a tarpaulin over them, he knew that they were about to be drenched. The noise they'd first heard as little more than a whisper was now close to a roar. Keb in hand, Colbeck used it to rake the bed of the canal. They'd been told that Smayle's body had been dumped close to the point where an underground spring had broken through the roof and cascaded into the canal. In the stifling darkness, the thunderous gush of water was intimidating. Before they reached it, however, Colbeck felt the keb hit something big and solid.

'I think I've found him,' he shouted, barely audible above the roar.

'Do you need a hand, sir?' asked Leeming.

'I will in a minute. He must have something tied to him to keep him down there. I'll have to go in and cut him free.'

'You're going into the *water*?'

'Someone has to.'

Leeming was astounded. Colbeck was very particular about his clothing. Though he was no longer wearing his usual immaculate apparel, he was still dressed in a suit. Tearing off his coat, hat and shoes, Colbeck plunged over the side of the barge and went underwater. It was little more than five feet in depth, enabling him to stand on the bottom. He groped around for some time until his hands eventually made contact with a body. By feeling his way around the corpse, he located a rope that had been tied around the feet. It was attached at the other end to a heavy boulder. Before he could undo it, Colbeck had to surface in order to take in more air. He reached for the knife he'd brought with him. After taking a deep breath, he went down again and began to wrestle with the rope, using the knife to cut through it.

Leeming was peering into the dark water when Colbeck suddenly popped up again. One arm around the body of Edgar

Smayle, he called for help. Leeming and the bargee felt their way towards him and hauled out the shepherd. Dripping with wet and gulping for air, Colbeck climbed aboard after him. Their search had been successful. They could now return the body to the Smayle family. For all his faults, they felt, the shepherd deserved a decent burial.

'It's just as well you can't see me, Victor,' said Colbeck. 'I must look like a drowned rat.'

'So do I, sir.'

'We've each had a wonderful new experience.'

'I'll have nightmares about mine for the rest of my life.'

Their laughter was drowned out by the thunder of the waterfall.

Edward Tallis was smiling for once. The sun was shining, his toothache had disappeared and he'd just read a full account of events in Gloucestershire. Having delivered Colbeck's report, Hinton had been able to explain what had detained both the inspector and Leeming.

'Good luck to them,' said Tallis. 'I wouldn't care to search for a dead body in a canal tunnel in complete darkness.'

'They'll go to any lengths, sir.'

'And so they should. I trained them to face every emergency. But you made your contribution as well, Hinton,' he went on. 'This report makes that clear. Congratulations are due.'

'Thank you, Superintendent.'

'I wasn't thanking *you*, Constable. The congratulations are mine. I was giving myself a pat on the back for having the idea to send you by way of reinforcement. Having an extra man seems to have made all the difference.'

Hinton knew that it was a decision made by Colbeck but he didn't dare to contradict the superintendent. Finding him in a mood of such benevolence was all too rare. It was better to enjoy it before Tallis lapsed back into his more usual bristling hostility.

'Do you know what a gongoozler is, Superintendent?' asked Hinton.

'Do I *need* to know?' challenged Tallis.

'I suppose not, sir.'

Hinton made an excuse and left.

Colbeck and Leeming were standing outside The Grange, taking their leave. Stephen Rydall showered them with praise. Though he'd suffered setbacks, there had been compensations and he was keenly aware of them.

'I may have lost a shepherd,' he said, 'but I've regained a son.'

'And Michael has regained a family,' said Colbeck.

'There are still lots of things to sort out, Inspector, but we're definitely talking to each other again.'

'That's good to hear.'

'What about the cricket team?' asked Leeming. 'Is Michael going to play for that again?'

'No, Sergeant,' affirmed Rydall, 'he most definitely is not. When he heard how Etheridge has been behaving towards me, he decided to stay well clear of him. Besides, he and Edith, his wife, have a daughter to worry about now. That will keep the pair of them busy.'

'I'm rather disappointed that I was unable to arrest the

squire,' said Colbeck with a grin, 'and I feel the same about the Reverend Cinderby.'

'I share your disappointment. By the way,' said Rydall, 'I've been asked by the Smayle family to pass on their thanks. They were so grateful for the way that you retrieved the body from the canal.'

'How are they?'

'They're distraught, as you can imagine. But I was able to soften the blow slightly. Since Annie and Will proved their worth during their father's absence, I'm letting the family remain in the cottage.'

'That's very kind of you,' said Colbeck. 'I have to admit that I never suspected the Dobles for one moment. I was beginning to wonder if that strange artist who haunted churches was behind it all.'

'I thought that Beckerton was the culprit,' admitted Leeming, 'but he was in the clear.'

'That doesn't make him an exemplar of innocence. Think of that rumour we picked up earlier down by the canal. A bargee was beaten up by thugs yesterday. The likelihood is that Anthony Beckerton was settling another old score. However,' he went on as Sidney Walters came in view, driving a carriage, 'it looks as if our chauffeur is here.'

There was an exchange of warm handshakes and farewells.

'It's a pity you can't stay another week,' said Rydall.

'Why is that?' asked Colbeck.

'Work is ahead of schedule on the crash site. Wait until next Tuesday or Wednesday and you'll be able to take a train that goes straight through the Sapperton Tunnel.'

'It's a kind invitation, Mr Rydall, but we'll have to decline it.'

'Why?'

'After our experience on the canal this morning,' said Colbeck, firmly, 'Sergeant Leeming and I intend to keep as far away from tunnels of all kinds as we possibly can.'